IF IT AIN'T ABOUT THE MONEY

Also by Saundra

Her Sweetest Revenge

Her Sweetest Revenge 2

Her Sweetest Revenge 3

If It Ain't About the Money

Hustle Hard

A Hustler's Queen

Anthologies
Schemes and **Dirty Tricks** (with Kiki Swinson)

Published by Kensington Publishing Corp.

IF IT AIN'T ABOUT THE MONEY

KENSINGTON PUBLISHING CORP.

www.kensingtonbooks.com

DAFINA BOOKS are published by

Kensington Publishing Corp.
119 West 40th Street
New York, NY 10018

All Kensington Titles, Imprints, and Distributed Lines are available at special quantity discounts for bulk purchases for sales promotions, premiums, fund-raising, and educational or institutional use. Special book excerpts or customized printings can also be created to fit specific needs. For details, write or phone the office of the Kensington special sales manager: Kensington Publishing Corp., 119 West 40th Street, New York, NY 10018, attn: Special Sales Department, Phone: 1-800-221-2647.

Dafina and the Dafina logo Reg. U.S. Pat. & TM Off.

ISBN-13: 978-1-4967-1196-0
ISBN-10: 1-4967-1196-3
First Kensington Trade Edition: February 2018
First Kensington Mass Market Edition: July 2019

ISBN-13: 978-1-4967-1197-7 (e-book)
ISBN-10: 1-4967-1197-1 (e-book)

10 9 8 7 6 5 4 3 2 1

Printed in the United States of America

Acknowledgments

Thank you, father God, for blessing me. Being able to live your dream is a feeling that I can't describe. I'm thankful. To my daughters, Dj and Cj, you were twelve and six when I started this writing journey. Now you are sixteen and ten—my how time flies. I love you both. To my husband, Jaye, thanks for continuing to support me. The work is just beginning. Let's push this one. Can I say book tour? Shout out to my mom, my sister, and my brother for traveling to two cities in 2016 to support me; you guys rock.

I would like to thank my editor, Selena James, for believing in me and pushing me to do my best. Also, thanks to the entire Kensington/Dafina family for their continued promotion and support. Screaming good luck and congratulation to One-sisha for following her dream and becoming a flight attendant in 2017. The sky is the limit. Your dad and I are proud of you.

Shout out to my family and friends Latunya, Denise, Saidah, Red, Shekie, Veronica, Lisa, Pamela, Shanta, Quatesha, Melvin, Mario, Roy Jr., O-Rayfo, Dad, and Mary. Also, my entire Housing Authority family. Last, but not least, shout out to all my reading fans. Without all your support, this would not be possible. I appreciate you!

Chapter 1

Secret

I swear the life I was forced into was some straight bullshit. No child or children on God's green earth deserved it. Nothing was ever legit. At least not in our household. There was never any food, and sometimes no lights or gas. And at that moment, no fucking laundry detergent. Gripping the All detergent bottle in an upside-down motion, I waited patiently as only two drops slowly fell from the bottle into the river of running water as it filled the mildly beat-up washing machine. Angry, I threw the empty container across the room with as much force as I could assemble; it smashed into the wall with a loud thud. I rolled my eyes as I watched the bottle spin in a circular motion before settling on its back. Having detergent to clean our dirty clothes shouldn't have been too much to

ask. But, to be honest, my baby sister Penny and I
were used to a lot worse.

Our mother, Jackie, was a full-fledged drunk,
which in turn caused her to be angry and abusive
all the time. Things had been this way since I was
about four years old, when Penny's dad, Ed, had
come into our lives. Before Ed, Jackie had been
pretty normal; she did simple things like fed me,
hugged me, and kept a job. But by the time Penny
was four years old, all that had changed drastically.
By then Ed was constantly abusing Jackie and
keeping her wasted. But even then she was able to
keep a steady job. At the time, I thought things
couldn't get any worse. Boy, I was wrong. When I
was ten, Ed was killed trying to rob a gas station for
a few measly bucks. After that Jackie started to
drink constantly as if it was a sport. If drinking had
been a job she would've had hella overtime. I'm
talking about sloppy drunk. Once she was so
drunk she sat on the kitchen floor, peed on herself, and slept in it. I was horrified and disgusted
all at the same time. Suddenly, she was always frustrated with Penny and me. In her eyes, everything
we did was wrong. That was when the abuse
started.

But we got smart real quick; in order to avoid
being cursed out or attacked we learned to stay out
of her way. I took on the role of caring for Penny. I
became the responsible adult in the house. But
that was difficult, seeing as how I was only a kid myself and there was never any food in the house, because Jackie sold off all of her food stamps so that
she could buy liquor. She could no longer keep a

job because she couldn't stay sober a full twenty-four hours straight. The smell of cheap whiskey seemed to pour from her once glistening, smooth skin. Sometimes the smell was so strong it caused me to gag. Simply put, it was too much for a child to be going through. But there I was, now fourteen, and Penny ten, and the shit was no different. Growing up on mean gritty 224th street in Goulds in Miami, Florida, was enough pressure for any kid. To add being beat and sometimes starved because your alcoholic mother couldn't kick the bottle was a whole other story.

"Secret, what are we going to eat? I'm hungry." Penny sat up on her elbows with a pout spread on her lips. She lay across her twin bed in the room we shared in the two-bedroom house we grew up in. The neighborhood we lived in was tough. There was a drug dealer, gangster, drug addict, or thief on every corner. Police sirens ran night and day, and that was as normal as taking a breath. But it was our home, so we feared nothing except Jackie and her constant drunken rages, which always caused her eyes to bulge out of the sockets like she had received shock therapy, all while screaming at us with spit flying out of her mouth. Most times that spit landed on us.

"I don't know." I plopped down on my bed and started to fold up the towels I had been able to wash and dry earlier. "Just chill for a minute. Jackie might bring something home." We called our mother by her first name, and she was cool with it. I chalked it up to maybe she knew she was a failure as a mother.

Penny sighed, rolled over, and sat up. "But I can't wait. I'm hungry now. I've been hungry for almost two hours. I want something to eat."

I rolled my eyes because I knew she was about to bug me until she got what she wanted. But she was ten; what else could I expect? "I'ma go in the kitchen and see what's in there." Throwing the towel I was folding on top of the bundle of clothes that still needed folding, I headed to the kitchen. I opened the refrigerator, and I was met with darkness. The bulb had gone out a month ago, and Jackie had still failed to replace it. Like I said, it was always the bullshit. My search proved what I already knew: There was next to nothing inside to eat. With not much choice, I grabbed the half-closed package of chopped ham and three eggs. Firing up the first front burner on the stove, I fried the meat and scrambled the eggs. By the time I was done cooking it all, my own stomach was growling.

"Penny, come eat," I yelled, as I fished out two plates and filled them with food.

Penny and I wasted no time devouring the food. Our plates were clean in record time. "Secret, I think that's the best piece of meat and eggs I ever had." Penny smiled.

"Ha, ha. You were just hungry."

"I was." She giggled. Just as I was prepared to giggle along with her, the doorknob started to jiggle and in walked Jackie. We both glanced at each other. Who knew if she was drunk or sober? The two brown grocery-like bags in her hands piqued our excitement, though. Penny stood without being asked and went over to assist with the bags.

Just as I was about to have hope that she was

sober, I noticed her steps were wobbly. Penny set the one bag she had grabbed out of Jackie's hand on the table. Pissed that she was drunk again, I walked over to the sink and started washing the plates we had used.

With my back turned to her, I could feel her closing in on me. I was not ready to deal with her madness. "Did you cook dinner?" She was now standing over my shoulder. Standing five foot nine, she was tall compared to me. Mixed with Italian and white, Jackie had once been beautiful. But the toll of drinking had dried that all up. The only beauty that existed about her was us, her two daughters, who were mixed with all her genetics but also our African-American father's.

"Yeah, we had some chopped ham and eggs." I was pleasant on the outside but boiling on the inside. I wanted to scream, *Why do you care?* But instead I chilled. Turning on my heel, I peeked into the bags she had just brought home. My eyeballs felt as if they would pop out of my head when I saw both bags contained cans of Budweiser and nothing more.

I turned to face her as she started to take off her run-down hot red high heels. I rolled my eyes at her with so much force my eyelids ached.

"Did y'all save me some?" she had the nerve to ask me.

I bit my tongue because I was too upset to talk. Sucking my teeth, I said, "It wasn't enough." She had some nerve. I wasn't surprised, though, because that was Jackie all the way, bold as fuck.

"I tried to do the wash but there was not enough laundry detergent. So only half of the dirty laundry is done." I kept my eyes glued to her, then eyed the bags on the table.

I could tell that had made her angry by the way she sucked in her bottom lip. "What the hell are you trying to say, Secret?" she yelled. "Watching my bags like you found a clue."

"That there is no detergent to wash the clothes." I looked at her, confused. What did she mean?

"You know what? You get the fuck on my nerves with that shit. Ain't never shit up in this raggedy motherfucker. Spend all of my damn money for this, fucking spend it for that. What the fuck am I supposed to do?" This time she screamed at the top of her lungs. I glanced at Penny and saw the fear on her face. "Shit, come at me with this bullshit as soon as I get in this damn house. I can't even sit down in peace and have a drink to calm my nerves. Hell, blame yourself ain't no detergent. You the one who used it all up. Same way you ate up all the damn food . . . Always cookin' and washin'. So just think of it this way. Until next time."

"I did not use it all up. I wash everyone's laundry with it. Not just mine." I gave her attitude on purpose. She was not about to blame me for this. Not that day. I refused. What I really wanted her to do was go to her room. I didn't need the drama or the aggravation. Bed was the best option for me, so I headed toward my room.

"Secret, girl, you better get yo high-yellow ass back here," she yelled to me. "Think you can talk shit to me in my house," she raved.

I turned around ready to match her with some truth. "We don't have food because you didn't buy any when you received our food stamps," I pointed out. I was no longer an eight-year-old kid. I knew what was going on.

Her eyes flashed bloodshot red. I had hit a nerve, and I knew what that meant. I almost tripped and fell as I turned to run. Jackie charged at me. What I didn't see was the high heel in her hand that landed in the center of my back. The pain was bad; it felt like I had been struck by a bolt of lightning, but I didn't stall because I knew from experience if she caught me it would be ten times worse. Inside my room I hurriedly shut the door and locked it behind me. And there was Penny on the floor, in a corner, crying her eyes out. I hated seeing her like this.

Out of breath, the hype of the moment left me drained. Dropping to my knees, I crawled over to Penny. Tears wet my face as I cried along with my sister. It took another ten minutes for the crazed constant knocking on the door Jackie had been doing to stop. I breathed a sigh of relief. But only for the time being. Like Jackie said earlier, *Until next time.*

Chapter 2

Isis

"It is the decision of this court that you be sentenced to ten years in prison." Every word that fell from the judge's big brown lips seemed to make a *boom* sound in my ears. The room seemed to grow larger and push me all the way to the back of it. My eardrums started to feel as if they were being ripped apart, the pain was so intense. My entire body seemed to be on fire. The only reason I had that would explain these unusual feelings was pure shock.

"Please, nooo!" I yelled at the top of my lungs. I jumped up and made a dash for my mother's side, swiping past the female officer who stood next to her. "Mama. You can't go," I screamed. "I need you." I reached for her, but her lawyer and another short, stocky police officer held me back. I kicked and yelped for dear life. How could this be happening?

"Let her go," I heard my mother yell. "I'm sooo sorry, baby," she apologized. But I could no longer see her as I felt myself being pulled backward out of the courtroom. "Take your fuckin' hands off her," I heard her yell one last time before I was completely out in the hallway. Onlookers gazed at me as I tried to fight my way back inside the courtroom.

"Listen, sweetie, you have got to calm down." A female officer approached and waved away the other two male officers who had been trying to block me from going back into the courtroom.

With my fist balled up I looked at her with all the hate I had inside of me. "Who the fuck are you?" I barked.

"I'm Officer Smith," she announced—as if I gave a fuck. There were cops in every direction I glanced. But she wanted to take it upon herself to think her name mattered to me. I would have laughed at her, but I was distraught.

Upset and feeling defeated, I looked at her and walked away. She tried to stop me, but I kept stepping until I was outside in the beaming Miami heat. With my head held to the sky, the sun threatened to blind me. Tears flooded my face; my chest heaved up and down with so much force I felt as if I could barely breathe.

I turned and looked at the door to the court and realized that my mother, Felicia, would not be coming out. This would be the first time she didn't leave the courthouse with me. After all these years of stealing, this was it. She had been stealing and taking me along with her since I was old enough to remember. My mother, Felicia Payne, was one of the baddest thieves Miami, Florida, had to offer. She boosted everything from clothes, shoes, jewelry, to even seventy-inch televisions. I don't mean off brand TVs, I'm talking about top-of-the-line electronics. A career thief is what she was, and honestly, she had only been caught a few times. Unfortunately for her, the times she did get caught it was high-dollar shit. This time the judge made his point. Here I was, fourteen years old, left without a mother. And I never knew my father; it had always been me and her.

Clueless and hopeless, I ran all the way to the bus stop, where I boarded the bus headed for home. Throwing myself on the couch, I cried long and hard until I felt as if I would throw up. My throat was on fire. Someone knocked on the door, and I was too weak to stand and answer. Praying they would go away, I lay as if I were lifeless on the couch and felt relieved when the knocking abruptly stopped, but suddenly it started back up again. I dragged my whole body to the door, and I snatched it open, ready to scream at whoever felt the need to continue banging on it. To my surprise, it was a chubby, middle-aged white lady with her hair swooped into a tired bun. She was accompanied by two white police officers with flushed red cheeks. The one on the left either had a slight limp or she missed a step when she walked, I wasn't sure which. But she had a scowl on her face to die for; I guess that was to scare me. If only she knew it would take more than that. If only she knew what I really wanted to do was laugh in her face. But it would take too much energy to do all that.

I eyed the cops from head to toe. I was used to them coming to the door looking for my mother, even though most of the time they didn't have enough evidence to take her to jail. "If you looking for Felicia, you can find her down at the county jail where she'll be for a while." I sucked my teeth and sniffed back a few tears. I tried to play tough and appear unfazed, but really I wanted to lie down in the floor and kick and scream for my mother.

The chubby lady turned and glanced at the police officers then slowly faced me again. Further investigation of her made me discover she had a lazy eye and a brown birthmark on her left forefinger. Growing impatient of their presence, I sighed.

"Isis Payne, my name is Cindy Martin." Confused as to how she knew my name, I gave her a suspicious look. She glared at me as if she were trying to see through me or something. Nothing was there for her to see, though, except hurt and pain. I hoped she saw a clean picture of it.

"How do you know my name?" I questioned, my arms now folded in defense mode.

"I'm with the division of Child Protective Services. And we are here to pick you up. We are going to place you in a safe home until your mom gets out."

"I don't need no safe place. I can stay right here. My mother paid the rent up for four years," I lied. Really it was paid up for three years. But she had figured if she went to prison, I could get a job and save up to start paying rent by the time it started being due again. Only neither of us ever believed she was actually going to prison.

A fake smile spread across Cindy Martin's face. "That was a good thing your mother did. Noble, even. But, Isis, you're only fourteen. And you can't live alone; there are laws against it, and according to the information we have, you have no family to claim you. So we have to take you with us." I looked at both of the cops. I could tell they were ready to handle me if I acted up. "Go and pack your things," she ordered as if she had won.

Feeling angry, scared, and helpless, I rolled my eyes at her and stomped my right foot before marching off to my room. The ride in the car was horrible; the tears would not stop falling. A few times Cindy glanced in my direction. I wanted to scream at her and call her a fat pie-eating bitch. But the fight was leaving me by the minute. Finally, we pulled up to a ranch-style brick house with a blue car in the driveway. Cindy shut off the ignition to her car. I sniffed and blinked back more tears that threatened to fall.

"Isis, this here is where we are going to place you for the time being. I know you think we are doing this out of meanness. But you'll see it's for your own good . . ." She paused. "This is a good pick for you." She nodded at the house. "Your foster mother is very nice. And don't worry, someone from the department will drop in often to check on you, until you are placed somewhere permanently."

She walked in front of me and rang the doorbell. A tall, skinny, brown-skinned, middle-aged woman opened the door. "You finally arrived. I've been expecting you for almost two hours." The lady smiled at us.

"Sorry about that, Martha; we are running a bit behind schedule," Cindy explained. I gripped the handle to my roller suitcase tighter. I didn't want to let that suitcase go; it was like my lifeline back to my mother.

"I figured as much."

"Isis, meet Martha Tate, your foster mother. You can call her Mrs. Tate." Ha! I didn't plan on calling her anything, because what they didn't know was I didn't plan on talking. I had nothing to talk about.

"Hi, Isis. Come on in and make yourself at home." Mrs. Tate reached out for me as if she was reaching for my hand. I look at her hand as if it were a bug I wanted to swat.

"Well, I better get going," Cindy announced. Mrs. Tate bid her goodbye. I didn't so much as glance in her direction. I hoped to never see her again. Mrs. Tate had gestured for me to come inside; this time she ushered me inside. Reluctantly, I put one foot in front of the other and stepped in.

I followed Mrs. Tate as she took me on a full tour of the house. It was simple but nice. There was a welcoming, homey feeling that I picked up on right away. She made my new room the last stop on the tour. The room was huge with a big walk-in closet.

"Well, Isis, it's lunch time. I think we should head down to the kitchen and grab something to eat. Just push your suitcase into your closet for later," she instructed. Back in the kitchen she reached inside the refrigerator and pulled out a tray of sandwiches. Placing the tray on the table, she scurried back over to the stove, where she pulled the lid off a piping hot pot, and started spooning what appeared to be tomato vegetable soup into a bowl. "This is going to be delicious," she said.

"I . . . I'm not hungry." I swallowed to rid my throat of the lumpy feeling. Then I quickly braced myself for what she might say next.

"Are you sure? My vegetable soup is award winning." She smiled, and this time I saw a very small chip in her front left tooth. It was small but noticeable. I looked away, not wanting to make full eye contact. I glared out of the kitchen window that looked out into her backyard. The yard was filled with beautiful flowers that were clearly tended daily, just as her front yard appeared to be. I wasn't used to that in the hood. Sure, people's yards were full of grass, but nothing special or cared for. In most cases, it needed to be mowed. "Come sit down and try a bit. You have had a trying day. And you need to keep up your strength." I watched her place a bowl with soup on the table, along with a plate, then she placed two sandwiches on it.

The sight of the food caused my stomach to growl. I hadn't eaten anything all morning, but there was no way I could eat. The lump that sat in my throat would not allow it. Placing one foot in front of the other, I made small strides to the table, where I sat down in front of the food and attempted to eat the soup. Mrs. Tate sat down across from me and ate. She attempted to make small talk but after asking me a few questions and receiving no response, she gave up.

Then suddenly that smile that had been on her face earlier reappeared. She stood and made her way over to the refrigerator, where she pulled out a cake. Walking over to me, she set it down on the table next to me. It read "Happy Birthday, Isis." My eyes scanned the cake in confusion. "It's for you. Happy birthday . . . Oh, I guess you're wondering how I know it's your birthday. Well, this morning when your file was delivered to me I instantly recognized today was your birthday. So I ran out right away and bought you a birthday cake."

Not knowing how to react to her seeming act of kindness, I sat there and glared at the cake as if it were a brick being offered to me. Turning my attention back to my plate, I pretended to eat again. Who was this stranger that thought she had the right to celebrate my birthday? She didn't even know me. Honestly, with all that was going on I had not thought about my birthday, except for when my mother had surprised me this morning with two brand-new pairs of Jordans and some clothes. Even then I didn't feel like celebrating, knowing we were on our way to the courthouse. And now here this woman was reminding me that I would be celebrating without my mom. Unable to hide my frustration I slammed my spoon down beside the bowl. Mrs. Tate took a seat beside me.

"Listen, Isis, I won't sit here and tell you that I know what you're going through. Because I don't . . . mean, I won't pretend I don't know all about heartache, because I've been living a mighty long time. So I do. But what I will say is that while you are here with me in my home, know that this is your home, too. And I'm going to treat you as such.

While you are here I'm going to treat as if you belong to me . . . I know I can't replace your mother . . . But if you need anything, just know that you can always come to me. The door is open."

This stranger was once again acting as if she knew me, trying to be nice when she didn't know anything about me. I turned to her. "You don't have to worry about me. I will stay out of your way. Because I don't need you or no one." Angry, I pushed my chair back and ran to the room I would be occupying. Throwing myself on top of the bed, I cried, kicked, and punched the mattress until I was worn out. Before long, I was asleep. Feeling as if I was being weighed down by something, I attempted to toss and turn but couldn't move. I heard myself screaming and squinted my eyes to see what was in front of me, but it was foggy. I opened my eyes to darkness and realized that I had been dreaming. A bright light came on and Mrs. Tate stepped into the room.

"It's okay, sweetheart, you were only dreaming." She rushed over and sat down on the bed next to me and placed her arm around my shoulder. The dream had terrified me; my heart was beating fast, even though I was awake and could see everything was okay. I was still shaken. With tears flooding my face, I sat up and placed both my arms around Mrs. Tate. She hugged me so tight. Instantly, I could feel the love. "Like I said earlier, I'm here for you, Isis." This time I believed her. Until I was placed with a permanent family, I was home.

Chapter 3
Secret

Four Years Later

The heat was not playing with me today. It was beaming down, beating the shit out of me. And after working an eight-hour shift at Taco World, I was not up for the fight. I smelled like straight tacos and sweat; it was enough to make anyone want to puke. It was days like this that I prayed for a car. The bus line was not working for me. It only took you so far, and you had to hike it the rest of the way. But what choice did I have? I had to work or Penny and I would be up shit creek without a paddle. Jackie couldn't give two fucks about Penny and me.

Stopping by Ike's snow cone stand, I ordered a large bubble gum flavored snow cone. I needed it. I had to eat it in record time, though, or the sun would melt it to piss. That cool feeling that the snow cone provided was refreshing, but it only lasted for a few more minutes before I was back in misery. I was just about to give up.

Screecchhhhh. I almost jumped outta my skin as a brand-new black Dodge Charger pulled up next to me. For just a brief second I closed my eyes. Drive-by shootings and robberies were known to happen in this neighborhood; I figured it was my turn. "Mane, what's up, Secret?" I opened my eyes as I recognized the voice.

"Kirk," I whispered, surprised. He was older and definitely looked different, but I would have known him anywhere. Kirk and I grew up together; he was my neighbor most of my life. But he had been gone off the grid for a minute. "Kirk, why the hell would you ride up on me like that?" I laughed.

"Shit, you were scared straight." He chuckled. "What the hell you doing out here in this damn Miami heat wave. You should know better. This ain't the tan you want."

"I know, right," I agreed. "Just got off work. Ain't got no car, so . . . It is what is. That bus life." I grinned. He knew what the bus was like; he had ridden it enough growing up.

He glanced at my shirt. "So you over at Taco World, huh?"

"Yep, trying to get this money, and Taco World serving it up, so I'm there."

"No doubt. That's called hustlin'. You do what you gotta do to make that dough. Nobody knows that better than me."

I nodded my head in agreement. "But what's up wit' you, nigga? Where you been hidin' at for a billion years? Comin' back like you George off the Jeffersons," I joked. I thought about the old television show; just by looking at him you could tell he had moved on up. Really, he had only been gone for about two years. But even that was too long. "And whose car you driving? Or stole?" I pried as I checked it out. Brand-new twenty-inch chrome rims. It was nice.

Kirk started laughing. "Stole. You got jokes. Nah, this all me right here," he assured me. He looked around the inside of the car like he was seeing it for the first time himself. "Yep, drove this bitch right off the showroom floor a few days ago." I couldn't believe it. I was definitely impressed and excited for him at the same time. Kirk had grown up just like me: with nothing. His mother had ten kids, and most of them had different daddies. I couldn't remember her ever having a job. All she ever did was stand in her doorway, smoke Newports, and curse. They lived straight off the county. Kirk used to come to school with holes in his pants. He ended up in so many fights at school defending his honor that he stopped coming. Then suddenly he was gone. But here he was back and in a major fucking way. I was wowed.

"Would you like a ride home?" he offered.

I almost screamed, *Hell yes*. But the pride in me said no; I hated being needy. Plus, I didn't want to mess up his nice new car. I smelled like tacos and sauce, and while I loved to eat Taco World food, I knew it could smell awful bad after you slaved in it for hours. But fuck that. I was not about to turn down a ride. Not today, it was too damn hot. "Dude, as hot as it is out here. And you gotta ask." I wasted no time walking around to the passenger side and climbing in. Letting his window up, Kirk pumped the AC right up. It felt so good as I leaned back in my seat. This was living. "I swear you have no idea how good that air feels. I thought I might die a few minutes ago when I was walkin'." I laughed, but I was serious.

"Yo, I remember those hot-ass walkin' days. You ain't gotta tell me." He chuckled. Kirk glanced at my Taco World cap lying in my lap. "Yo, what's up with you working at Taco World for real, though?"

"What you think? Who else gone feed Penny and me? I think you know the score on Jackie. Ain't shit changed over that way." I kept it real.

"Man, she still on that bullshit?" He seemed a little shocked.

The mention of her made me bitter all over again. "She still Jackie." My tone was full of sarcasm on purpose. Her name left a sour taste in my mouth. But I didn't want to talk about Jackie. She was the last person I wanted to discuss. It was bad enough I still had to live with her. I changed the subject. "So what's up with you and school? How you just gone leave like that after you made it so far? You could have at least stuck around for graduation; it was cool." It had been a few months since I had graduated, and no matter how hard the struggle was with my home life, I was proud that I had finished.

Kirk still had not answered my question. I glanced at him for a brief second. His eyes were focused on the streets, but the distant look they held told me he was thinking of something else. "You know I thought about graduation a few times. What it might feel like to walk across that stage." He paused. "But I had other stuff to do like chase this paper." He gripped the steering wheel.

"Yeah, I see, and it looks like you being successful at it." I glanced around his new Charger.

He looked at me and smiled. "So what's going on with your girl Isis? Y'all still best friends?"

"You know it." I grinned.

"I swear y'all was thick as thieves back in the day. Damn, Doublemint twins." He chuckled.

"And ain't shit changed. That's forever."

We were getting close to my house; I could see it from a distance. The ride was so comfortable I didn't want it to end.

"Aye, are you really happy with Taco World? I gotta know." He sounded as if something counted on it.

What was with him and my job? He kept jumping on the subject. "Yo, why are you trippin' off my work?"

He pulled in front our house and put the Charger in park. "Naw, I ain't trippin', just tryin' to see if you straight."

I gazed at our house, and the thought of going inside suddenly seemed overwhelming, but it was my reality. "Like I already said, it feeds Penny and me. And that's survival." I hoped that was enough to end his interest about my job. Because I was really tired of him asking.

"A'ight. Well, check this out, if you really want to get paid. Really get money and not just survive," he stressed. "You need to holla at me. Real talk."

"Holla at you?" I gave him my undivided attention. "You gone be my employer or something?" I giggled. "So what's the job?"

"Don't worry too much about that. Just know that when you are ready, I got you. All you have to do is say the word. We gotta hold each other down from the old neighborhood. Shit, Miami small so your circle need to be even smaller. Trust me, mine is, and niggas lining up to be me. I make dreams come true and fatten pockets."

I thought about his car and the nice clothes he wore. Could that be me? It all seemed too good to be true. *Yes, hook me up,* was on the tip of my tongue. Instead, "Nah, I'm good" is what came out of my mouth.

"A'ight. But take my number, and if you change your mind or even if you just need something, just hit me up, anytime."

"No doubt I'll hit you up, I promise. But I gotta go. Thanks for the ride." Reluctantly, I put my hand on the door and exited the luxury. I really wanted to fall back into the seat stake my claim and cry to never to come out.

The deeper I made it into our yard and the closer I got to our front door, the more I could hear Penny yelling. Her words were muffled so I couldn't exactly make out what she was saying. But I could tell she was arguing. I turned around to look behind me to find Kirk still sitting there. I guess he was making sure I made it inside. With a fake smile I waved him off. Finally he pulled away. I made a heavy sigh before opening the front door.

"I don't know what you're talking about. There ain't no money hidden anywhere in this house."

Penny's tone was shaken. It sounded as if she was in the kitchen. Without being certain, I made it my destination. I found Penny in the corner with Jackie standing directly in her face, yelling.

"Don't be tellin' me no fuckin' lies. That's all your ass ever do is cry and lie. And the shit is really getting on my last damn nerve." Terror was written all over Penny's face. Once again Jackie was being a bully.

"Jackie, get away from her. You ain't gotta be in her face like that," I yelled. She always took things too far. Her bullying was on ten.

"You don't tell me what to do, girl. This is my house," she replied without even looking at me. "Hiding money in my house and I want to know where!" she screamed.

"No, it's not true, ain't nobody hiding money from you," Penny cried. "I don't know what she talkin' about, Secret." I couldn't see Penny clearly, but I knew she was begging for my help.

"Just get out of her face, Jackie. Ain't nobody got any money up this house to hide from you, this is just crazy. Trust and believe if I had money we would be out this dump in no time."

"Secret, stay your narrow ass out of this and just shut your damn mouth. Because if I find that money, there is going to be hell to pay for the both of you. Now you take that and trust and believe," she threatened.

"Well, good luck on your search. Now move away from Penny!" I shouted. But Jackie didn't budge. I tried to reach around her to pull Penny out of her reach, but she blocked me. Frustrated, I tried to pull Jackie out of Penny's face; that's when I could tell her face was red on the left side. I knew then that Jackie had slapped her. Just like she had done time and time again. Rage took over. I was tired of the hitting. It had to stop.

I shoved Jackie so hard she stumbled back, almost falling over, but she threw her arms out sloppily and tried to catch her balance. I rushed over to her and put my finger in her face. "Why you put your fucking hands on Penny?" I demanded. "Huh? Why the fuck you have to hit her?" Penny grabbed both my arms from behind and start pulling me away. Now steady on her feet, Jackie quickly ran up on me.

"Who do you think you are, Secret? You think you tough now? Huh," she barked. "Don't you ever put your hands on me, girl! I will fuckin' end you." Spit flew out of her mouth and landed in midair. The smell of liquor poured from her skin. As usual, she was overly drunk; that was the backstory to her stupid-ass money hunt. She reached out and tried to push me down. I pushed her back in resistance.

"Stop, y'all. Please stop it," Penny screamed and cried at the same time. Jackie and I continued to tussle. I did everything in my power to keep from striking her. Finally, pushing her away from me, I ran over to check on Penny. She fell to the floor with grief. Looking at Penny's red, swollen face, I realized for the first time in my life I had had enough; this was it.

"Get up, Penny," I demanded as I stood up first, then reached for her trembling hand. I turned to Jackie. She was breathing so hard she was almost out of breath. "Penny and I are leaving. And I mean for good. This will be the last time you *ever* put your hands on either one of us again." I stared her down with disgust.

"Hah," Jackie laughed. "Leaving, where the hell do you think you going? Don't nobody else want you." I guessed that was some type of damage control. "Last time I checked didn't nobody do shit for either of you but me." For that lie I could have laughed.

"Come on, Penny, grab a few things." I decided not to respond to her; entertaining her would only be a waste of breath. Arguing and going back and forth with her only fueled her fire. Whenever she got that drink in her, only one of two things could happen. She could pass out, which was scary, because you didn't know if she was alive or dead. Or two, she could remain awake and wreak havoc on us. This was number two. So whenever she was passed out drunk, we took turns watching her just to be sure she was still breathing. After all, she was still our mother. But at this point I didn't feel anything toward her but hate and resentment.

"Go ahead and leave then!" she yelled from the hallway. "You'll be back. Who else gon' take care of your ungrateful asses?" While we were in the bedroom, each throwing things into a bag, she could still be heard rambling nonsense. "So go right ahead don't let the door hit you where the good Lord split you," she sang in her drunken tone.

Each of us with a bag in our hand, we stepped past her in the hallway where she was still sitting on one knee. But I paused for a minute and looked her in the eyes. There was something I needed to make clear. "Jackie, you have never taken care of us. And after today you won't have to." I nodded my head at Penny signaling her to follow me and we made our grand exit. It was now or never, us against the world. I was eighteen, which meant legally I was an adult. I had to take Penny up outta there before she ended up in foster care. Not once but twice had CPS been to our home because of Jackie's drinking and apparent abuse. Each time we were lucky they didn't take us. Not lucky that we got to stay with Jackie, but lucky that CPS hadn't dragged us off to the system and separated us. We had heard about it happening all the time. I feared the next time they came out it might be a wrap. They would take Penny. All we had was each other, and I could not let that happen. From now on, I was our guardian.

Chapter 4
Isis

"Are you okay? Because you look really tired." I noticed the exhausted look on Mrs. Tate's face as soon as I walked into the kitchen. She was sitting at the kitchen table having a cup of coffee.

With her right hand, she slowly rubbed her left shoulder. "I'm fine. Just a little tired. I baked all those cakes for the church last night, remember? That kept me up most of the night. I ain't no spring chicken no more." She gave a weak grin.

"I had forgot about that. Well, now you can get some rest. And tell Pastor Fist the next time he needs all those cakes to call Martha Stewart," I joked, opening the fridge to retrieve a bottle of water.

"I think I'll do just that," she cosigned. We both knew she would never do that; when it came to that church, Tree of Life, she would go above and beyond. Even if that meant overdoing it, there was no stopping her; never once had I heard her utter the word "no" to them. "What are you up to today?" she asked, then slowly sipped from her cup. I could see the steam rising from the coffee mug.

"Out to meet up with Secret to have our nails done. Can I use the car?" I don't know why it was taking me so long to cop a whip, but that would be my next move. It was a must: I had to have my own car. Besides, it would keep me out of hers.

"Of course. I'm done for the day. I don't want to be leaving the house again; this Miami traffic gets more vile by the day. Back in my day people drove as if to enjoy their automobiles. Now, everybody is just in a rush to be nowhere. Sometimes I consider hiring a driver." She gave me another feeble smile.

"I know. Everyone just seems to be full of road rage. Except me, though." I chuckled, knowing I was sometimes guilty of what she accused.

"You better behave." I noticed again that her smile was a bit weak.

"Can I get you anything before I head out?" I couldn't help but be concerned. I wasn't used to her sitting down. In the past four years since I had been placed with Mrs. Tate, she was always up, moving around nonstop, and full of chit chatter. At sixty years old, she had more energy than a thirty-year-old. I couldn't remember the last time I had actually witnessed her sit down to enjoy her coffee. Most days she drank it during the hustle and bustle of her daily household chores or doing errands for others.

"No, baby. I'm fine. Go on, and I'll see you at dinner tonight. We're having oven cooked pot roast and grilled cheese, so don't spoil it eating fast food," she warned me. I had a habit of picking up fast food whenever I was out and got hungry.

"I promise I won't." I smiled. In the hallway I seized the car keys from the key rack. I waited until I was half-way down the block before I turned up "I'm a Flirt" with R. Kelly, T-Pain, and T.I. Mrs. Tate always fussed about me playing loud music when driving; she said it was a distraction. And with that I did not agree, so I tried not to get caught. We only had one car, so when I was gone, she was home. The only way she could catch me would be if a friend or church member rolled up on me, or if I forgot to turn it down when I pulled up to the house. But I had trained myself to never forget, and so far I had been successful. Loud music was my vibe when I hit the block. I could not wait to meet up with my girl Secret. Secret and I were more like sisters than best friends. We grew up together. We lived directly across the street from each other until I was placed in foster care.

Our lives were somewhat similar, but different. While my mother was a habitual thief, she cared for me, loved me even. She made sure I had the things I needed to survive. Secret and her younger sister, Penny, on the other hand—their mother was a drunk who beat and neglected them all the time. It was my mom who provided Secret and Penny with clothes and shoes when she was free. She had also fed them when she could. But truth be told, both our households came with their share of trials and tribulations that I would not wish on my enemy.

Pulling into Pretty Nails, I found an empty parking space with no hassle, which most times was hard to do. I turned off the ignition and made my way inside. Observing the faces in the nail shop, I didn't see Secret anywhere. I pulled out my cell to dial her number, and just as I hit talk she strolled in with a smile spread across her lips.

"I was just about to give you the business. You know I hate to wait," I scolded her for slight revenge. Normally it was me running behind, but today was her day to get fussed at. I was enjoying every moment of it.

"Really, Isis? I swear you petty. I'm like a minute late." She glanced at the time on her cell phone. "Yep, you petty," she repeated with a grin. "But I ain't even tryin' to hear that."

Mae, one of the nail technicians, asked us what we were getting. We both replied, "A fill." She gestured for both of us to have seats. I sat at Mae's booth and Secret was right next to me with Sue. They were both good at what they did, which was a must. In the hood you could always find somewhere cheap to get your nails done. Unfortunately, the results were not always good. At Pretty Nails, though, they were on their shit, but they were always busy. You had to get in there early, like afternoons. So Secret and I made that our time to go whenever we shared a day off.

"So how is the new apartment going?" I was so thrilled for Secret and Penny. Recently they had moved away from their mother, Jackie, and into their own apartment.

Secret observed her nails as the technician removed the old polish. "Great. We're loving it. Who wouldn't love being away from Jackie? Shit, I would damn near sleep in a pothole on the street rather than live with her." She gave a light chuckle. But I knew she meant exactly what she had said. "It ain't Beverly Hills. But it's cool for us."

"That's all you guys need for now. You can look for another place when it's time. Right now stability and feeling safe is what's most important."

"Yeah, I know, and I have been working a bit of overtime to keep up with the few bills without being totally busted. But the shit is worth it, like I said; anything to be away from Jackie's messed up ass. Now I can leave the house and not have to worry about Penny at home being terrorized if Jackie gets into one of her bullshit drunken moods. That unnecessary shit was becoming helter skelter."

"No doubt. You know I know what's up," I added. Jackie was a trip. I had witnessed her on many occasions in action. She had even flipped on me a few times during the years. Only she had never hit me. However, I had ducked a few blows that were aimed at Secret.

"It's just so fucked up that she chose an alcohol bottle over us, her own kids." Secret shook her head side to side with disappointment. I knew that feeling. That's exactly how I felt about my mother, Felicia. She had chosen her life as a thief over me. But she claimed it was all in the name of her love for me. My response to myself for that was simple: *Fuck outta here.*

"How's Penny doing? I know she got that soft spot for Jackie. She ain't cryin' to go back yet?"

"She's good. I don't think she misses Jackie at all, but aye, I could be wrong. I will say the move has been good for her, though. Her grades are getting better. And she ain't mad all the time. I'm telling you I made the right choice, and I ain't never regretting that shit." That was one thing I hundred percent agreed with her about. "Living here with Jackie was do or die. It was time for us to sleep tight and breathe without sucking in heat. Some people take peace for granted. But from now on I'm going to cherish it. Penny ain't said so, but I'm sure she does, too."

"You definitely made the right choice. Something had to change and right away for both y'all sanity." Their home life was affecting Penny the most; being the youngest, she was still somewhat tied to Jackie. She allowed Jackie to play on her emotions, whereas Secret's guard was always up, so Jackie could never get close. "Is Jackie still calling you like a mad woman?"

"Hell, no. I guess she finally got the message since I wouldn't answer. Girl, she probably somewhere drunk, outta her mind right now. We're over here straight, though. She can do whatever she likes. All I ask is that she leave Penny and me alone."

"Shit is crazy. I feel you, though."

"So what's up with your birthday? Do you realize you about to be eighteen?" Secret was excited. I already knew what was on her mind. She loved to party.

"Yeah," I said calmly, with a slight smile. I was excited about my birthday, but with it being such a milestone, I felt as if something was missing. I just didn't want to say what I thought was missing, mainly because I didn't want to face it. So I ignored it and waited for the surprises that would surely come on my birthday. I didn't know what they were, but I knew they would come.

"Bitch, you don't seem happy at all. Ugh. What's up? Where the party gone be at?"

I laughed out loud; just as I thought, she had party on her mind. "For real, though, I ain't planned nothing. But I ain't worried. I'm sure you'll make sure I'm straight. People gon' swear it's yo birthday instead of mine."

"Damn right. Jell-O shots and more." Secret snapped her fingers for reassurance and couldn't stop beaming. Sue gently reached for her hand and placed it back under the gel light. "Wait, that's if Mrs. Tate lets you out the house. You know she think shit ain't safe. That lady don't trust nothing, I swear."

"I know, right." Mrs. Tate was real protective of me. Anyone would believe she was my biological mother. "But real talk, I think she's doing something for me. I don't know what, but I wouldn't be surprised if she tried to take me on a trip or something."

"Man, I swear that would be messed up. But I can't front, that's what's up? Well, just in that case, we need to celebrate tomorrow. I'm off work so I can throw a set at my crib. 'Cause we got to get it in."

"A'ight, I'm wit' that. Just as long as you invite that fine-ass Steven over."

"You still psyched off that black-ass nigga?"

"Shut up. Don't be callin' my future man names. It's disrespectful." I laughed.

"Real talk, I got you, though. He'll be there and that's a promise. Any other special request?"

"Nah, I'm good. Just make sure I enjoy myself and get some hot wings with carrots."

We sat and joked while Mae and Sue put the magic touch on our nails. Afterward, I decided to go home early and help Mrs. Tate with dinner. Originally, I had planned to do a little window shopping. But I figured I could help her with the grilled cheese, because she had really seemed tired when I left. I was so grateful to have her: she had kept her word when she told me all those years ago when I came to her that she would be there for me. I thanked God every day that no one had adopted me, because Mrs. Tate had been a lifesaver, and I could never thank her enough. To add to my delight was the fact that in two days I would turn eighteen, which meant I didn't have to ever worry about being adopted by another family. While she had not told me what she had planned, Mrs. Tate had made it clear that we were going to celebrate and in style. I would be thrilled to find out her surprise.

"I'm home," I announced as I dropped the keys to Mrs. Tate's Nissan Altima on one of the coffee tables in the living room, then headed to my room to take off my sandals. My feet were in the mood to feel something soft under them. I opened the top drawer on my dresser, which served as my sock drawer, and pulled out a pair of pink footies and slid them onto my feet one after the other. Wiggling my feet around the carpet, I suddenly realized Mrs. Tate had never responded when I announced I was home. That was a bit unusual; normally she'd be at my bedroom door before I was settled in good.

I also didn't smell any food cooking. Pushing

myself to my feet, I made my way to her room. I guessed she had decided to take a nap after all. But I also knew she would be upset if I didn't wake her up to cook dinner. "Mrs. Tate, it's time to get up," I said as soon as I opened the door to her bedroom. But her bed was empty. Walking farther into the room, I saw her bathroom door was open, and she didn't appear to be inside. I stood still for a moment. For some reason my heart skipped a beat. The kitchen became my destination as I walked fast.

I heard screaming, not realizing it was coming from my own mouth. There was Mrs. Tate laid out on the floor on her right side. I rushed to her. "Mrs. Tate, wake up," I cried, feeling helpless. Reaching in my back pocket, I pulled out my cell phone and dialed 911. "Please, please, send someone quick!"

Chapter 5

Isis

The previous four days had been surreal. I still could not wrap my mind around the fact that Mrs. Tate was gone. The doctors had said it was a heart attack. I couldn't help but believe if I had gotten home earlier, she would still be alive. She was still breathing when the ambulance arrived to pick her up. But by the time we arrived at the hospital, she was gone. The doctors announcing she was gone had sent pure shock through me. I fell to the floor and I couldn't stop screaming . . . I couldn't stop crying. I was a vegetable. It was so bad the doctors had to sedate me.

It wasn't until the next morning, once the medicine wore off, that they were able to get any information from me about Mrs. Tate. Even then I felt like a zombie. But I pulled myself together and called Secret so that she could catch a ride to the hospital and then drive me home in Mrs. Tate's car. There was no way I could drive. One look at the house, and I broke down all over again; the sight of Mrs. Tate lying helpless on the floor was all I could think of. Secret hugged me until I calmed down a bit. Inside the house I slowly walked into Mrs. Tate's room. It took everything in me to be strong as I looked for her cell phone. Scrolling through her contacts, I dialed her sister, Mona, and broke the news. It was awful.

That had been four days ago, and I was still in shock. My head didn't seem to be on straight. I thanked God when Mona finally arrived. She had jumped on the first flight headed from Baltimore straight to Miami. Mona was Mrs. Tate's one and only sibling, but they hardly saw each other because Mona was a workaholic. Just like Mrs. Tate, Mona was alone; she had been married but had divorced when she was young. They had one son, but he lived in Germany, and he only came home on holidays. So I felt bad for her, but I still needed her to be the strong one. I couldn't even get out of bed; the only thing I had been able to get down were fluids. As a result I had lost a few pounds. I was plain devastated. I couldn't understand why everyone I loved left me. First my mother, and now Mrs. Tate. With her gone I felt alone. The only person I had was Secret. She had been there for me as much as she could.

"Isis, it's not healthy for you to be in this bed this much. Even more, you have to eat something or you will get sick." Secret was worried about me.

"But I'm not hungry." I had my back to her with my hands under my head staring at the wall. I wanted my mind to be blank, but a million thoughts were running through it.

"Yeah, well, if you don't eat you're going to end up in a hospital bed; the doctor warned you already. Now is that what you want?" I wanted to answer her, but that required talking, and I really wasn't in the mood. I had said enough already. But I also knew Secret wouldn't give up until she got what she wanted. "You have to get up, Isis," she continued to beg. "You know today is the funeral . . . You have to get up. You don't want to be late for that." Her constant nagging was getting on my last nerve. Couldn't she see I just wanted to be left alone? I had already decided I couldn't go to the funeral. Trying to sleep was what I wanted, I mean needed, to do. I pulled the covers over my head praying this would drown Secret out. "Isis, come on now. I know you hurtin' . . . but . . ." She gently pulled the cover back. I'm really not sure when the tears fell but once the air hit my face I could instantly feel the wetness. Secret's eyes teared up as soon as she saw my face. Sitting down on the side of my bed, she bent down and hugged me. I cried on her shoulder. "Listen, you got to be strong. Mrs. Tate would want you there today . . . And I'll be there with you every step of the way; I promise you will not be alone." The tears continued to fall. I sat up.

"You're right." I threw the covers back and placed my feet on the floor. This was Mrs. Tate's day, and I could not let her down; she wouldn't expect any less of me. "I can do this . . . I will do this," I said with confidence, but really I was giving myself a pep talk.

It was extremely hard, but I made it the through the services in one piece. A piece of my heart was broken that I would never get back. But I tried to be strong.

Back at the house a few people came by to eat and pay their final respects. I wasn't in a sociable mood, so I stayed in my room. Secret joined me; she was determined not to leave me alone. We sat in silence; her just being there was enough. A knock on my bedroom door startled both of us. "Come in," Secret replied.

Mona walked into the room. The look on her face confirmed the way I felt: it had been a long day. She had been very strong, but I could tell it was weighing on her heavily. Although they didn't see each other very often, Mona and Mrs. Tate had been really close. "Well, everyone is gone . . ." She sighed with a hint of exhaustion and hunched her shoulders.

"I'm sorry I couldn't be out there. I just didn't feel like talkin' or hearing anyone say the word 'sorry,' " I admitted. I felt bad for leaving Mona alone to deal with the guests.

"It's fine, sweetheart," she assured me. "You've been through a lot." She attempted to massage her right shoulder with her left hand. "I wanted to come in here and just let you know that my sister loved you dearly, just as if you were her own. Every time she called me up you were the highlight of her conversation . . ." Tears started to slide down both Mona's cheeks. "And I'm just glad she got the chance to have you here with her. She always wanted children but couldn't have any. Guess you can say it just wasn't in the cards. That's the reason she went into fostering children. But you were the one child she became attached to. In fact, without you knowing, she had attempted to adopt you a few years back. And she would have been able to. But because of her heart condition she was turned down. Needless to say, she was devastated. It all worked out, though; God had other plans, and look, after all this time you were still with her." Mona smiled at me.

I couldn't believe my ears. I never had any idea that Mrs. Tate had tried to adopt me. However, it was what she said after that that really took me by surprise. "Wait, she had a heart condition? I never knew." That bit of information was really a surprise. How had she hidden that from me all those years?

Mona dropped her head for a brief second. Slowly raising it again, she looked at me. "I'm sorry, but she didn't want you to know. She never wanted you to worry. Her exact words were that you 'have been through enough.' "

Once again tears invaded my face. That sounded just like Mrs. Tate trying to protect me. She had been my guardian angel come to life. I would never forget her. "I loved her, too." I sobbed uncontrollably. "But I wish she would have shared it with me. Maybe I could have helped."

"You can't worry about that, sweetheart. So don't beat yourself up about it. Just know that she enjoyed the time she spent with you." Mona slowly wrapped her arms around me. I cried on her shoulder.

After she left the room, I decided I needed some fresh air. Secret agreed. The sun had gone down, so I prayed for a cool breeze. "I'm going to miss this neighborhood." I looked around at the tall trees and houses in plain view.

"Did Mrs. Tate leave the house to Mona? Does she plan to sell it? I'm sure she's not planning to uproot to Miami," Secret said.

"No, she's not moving to Miami. Her flight leaves tomorrow. As for this house, the bank has control. Mrs. Tate took out a second mortgage a few years back to get some house repairs done. So . . ."

"I see. So basically the house will go back to the bank," Secret answered as if what I said had just sunk in.

"Yeah. I don't know what I'm going to do." I couldn't believe I was really saying it. Here I was again faced with being alone. But this time I was eighteen, so whatever I decided would be my own choice. I found little comfort in that.

"What do you mean, what you're going to do? That's easy. You'll move in with Penny and me."

"Nah, I can't do that. Your place is too small, and I won't crowd you and Penny like that. It's not fair."

"Now, Isis, don't you start that shit. This is for the best. So don't even think about arguing with me. Because you will not win. This decision is final."

And boy, did I believe her. Secret was like a drill sergeant once her mind was made up. There was no changing it. I was tired, drained, and stressed. Therefore, I was not in the mood to be arguing. "A'ight, if you say so. But we need to get something larger. All three of us cannot stay in that one-bedroom icebox apartment."

"Oh, so you got jokes." Secret laughed. An unexpected chuckle escaped my throat.

"No, real talk, we need a place just a bit larger. We can't be walkin' all over each other. Besides, I can use the money Mrs. Tate left for me to make a down payment."

"She left you money?" Secret was astounded.

"Yep, a few thousand dollars." Secret's jaw dropped. Honestly, I was also in disbelief when Mona had told me when she arrived. I never had any idea Mrs. Tate had any money. It wasn't much, but fifteen thousand dollars could do a lot to help me out. I was grateful.

"Dang, Isis. She really did care for you."

"I know." I wiped a tear that slid quickly down my left cheek onto my shirt. "So that's settled." I sniffed. "We can start lookin' for a place tomorrow. Another new beginning." The tears and heartache caught in my throat. I turned on the balls of my feet to face the house. I couldn't believe the words as they left my mouth. Four years of my life in that house. And now it was all memories.

Chapter 6
Secret

Two Years Later

"Penny, get up," I said for the third time since I had entered her room. I knew she heard me. Every morning she played the same game. She would stay up late at night then feel brand-new when I tried to wake her up for school. But I knew how to get her up. "Penny!" I shouted. This time I yanked the covers off of her. That was a sure way to get her moving. She hated being cold, and we always turned the air to at least seventy at night, which meant the apartment was freezing by morning.

Only half sitting up for a brief second, Penny tossed her pillow at me. I dodged it. She swiftly flipped back over onto her stomach. "Get out, Secret, I know what time it is." The tone of her voice was muffled as she had her face down on the mattress.

"Girl, you better get your butt out of that bed before I drag you," I threatened, but I knew she didn't take me seriously.

"Ahhh," she grunted with annoyance.

"Come on, get up," I demanded. This time I grabbed her by both of her ankles and started pulling her toward the edge of the bed.

"Stop, Secret. I swear you annoying." She grabbed the fitted sheet on her bed, trying to hang on. I had to hold my breath to keep from laughing out loud.

"You better not be late for your first-period class. Or we gone have a conversation," I threatened again.

"I'm never late." She turned over and sat up. Gazing at me, she raised her right eyebrow. That look meant she would get me back. But I was not worried. She tried to reach for the covers at the foot of her bed. I snatched them out of her reach. "Ugh," she grunted.

"Ha ha, and you didn't think I'd know you would try that?" I taunted her for the fun of it.

This time she threw her legs over the bed, feet touching the floor. "I swear I can't wait until I graduate. I'm moving out. Then I won't have to worry about you torturing me in the morning."

"Don't be so sure. I make house calls. For free."

"Trust, you will not have a key." She dragged herself out of bed and over to her dresser drawer and started fishing out underwear.

"Oh, so that's how you livin'? Lockin' your big sis out."

"No, I'll be lockin' out all trespassers." She shut

the dresser drawer. "And you, my dear, will happen to be a trespasser." She smirked.

"Ha ha. You know you can't live without me. And stop being in a hurry to grow up. I'll miss my baby when you are grown." I grabbed hold of her and squeezed.

"Secret, get off. It's too early. Why don't you go back to sleep or something?" she whined.

"I swear you're such a grouch in the morning."

"Whatever, I'll be in the shower." Walking with her shoulders down, she sleep-walked to the bathroom.

"Hey, don't be in there long. Make it snappy," I reminded her. Once I had found her asleep on the toilet. The girl truly was not a morning person.

Next up, I banged on Isis's bedroom door. She was another one who was hard to get out of bed first thing in the morning. But I enjoyed dragging both of them out of bed. I was just glad we were all together. Since Mrs. Tate had passed, we had found a three-bedroom apartment so that we could each at least have our own bedroom. We were still in the hood, but it wasn't all bad. Besides, it was the environment that we grew up in, so we were accustomed to it. Although we didn't discuss it, deep down, we all craved better. But this is where we were. And honestly, there were a lot of reasons we couldn't complain.

"Secret, get away from that door. I'm up," Isis shouted.

"Are you sure?" I chuckled.

Now that I had woken everyone up, I went back into my room and got myself dressed. By the time I was done, Penny was coming out of her room, ready to go. We left out the house at the same time, her to get on the school bus and me to catch the city bus to my second job at Chic Clothing, a cheap knock-off clothing store in the neighborhood. I had been working there for the past year while still holding down my job at Taco World. As soon as I opened the double doors of Chic Clothing my stomach turned. I hated it. My coworkers, for the most part, were ghetto, trifling, lazy-ass bitches. Not that I was top employee, but it was some shit I felt could be avoided. And that was working hard and not smart. It seemed no one ever did their fucking job on their shift, which meant it was left for the next shift. I was not having that because I didn't believe in doing anybody else's work.

As soon as I started strolling down the aisle toward the back of the store, it was clear to me that the night shift hadn't done a thing but go home. I'm talking about shit everywhere. There were more blouses on the floor than on the racks. To make matters worse, the first person I saw standing by the time clock was Tasha, one of the most ghetto, ninety-nine-cent, purple, blue, raggedy braids, and extremely lazy hos you ever want to meet. I could not stand her ass. Period. And she knew it, so she didn't like me either. But that I could give zero fucks about.

"Hmmm, it's nine-twenty," Tasha let slide off her big pink lips. I hated her lips; they looked like they had been burned then painted with pink lipstick. Ugh.

"I guess if I needed to know what time it was, that would help," I said and kept walking.

"I guess Ms. Girlie got an attitude this morning," she said. "It ain't no need to have no attitude with me. I was only pointin' out you late." My head almost jumped off my neck. This girl had the nerve to be checking me on my time.

"First off, Tasha,"—I allowed her name to roll of my tongue as if it tasted nasty—"I don't need you to clock my time for me. I got that, boo." I rolled my eyes. "Second, why should it matter if I'm late? It ain't like the people that's on time do shit." I pointed toward the messy aisles. I wanted to be clear I was talking about her. It had been her and her other lazy night crew people who had left the floors that way. "So maybe before the next time you decide to check my time, you could be checking those damn aisles first. You are a lead, right?" Again I rolled my eyes and switched away with so much force I wished she blew down. I almost called her a bitch but I chilled.

Work seemed to drag by, but as soon as it was over I jetted out of the building, hopped on the bus, and headed home. All I craved was a blunt and some peace. Unlocking the front door, I was a bit taken aback when I found Penny and her so-called boyfriend, Dwayne, sitting on the living room couch. They had recently declared they were in a relationship. But I still wasn't sure I was agreeable with that. I understood that Penny was seventeen, but I wasn't sure if I was ready for her to date yet.

"Hi." I gave him emotionless eye contact.

"Hey," he responded. He seemed a bit nervous.

"What's up, Secret?" Penny chimed, a huge smile on her face.

"Can you come here for a minute, Penny?" Her eyebrows raised. "It'll only take a minute," I added. She knew I was about to start nagging. She told Dwayne she'd be right back, then followed me into my room and shut the door behind her. I had to count to ten so that I didn't yell at her. Slowly I turned around to face her. "Why is he here?" I asked.

"I invited him over. Remember, I told you I was going to and you said it was cool."

"When I'm home is what we agreed."

"I know that. But Isis got here before you. So I told him to come on over."

I took a breather for a minute. I had assumed they were there alone. "Where is Isis?"

"In her room." Her tone told me she was annoyed. "Look, Secret, you have got to stop treating me like a baby." Before I could open my mouth, she turned and stormed out of my room.

I walked down the hallway and tapped on Isis's closed bedroom door. "Come in."

"What are you doing home so early?" I asked, then bounced down her bed.

"They cuttin' hours again." Isis sounded annoyed.

"These jobs are full of shit," I replied.

"So what's up?" Isis put down the book she was reading.

"I think I just pissed Penny off." I beat around the bush. I had definitely pissed her off.

"What happened? What did you do? She was just fine a minute ago when I saw her."

"Well, I kinda wanted to know why Dwayne was

here." I hunched my shoulders as if I was innocent.

"Wait, why trippin'. She told me she was callin' him to come over. You know she don't be doin' no crazy stuff."

"I know but . . . I don't know." I hunched my shoulders nonchalantly. "She growing up too fast, Isis. She about to graduate soon, and I just don't want her to mess up. Getting all serious in a relationship could throw shit off track. You know how it is," I stressed. I really was hoping Isis would agree with me.

"And I feel you. You know I do. But Penny's a good kid for her age, especially growing up in this crazy-ass neighborhood. You gotta let her grow up, Secret."

"Whatever." I stood up, annoyed. "I'm about to roll up. You in?" A blunt would rationalize all this for me. But deep down I knew she was right.

"And you know this." Isis grinned.

Chapter 7

Isis

"Dang, baby, you enjoying that burger, right?" Bobbi, my boyfriend, laughed as he took a napkin and wiped at the mess on my right cheek that the burger I was devouring made. What can I say? The burger was the bomb. It had just the right amount of grease to make it tasty.

With my mouth full and chewing at the same time, I giggled then replied. "Yes, babe, it is so delicious." Top Burgers was one of the best in Miami. We ate burgers from here often. They had the sloppiest, greasiest burger on planet earth. And I think it was fair to say I was addicted. Bobbi said if I kept eating them so much, my thighs were going to spread.

"Next time we gon' have to get you a salad or some. I got to help you watch your figure," he joked.

"Boy, don't even try it. I promise you'll be in the doghouse until you beg and grovel." This time I opened my mouth wide and took another huge bite out of my burger.

"Damn, you look sexy when you do that. Come on, let me bite it." Bobbi leaned over the table like he was trying to bite my burger.

"Babe, you always trying to eat my food. Eat your own burger," I whined.

"A'ight. Treat your man like that." He chuckled, sitting back down. Bobbi and I meshed together like glue and paper. I had met him two years ago; he was working on his friend's car in the parking lot of the new apartments we had just moved into. I soon found out that he was a known mechanic in the area. He fixed cars, motorcycles—name it, he fixed it. He really had gifted hands. Even though I thought he was cute as ever, I had turned him down twice when he asked me out on a date. He was in our apartment parking lot so much fixing his friend's car I was beginning to think he was breaking it just so he could fix it. Finally, he showed up at our door with flowers, and I gave in. A couple dates later my panties fell off. We were inseparable.

"Babe, so how much longer do you think it'll be before we can find our new place?" I sipped my strawberry milk shake and savored its creamy goodness.

"Hopefully soon. I'm ready as hell to get off Melvin's couch. Shit fuckin' wit' my organs." Melvin was his cousin. They had been living together for the past three years, because for a while Bobbi couldn't find steady work as a mechanic. But a year ago he had finally landed a job at a mechanic shop. It offered good pay, full-time hours, and benefits. And things had been going good for us. For the past six months we both had been working really hard and saving our coins so that we could get our own place. I couldn't wait to move in with my man and wake up to him every morning.

"Wait, he ain't got bedbugs, does he?" I questioned, suddenly worried. I spent a lot of time over there myself, and the last thing I needed was to take home bedbugs, or any bug.

Bobbi's eyeballs bugged. "Hell, naw, he don't have bedbugs. Shi'd, he better not have any." He didn't sound so sure. "I'ma fuck him up he if he do. 'Cause he ain't told me 'bout it." He got hyped, his voice booming. A few people glanced in our direction. I was embarrassed.

"Keep your voice down, babe," I whispered to him.

"My bad." He glanced around then leaned in a little closer. "I done told him about them ratchet, two-dollar hos he be bringing home, though. Ever since the last time I snapped he chilled, though. Remember I told you about the girl who had roaches crawling out of her purse? That shit pissed me off; I put her ass out my damn self. Fuck out here with that. Nigga act like he don't know no decent females."

Bobbi was getting angry just talking about it. I laughed so hard I had to cover my mouth to keep my milk shake from spewing out. "Yep," I said. But I knew firsthand he was telling the truth. "Remember the girl with the big brown greenish looking stain in her drawers?" I reminisced. The girl had decided she wanted to take a shower; apparently she forgot her underwear in the bathroom. I went in to use the bathroom, and there were her stained panties laid open for the world to see. I nearly threw up in my mouth. From that point on I stopped using the bathroom over there. It was just recently I felt safe using it again.

"That was some repugnant shit." Bobbi chuckled.

"Let's go." I laughed. "I can't be late for work." I loved spending time with Bobbi; we always had a good time. He kept a smile on my face, and I loved him even more for that.

Pulling up to the mall, I kissed Bobbi goodbye before climbing out of his 2001 Cutlass Supreme. I always joked with him, calling it his mac daddy ride. Working at JCPenney wasn't exactly my dream job, but for the most part I received full-time hours and it paid the bills. Watching Bobbi pull off, I realized I'd much rather be spending my time with him. I wasn't crazy, though; I knew staring in my man's face all day didn't make money, so I ditched that fantasy quickly. With my Top Burger cup in hand still half filled with strawberry milk shake, I strolled inside the crowded mall, optimistic and ready to start and finish my shift.

The very next morning I rolled out of bed still tired from my eight-hour shift the day before. But I was on a mission: I was going down to the prison to visit with Felicia. After all these years, I still hated making this trip; for one, it was long, and two, I was never in the mood. The bars, the whole atmosphere was depressing, and I hated taking

that feeling back out into the real world with me.
The only reason I still went was because I knew it
was necessary. For all the resentment that I held
toward her, she was my mother, and I could not
leave her in there alone. I was all she had. It had
been six months since the last time I had gone, so
I knew it was time.

A cab delivered me to Hertz rent-a-car, where I
rented a car for the day. At the prison I checked in
and went through all the grueling checkpoints in
order to complete my visit. The rude-ass guards
with their comments were the worse part. Especially the women: every single one of them was on
a power trip for toughness. It annoyed the shit out
of me, but I was always able to keep my cool. After
being led to the visiting room, I took my seat and
waited. The scenery was old and redundant. I wondered if Felicia would come out with her usual
smile; as usual I wouldn't be able to return that
smile because of my bottled-up anger.

Over the years I had tried so hard to shake the
hostility I held against her, but every time I entered the facility the anger hopped on me like flies
to shit. I couldn't help but think she was in there
for her own selfish reasons. All I could reflect on
was how she had chosen material things over me.
How was I supposed to forget that? How could I
overlook the fact that she was the cause of our sep-
aration, of me having to drive hours to sit and talk
to her in a room full of strangers?

Observing the room, I saw kids who were much
younger than me hugging their incarcerated moth-
ers. My heart broke for them. I was a grown woman
and couldn't understand my mother being locked

away. I couldn't even imagine how those small children could. I glanced up at the clock; five minutes had passed, and still my mom had not appeared. I wondered if something was up. Normally she was out no sooner than I could take a seat.

"Hey, baby." She appeared just as I was about to ask the guard if something was up.

"Finally," I said with a sigh. "I was beginning to think you weren't coming."

"I'm sorry, a girl on my block was busted with contraband. So the guards held us up for strip search," she explained. "But I don't even know why they put us through that shit. It's the shady-ass guard that's bringing her that shit up in here. Ugh, I get so sick of this place." She sighed and looked around the room. I almost replied, but I knew it wouldn't be good so I kept quiet. "Sooo . . . how have you been? It's been a minute since you've been up."

"I come up when I can," I clarified right off the bat. It always pissed me off when she slick questioned me about my visits. As if my life revolved around visitation. "I've been working a lot of overtime lately," I said, but this time more calmly.

"It's okay, I understand. You don't have to explain. I get that you have other pressing issues. I just missed you."

"I'm not explaining, just stating the facts."

A smile was spread about her lips, but I could see I had hurt her feelings. "How are Secret and Penny?"

"They are cool. Penny's about to graduate soon, and Secret's still working. Same ol' stuff."

"Wow, I can't believe Penny is about to graduate

high school. My, my, has time flown." She shook
her head and held a distant look in her eyes. I assumed she was thinking about when we were all little kids.

"Yep," was my dry reply. Sometimes I believed
she thought the whole world was supposed to
have stopped when she went to prison. And it in-
furiated me.

"And how is Bobbi? It's been a while since you
brought him down with you. Are you two still together?"

That last part of the question annoyed me. She
knew we were still together; to ask was just plain
stupid and a waste of our visitation. And she knew
exactly why he didn't come: she hated him and it
showed, that's why he had stopped coming, so her
pretending to care was fake. "Yeah, Felicia, we're
still together. We've been saving, and soon we are
moving in together. So no, your dream has not
come true." I was sarcastic on purpose. I knew she
hated when I called her Felicia. But a year after she
had been locked up I realized a mother wouldn't
choose materialistic things over her own daughter.
So why honor her with that privilege? Felicia it was.
The grave look on her face told me that it broke a
piece of heart every time I called her that.

She looked down for a brief second then back at
me, her eyebrows raised. "I get that you care about
each other." That was her way of downplaying our
relationship. "But why do you have to move in together, Isis?" She was clearly not happy about the
news. "What's the rush?"

"What do you mean, why? What's the big problem with that? We love one another. Shouldn't that be enough?"

Again she looked away from me, and I knew she was trying to choose her words carefully. The last thing she wanted to do was piss me off and have me cut the visit short. I had cut the visit short on more than one occasion and wouldn't hesitate to do it again. "I'm just concerned about your future. That's it . . . You still have college to think about. It's been two years now since you have been out of school."

Here we were back on the college conversation again. "Well, college sounds nice, but I have real life to deal with." My tone was full of aggravation. "Besides that, I'm a foster kid, remember? We don't have it easy when it comes to all that paperwork. And just maybe if you hadn't been locked up in this hellhole. Maybe then I could have focused on college." The anger and hostility I was feeling reared its ugly head without refute.

Without any indication, she slammed the palm of her right hand on the table. "That's not an excuse." She finally got angry and raised her voice at me, and I could tell she instantly regretted it. I could feel all the eyes in the room on us. The two guards in the room gave us cold stares. "Wait, I'm sorry . . . I didn't mean to . . ." She tried to apologize, but the bells rang, prompting us that the visit was up.

With no words I just stared at her. I couldn't believe she had found the nerve to yell at me. It had been years since she had shown any anger when talking to me. Standing up, I turned and walked away without even a goodbye. She tried calling my name, but I kept stepping. I sped up my pace, not wanting her to see the tears traveling down my cheeks. But what I really wanted to do was turn around and throw myself into her arms. I missed her so much. But the contempt I held in my heart for her trumped all that. I didn't know if I would ever get over it.

Chapter 8

Secret

"That'll be twelve-ninety-six," I replied to the middle-aged lady who had just ordered three Mexican Bean Salsa Burritos. From the look of her she weighed easily three hundred pounds, so the last thing she needed were those burritos. But who was I tell her what to eat? I just worked here. She handed me a twenty, and I cashed her ticket out. "Your order will be up in just a few minutes," I said as I placed the change back in her waiting stubby right hand.

I fixed her diet drink as I waited for her order to come up. "Here you go, ma'am." I handed her her food and drink. "Thanks for coming to Taco World, come again." I smiled. For her sake I hoped she didn't take my advice. She should avoid Taco World and all other fast foods at all cost.

I was on my way to check the lobby when I saw Kirk march in like he was a boss. I couldn't believe it. "What's up, ma?" he said.

"You know me. Gettin' this money." I chuckled. I was glad to see him; he still looked as good as when I ran into him a few years back. Hell, not that that was even possible.

"I think you said that last time." He laughed. "But what's been up witcha? I thought you was gon' hit me up? My number ain't changed."

If only he knew things had become so crazy. Penny and I had moved out on our own. I had forgotten all about that. But I didn't even want to get into all that right now. I decided the best thing to do was to play it off. "Man, look, I been busy making these damn tacos." I gave him a fake laugh, hoping to ease out of that tight situation. It worked, because he laughed along with me. "What's your order? You and I both know that no one can come up in Taco World and not order tacos." And that was real.

"Yeah, no doubt." He smiled then ordered six steak tacos with the works. "Step over here for a second." He pointed toward the lobby. "Let me holla at you for a quick minute." We were over-staffed in the kitchen so his tacos came up fast. I handed him the bag before stepping around the counter.

"What's up?" I asked as we walked over toward a vacant table.

"Listen, no disrespect. But it's time for you to give up this petty money and get paid." He wasted no time cutting to the chase.

"Get paid how?" I asked.

"This ain't the place for that conversation. Just get at me. I promise I got you. But bet it's time you get up outta here. I ain't tryin' to knock your hustle, but this shit is wack." He looked around the restaurant. "Plus this shit is in the hood, so I know you be puttin' up with some rude motherfuckers."

"Damn now, that's real." I had to agree. "Just yesterday I had a chick come in here and call me a ho, because she thought her man was lookin' at my ass while I bagged their order. I swear on everything, Kirk, I was about to beat that bitch down and go to county. But two of my coworkers dragged me to the back."

"See, I already know. Here." He handed me a small piece of paper with a number on it. "That's my cell. Hit me up when you ready to boss up." With that he was out. I slowly walked back around the counter to my normal spot, all the while thinking about what Kirk had just said. And how good he seemed to be still doing.

"Girl, who was that? Was that nigga tryin' to holla?" Teresa from the kitchen interrupted my thoughts. I glanced up at her as she leaned over my shoulder, still gawking at the door Kirk had exited. She was cool, but I swear she was a ho.

I couldn't help but giggle at her question. "Hell, naw, he ain't tryin' to holla. That was my boy Kirk from back in the day. He like a brother to me."

"Hmmm, well, he fine as hell. I could barely make his tacos for checking him out. Shi'd, you need to hook a bitch up."

"Teresa, get yo ass back in the kitchen and stop being so thirsty. All that hot begging you doing," I chastised her. She was the last chick Kirk would

want to hook up with. Teresa already had three different baby daddies, and just thought she was
pregnant two weeks ago. I couldn't even take her
seriously.

"I just got this shit from the drive-through, and
it's all wrong." A young black girl came through
the doors all of a sudden, yelling and rolling her
eyes, with a Taco World bag in hand. I couldn't do
anything but sigh. Kirk and I had just talked about
this same mess.

Teresa made a beeline for the kitchen. I politely
reached for the bag. "I'll take a look."

"Take a look?" she screamed at me like she was
appalled. "Fuck that, y'all need to fix this shit over.
Asap." Megan, the girl from the drive-through who
took her order, eased closer to the drive-through
window as if she was trying to hide. I sighed. "Every
time I come to this motherfucker, you underpaid
bitches always fucking up my order. Bitches can't
do nothin' right." She continued to be disrespectful.

Unable to contain myself any longer, I jumped
over the counter and put my finger in her face and
demanded her to call me another bitch. Next thing
I know Megan, Teresa, and Sam, the night manager, were pulling me to the back of the restaurant.
It took a minute for me to calm down, but when I
did I clocked out. Fuck hours, they didn't pay me
enough for that bullshit.

As soon as I got home, the first thing I did was
jump in the shower. No one was home and nothing was on television, so I kicked my feet up on the
love seat. Reaching into my purse to pull out my
cell phone, I grabbed hold of the small piece of

paper with Kirk's number on it. Putting the number in my contacts, I contemplated taking him up on his offer. But I couldn't help wondering what it was. What was it that he could possibly turn me on to? I smiled to myself as I replayed in my head him calling Taco World "wack." And he damn sure was right. Low pay and disrespectful-ass customers didn't mix. I was up to my heels sick of the bullshit.

Reaching for my purse once more, I extended my hand inside and grabbed the swisher sweet I had picked up on the way home. Making a quick trip to my room, I lifted the mattress and pulled out that fire. Rubbing the plastic bag filled with the green substance brought me life. Back in the living room, I wasted no time cleaning out my swisher. I couldn't wait to inhale and exhale. Just as I licked and rolled the finishing touches, Isis strolled through the door looking exhausted.

"Damn, you must have read my mind," Isis boasted, throwing herself down on the couch across from me. "It has been a long day. Please hurry up with that and pass it to me." She referred to the blunt.

"Just hang tight, I got you." I smiled. Reaching for the lighter next to the ashtray on the coffee table, I lit it up. "You do the honors." I passed the blunt to Isis.

Wasting no time, she placed it between her lips, inhaled, and blew out. "That's what I'm talkin' about." Isis coughed a little bit and passed it back to me. "I so needed that."

One puff and I started to relax immediately. "I quit Taco World today." I released. "Well, I didn't officially tell them yet. I just kinda clocked out and left. But I made up my mind, I'm done with that bullshit."

"Ahh, hell, what happened?" Isis went in for her second round.

"Another bitch tried me up in there today. And I'm tellin' you if I don't get outta there I'm gone beat a bitch down for real, I swear. I just can't do it anymore."

"I feel you. You gotta do what you gotta do. I don't need that call from county talkin' 'bout come get you. Besides, you can't be havin' these ghetto hos costin' you money; that's where you gotta draw the line."

"And that's real." I chuckled. For the next couple of hours we sat and chatted and got fucked up. One blunt turned into two, and before we knew it we done ate up all the snacks in the kitchen. We were both laughing so hard by the time Penny came home she called us crazy and bid us a good night. The laughter turned out to be exactly what I needed while I juggled decisions around in my head.

A few days passed, and Kirk's offer kept clouding my mind and holding my concentration hostage. For some reason I felt as if I just needed to know more about what he meant. They say curiosity killed the cat. Well, my curiosity was nagging the hell out of me. That's what ultimately led me to make the call to Kirk. We agreed to meet up when I took my lunch break at Chic.

I ended up taking my break a few minutes later than expected because the store had gotten busy. But as soon as the rush slowed down, I exited the store and mobbed two doors down to Subway, where Kirk and I had agreed to meet. He seemed to be texting when I approached the table.

"What's up?" I said while pulling out my chair.

"Grinding," he replied, looking up from his phone. "I see you came through; for a minute I thought you had chickened out on me," he joked.

"Ha ha. No chicken here, never. The store just got busy. But I'm here like I said I would be. So what's good?"

"I got this work for you. All you gotta do is be ready when I call you."

"You keep talkin' about work, but you still ain't said what it is. So be ready means what exactly?" Kirk was my boy, but I was becoming a bit annoyed with him. Why couldn't he just tell me what the job was already?

"Private dancing," he blurted out. That cleared up a few things for me quickly. Like his hesitation to tell me what the job was.

"A stripper," I said, surprised.

"Nah, not a stripper. A private dancer for exclusive parties, or should I say gentlemen. All you have to do is show up, dance, and leave. Simple as that."

I was still a bit shocked; not once in a million years did I think that was what he had in mind. I never could have guessed. "I don't know about that, Kirk. Dancing at parties." I hunched my shoulders. I know he tried to clarify private dancing as not being a stripper, but at this point I wasn't sure what the difference was. "It just don't seem like nothin' I would do." I had to be honest. I considered myself to be bold, but I didn't know if I was that bold.

"Listen, it's safe. I set the whole thing up. Everything goes through me so you have nothin' to worry about. And the money good, you'll make more in one night than you'll make in one week at fuckin' Chic." He waved my job off like it was nothing but a name. "I can promise you that."

The money part had my attention, but I just wasn't comfortable with dancing for anyone. At least not when all attention would be directed at me. "What's in it for you?" I had to ask. Him setting everything up sounded like he was the employer. But in the world we lived in, not even an old friend from the neighborhood hooked you up for nothing. Strings were always attached.

"Just the standard fifteen percent." And that was the string. Kirk was trying to get paid. But I couldn't blame him; he had to make a living, too. However, I was still a bit perplexed by the offer. I wanted to make money, but I equally wanted to feel comfortable and safe. I had to think about it. Kirk was eyeing me hard; it was evident he wanted immediate answers. "What you think?"

"The money sounds enticing, but I don't know, Kirk. I ain't sure if this is the road I want to travel."

"Aye, I know this different for you. But look at this way, it's about the hustle, the grind. Simply getting paid," he stressed. "I'm tryin' to see you straight with your pockets laced. Trust I got you." He was dead serious and I knew it.

"You always been real, Kirk, and I appreciate that." I really didn't know what else to say. But my lunch break was just about over, and I had to get back to work. "Yo, time is about up. I gotta get back to work. Thanks for coming through."

"No doubt, anytime. I'ma get back on this hustle."

I walked back over to Chic in a fog; my mind was clouded with all types of thoughts. But one thing I was almost sure of was that I couldn't be a private dancer. The last thing I wanted was some turnt-up asshole too close to me. Not to mention I could be so mean at times no guy would buy that I was seductive. Back in front of Chic I reached out to pull open the entrance door; at that exact moment my mind was made up. There was no way I could do it. I just wouldn't be good at it.

After clocking back in, I tried to jump right back to my routine, but for some reason I couldn't seem to get it together. The entire store seemed to be a complete mess. I had only been gone to lunch for an hour and shit was everywhere, as usual. For the life of me I didn't understand why people went crazy over all this knock-off shit. Rock A Wear at that. That shit had been played out. Broke as I was, I could not afford any name brand at all and I still didn't rock this shit. I preferred to stick to places like Charlotte Russe, where labels were nonexistent. But I'd be damned if I wore fake name brands. Especially if I had to shop in pure chaos to get it.

As usual the lazy bitches at my job never did shit. Since I had been back from lunch I had picked up at least five pair of pants off the floor and placed them back on a half-empty rack. Then there was the fake-ass US Polo crap spread about the store, and it just seemed as if no one was picking the shit up but me. Everyone else seemed to be running around chatting, laughing, and chewing fucking gum. The last straw was a blue knock-off Polo shirt that damn near got tangled around my leg and threatened to trip me.

"Fuck this bullshit," I said to no one in particular, holding a pile of fake US Polo t-shirts in my hand and two pairs of shorts. I dumped it all on the floor into a pile with so much force my shoulder hurt. With fast strides and full of anger, I marched straight toward the time clock and clocked out. This was for the fucking birds, and I was done. In that split second my mind had changed. It was time for me to get money by any means necessary. Private dance, slide down the pole, or drop that ass in a baller's lap, this dead-end Chic with fake labels was over for me. This was not going to be my life. I was meant for better.

"And just where do you think you're going? You just got back from lunch and yo shift ain't over for another three hours." Tasha appeared from behind a rack of body dresses like the serpent she was. I wasn't surprised, though; her ass was always somewhere lurking and not doing shit. I think that was a part of her job description. I was over her, though, too.

"Not that it's any of your fuckin' nosy-ass business, I'm going home. It's time for me to roll up." I kept walking toward the entrance with an added swish to my walk.

To my revelation she chuckled. "And who do you think is gon' finish your shift?" she added a little bass to her voice.

That was enough to make me want to chuckle out loud. But I was sick of her damn mouth. She never got tired of being a mean, nasty bitch. I hated her ass. Turning on my heels, I planted the meanest scowl on my face I could muster. "Bitch, I really don't give a fuck. I mean, does it look like I give a fuck? Shit, how about you do it? Lazy, trifling ass." I rolled my eyes. With that I was out. Her jaw dropped to her chin. For the first time ever, she was at a loss for words. Stepping outside the store, I saw the sun setting behind the clouds and I realized I was free of the bull. I prayed to never see Tasha's lazy, sloppy ass again.

Chapter 9

Isis

"I love this part." I laughed so hard my stomach hurt. I was chilling at Bobbi's crib. It was my day off, so we were sitting back on his cousin's raggedy orange living room sofa watching *Good Times*, which happened to be one of my favorite golden-oldies sitcoms. It was one of the things I enjoyed most, that and lying in Bobbi's arms; whenever I was in his arms I was home. I couldn't wait until we had our own place and could do this all the time. Bobbi's favorite part, of course, was getting me out of my clothes. His right hand slowly started to travel under my shirt. I giggled like a schoolgirl. "Stop, babe, you're going to make me miss my part." I playfully moved his hand back to his lap.

"That's the plan." His lips found the crease of my neck, and his hand slowly traveled back up my shirt, where he freed one of my breasts from my bra and played with the nipple. No longer interested in *Good Times*, I turned to him, and he wasted no time sticking his warm tongue in my mouth. The ringing of Bobbi's cell phone killed the vibe.

"Come on, Bobbi. Who is that?" I pouted. His phone was famous for interrupting us just as we were about to get busy. And most calls were emergencies. On his days off from his real job, Bobbi had started up a side business where he would fix cars wherever they broke down. Sort of like a mechanic on wheels. Who could have known how many people's cars could break down in one day in strange-ass spots? Just the other day he got a call from a chick whose motor had fallen out while she sat at a red light. His idea had been genius, and it was bringing in lots of money. But while I was all about him stacking dough, I hated missing time with him. The shit was getting old and fast. My feelings were quickly becoming *fuck a mechanic on wheels*.

"Hello." He answered the phone. "A'ight, text that address to my phone. Yep, next half hour. I'm kinda in the middle of something." He eyed me and grinned. But I wasn't smiling. I knew it was about somebody's raggedy-ass ride.

I sighed, making sure it was full of annoyance as he ended the call, and turned my attention back to the television. "Who was that?" I asked him, just to make him say it to me.

"Baby, don't be mad." He pulled me to him and kissed my neck again.

"Nope, don't do that. Don't start what you can't finish." I pouted.

"Aye, you know I don't want to go. I'd rather be here with you all day. But I'm tryin' to get this business going, the right way. If it keeps on the way it's going, I'll be able to open up my own garage. Real soon." He sounded excited about his accomplishment.

"I know." I softened. I didn't want him to think I didn't hold him down. You know, stand by your man, as the saying goes. But I can't front: it was complicated as hell.

"Tell you what. I'll come by later tonight, and we can finish all this." For good measure he pulled up my tee and gripped my breasts in his mouth one by one. I almost ripped his clothes off right there.

"Okay, I'll be waiting." I said, my voice shivering from pure pleasure. But I also knew that when he started working on a vehicle, there was no guarantee what time he would finish. And in most cases he'd be dog tired when he was done, depending on what he had to do. Again I tried to remember that it was for our future. Suddenly my cell phone rang. "Hey," I chirped.

"What's up? Where you at?" Secret chimed on the other end of the phone.

"At Bobbi's crib. We were chillin', but he about to drop me by the house, though. What's good?"

"Why don't you have him drop you off at Los Lita we can grab some lunch, on me." That's all I needed to hear.

"Hey, if you payin', I'm there."

"Bet, I'm headed that way. See you there."

Twenty minutes later, Bobbi was pulling in front of the restaurant. I didn't even realize how hungry I was until I was inside. Secret was already there sitting down at the table munching on tortillas and salsa. Sliding into the booth, I couldn't wait to dig in. "What's up, chick?"

"Shit, I got the munchies, 'bout ready to eat these people's restaurant up." Secret chuckled. One look at her bloodshot red eyes, and I knew exactly what she meant.

"Why you blazin' without me? See you ain't right, but it's cool."

"Aye, when I woke up, you were already gone. Told you 'bout gettin' up with that nigga on your brain. You miss out on that fire and ain't nothin' worth that." She dipped her chip and munched down on it, grinning.

"Shut up." I laughed as I reached for a chip and dipped it in the salsa. "Besides, I thought you had to work this morning." I pushed the chip into my mouth and chewed. The waitress approached the table and took our orders. I got my favorite, cheese chicken enchiladas. Secret ordered her favorite, steak fajitas with extra sour cream.

"That's why I brought you out." Secret started to ramble again as soon as the waitress sauntered off. "I quit Chic the other night."

"The other night, why you ain't say nothing? Always tryin' to hide some shit."

With another chip in her mouth, she chewed like she was thinking then hunched her shoulders. "I guess I just wasn't ready to discuss it. I needed a break from even saying that damn store name. It leaves a spoiled taste in my mouth." She groaned as if she was exhausted.

"Well, I hope you didn't forget we still have bills. You already quit Taco World," I reminded her. I couldn't believe she had up and quit both her jobs, and to be honest, she didn't seem the least bit bothered.

"I know that, Isis . . . Look, I had to get out of there right then, I was just tired of it." Her cheeks were becoming flushed and her voice cracked. It became clear that she needed my understanding at that moment.

"I get it. You did what you had to. And I'm okay with that."

"I definitely had to do it." Relief was imprinted on her face.

"Aye, but job or no job, you paying for this damn lunch," I joked, then bit into a chip. A part of it crumbled into my greenish colored mini bowl full of salsa.

"Dang no sympathy for the unemployed?" We both laughed. "Hey, so guess who I ran into the other day?"

"Wait, please don't tell me crazy-ass Chris?" Chris was the first person to come to my mind. He had been Secret's on-again, off-again boyfriend for a year. Turns out dude was Secret's real-life fatal attraction. Nigga could not understand the word "no" or "fuck off." It wasn't until Secret shot him in the ass with his own gun that he got the picture not to fuck with her. He wanted love and didn't understand that she was not cut out for it. I had never met a dude yet that she dated and loved. For her being with them was only fun and a pastime. That was it. It was probably safe to say Secret's "fall in love with a guy" button was turned off or didn't exist.

Secret's mouth flew wide open, and she caught

her chest. "Wait a minute, who?" she asked, surprised. "What made you think of that fucking stalker freak? I wish that nigga would come within an inch of me. He and I both know he would get bodied on sight. Ugh, Isis." She grunted.

"Don't get your panties all in a bunch. Heck, you said guess. I just thought I would start with the person I would least expect. The one that's always on your shit list." I chuckled. "Since I'm making bad guesses, should I leave Jackie out, too?"

"I think you should stop guessing. Shit, you take it straight to the devil himself." Secret took a long, deep swig from her drink. "Damn, you made me thirsty bringing up Chris."

"My bad. But if not them two, then who?" I hunched my shoulders and waited, because at this rate I had no idea who she could be talking about.

"Kirk," she dropped.

I had to think for a brief second. Then it hit me. "Ohhh, Kirk from the old neighborhood." That was a surprise. I would have never guessed him. I hadn't seen Kirk for years, probably even longer.

"Yep," Secret confirmed with a grin.

"Wow, where you seen him at?" The last thing I remembered about Kirk was that he had kinda disappeared from the neighborhood. No rhyme, no reason.

"Well, he came into Taco World a while back before I quit. Really it was the same night I quit."

"For real? It's good to hear that he still alive. Dude sort of fell off the grid. Stop coming to school and everything."

"Yeah, well, he back and in full effect. I never told you this, but I actually ran into him a few years back. It was around about the time Mrs. Tate passed; it kind of slipped my mind."

"Yeah, it was a lot going on then." It still made my heart drop a bit when I talked about or thought of Mrs. Tate. I really missed her. "So what's up with him?" I asked.

"He good . . ." She paused as the waitress set her hot, sizzling plate in front of her, then mine followed. I wasted no time digging in. "He good, though . . ." she repeated. "Doing good for himself and he lookin' fine as ever. I mean he all grown up," she added with a smile, while placing the steak and vegetables inside her corn tortilla.

"That's what's up. Kirk was always a good dude."

"True that. Get this, though: he offered me a job."

I wasn't sure if I had heard her right. Her mouth was full of food. "Did you say he offered you a job?" I asked for confirmation.

Secret looked me straight in the eyes. "Yes, he offered me a job," she repeated clearly, so that I was sure not to misinterpret.

I laughed. "Damn, Kirk got it like that," I crowed. "Hmmm, what kind of job is it?"

Secret continued to chew the food in her mouth, swallowed, then took another bite and chewed. The food was so delicious we both found it hard to talk and eat. "Doing private dances," she said really fast in between grinding her teeth and belching.

"Ummm, what?" I was confused. "Private dancing. You mean like what?"

"Listen, I know how it must sound, but it's really not like what you might think. It's for exclusive parties and/or gatherings. Not like a stripper at a club or nothing." Her demeanor was a bit too non-chalant for my liking.

It really didn't matter to me how it sounded, though; that shit was a no go. "Hell, no, you can't be doing no shit like that, Secret," I said flat out.

"Isis, it's not what you think. I promise it ain't. Plus, it's safe. Kirk set up all of the dances. Not only that, the money's good. Kirk said I'll make in one night what I make in a week at Chic. And I don't have to put up with bitchin'-ass customers." She said that as if it was a selling point.

"I don't know." I was still not convinced.

"Yo, it is what it is. I'm tired of slaving for pennies. And you should be, too. How we ever gon' get ahead?" That statement made me pause. I thought about that all the time. But nothing different had ever presented itself. Not only that, I only had a high school diploma, and I didn't think that would get me far.

"You know that I want more, too. But I figure what else is there, you know . . . Listen, you do what you feel you got to as long as it's safe. Just don't get too caught up in it." There wasn't much more for me to say; her mind seemed to be made up.

"Shi'd, you ain't got to worry about that. I ain't stupid. Why don't you do it with me? This way we stack money at the same time." My tongue went dry. The girl was losing all her good sense right in front of me.

"Secret, now you know better than to ask me that crazy shit."

"It ain't crazy. What's so crazy about it?"

I was not about to break it down for her. "Nope, I can't do it. That's it." I shook my head. "Besides,

Bobbi wouldn't go for no mess like that. Or did you forget I have a man?" I reminded her.

"Isis, damn, you don't have to tell that nigga everything. Dammit." She got upset, her tone full of aggravation. Secret tolerated Bobbi, but she had never been a fan of him, and she made sure he knew it.

"Like it or not that's my man. And we have plans. Plans to live together, remember, and soon. We tryin' to build something together."

"Well." She rolled her eyes, still pissed. "Build it." She was sarcastic.

"Even if I were to agree to a ludicrous idea like this, how do you propose I hide that from him? Huh." Now I was aggravated and no longer hungry.

"Okay, you made your point." She sighed. "I don't know how you would hide it. But look at it this way, the money you could make would put enough quick cash in your pocket to help you move faster. And possibly help him with his dream of getting that shop he want so bad."

I had to admit she had a point, but Bobbi wouldn't give a damn about that. He would not want no other nigga drooling all over me. Period. "The answer is still no." My mind was made up. There was no way I was going to risk Bobbi finding out that I was doing private dances for money. No fucking way. "Furthermore, did you forget we both still have Penny to consider?"

"I am considering Penny. And she gon' be straight. Matter of fact, I'll be able to do more for her. Things will only get better for her." She dropped her head for a brief second from frustration. "Isis, I'm just fed up with these dead end–ass jobs . . . Hell, I been working my ass off at them two damn jobs all that time, and I still can't even afford a car." She sucked her teeth. The disgust was on her face. But I still didn't want her to use that as an excuse.

"Maybe we just need to work harder."

"Work harder?" She spit my words out as if they had a bitter taste. "Fuck working harder, I want more than just a minivan . . . I refuse to end up . . . broke and drunk like Jackie. That is not going to be me. Trust this is the best way. " Desperation was in her eyes.

It was clear to me there was nothing else for me to say. Back at the house I lay across my bed thinking about Secret's new gig. After giving it some more thought, I wasn't as worried as when she initially announced it. I knew Kirk would take care of her, and for a brief, weak moment, I played with the possibility of taking Secret up on the offer. But Bobbi crossed my mind along with all of our late-night sessions of planning our future. He loved me and I loved him, and I wasn't prepared to risk it all for any amount of money.

Sitting up in my bed, I suddenly had the taste for some strawberry ice cream. In the kitchen I grabbed a bowl and the ice cream scooper. Drowning my skepticism in ice cream always helped.

"Hey." Penny skipped into the kitchen.

"What's up, you?" I smiled. Penny's presence was always pleasing. She was the baby sister I wished my mother had had.

"About to grab some of that strawberry ice cream like you. It looks delicious." She peeled back the cabinet door and retrieved a bowl.

"Oh, and it's about to be." I stuck the ice cream scooper into the creamy goodness, filling my bowl with four huge scoops.

"Why don't you watch *Set It Off* with me? Secret actin' all anti-social."

"Sure. I ain't doing nothin' else. I'll see you in there." I handed her the ice cream scooper then went into the living room. Sitting down on the couch, I decided to call Bobbi real quick before the movie started. I hadn't seen him since earlier when he dropped me off at the restaurant to meet Secret. And I was missing him like crazy. His cell phone rang until it went to voice mail. Tossing the phone to the side, I dug into my ice cream. I couldn't wait to see Queen Latifah taking all those bullets at the end of the movie. I swear she was a straight up G for that.

Chapter 10

Secret

It had taken one full week for Kirk to set up my first "private dance" session. According to him, it had taken so long because he wanted to be sure I was not going to change my mind. I admit I had been a bit nervous, but not once did I even think about changing my mind. No, I wanted to do it. No, I needed to do it. Living hand to mouth was soon to be in my past, and I welcomed it with open arms. The only regret I had was Isis not going along with me. She was my best friend, and I wanted her to cash in on this opportunity as well. I had to respect her wishes. But who was I kidding? Deep down I knew she wouldn't go along with it anyway because of that fake-ass Bobbi. It did piss me off just thinking that if it hadn't been for that fuck boy who she called her man, she might have joined me. But, oh well, I refused to dwell on it.

Tonight was my first dance. Kirk had come by earlier and took me shopping so that I could pick up an outfit to do my dance. I was glad because I didn't have shit to wear that was decent, or should I say nothing enticing. Next he took me to his friend Tiffany's house, who did makeup, and I gotta admit she beat my face to the gods. I was cute as hell. As we pulled into the gentlemen's club where I would be doing a thirty-minute dance for the club owner and two of his business partners, my nerves kicked in full speed. I didn't understand why a man who owned his own gentlemen's club would pay money for a private dances when he already had women who could provide that exact same service working for him. According to Kirk, it wasn't about that; they wanted innocence and someone unique, not the regular Joe hos or dancers that everyone in the city knew. I still was a bit confused, but fuck it. It was their money, so however they chose to spend it was not my business.

Inside, Kirk led me to the dressing room where I would be getting dressed. I sat down in the chair, and before I knew it ten minutes had passed and I had not moved. A knock at the door caused me to stiffen. The second knock pulled me to my feet. I was not sure if I wanted to check to see who was at the door or hide. I tiptoed over to the door.

"Who is it?" I asked.

"Me." Hearing Kirk's voice, I instantly relaxed and breathed in a deep sigh.

I opened the door to see him with a huge smile glued to his face. "I brought you a drink. Thought it might help with the nerves."

"Nerves? What makes you think I'm nervous?"

"The look on your face. That's why I got you this drink. A few sips and you'll be good, I promise."

"How much longer do I have?"

"About twenty minutes. Look, I don't want you to worry, just let it flow naturally. I'll be right out there, sitting at the stage chillin'. By the time you're done with the dance, I'll be back out here waiting. I got you. But for now I'm 'bout to go out here and throw some money and pay some bills," he joked, insinuating he was going to throw money at the strippers.

"A'ight." I giggled then reached for the drink in his hand. Closing the door behind him, I wasted no time taking my first swallow of the brown liquid, quickly followed by the second. The warm tingle in my toes must have traveled to my brain, because all signs of nervousness evaporated. I slid into my outfit, and I looked myself over in the mirror for approval and was satisfied with what I saw. It had been a long time since I had taken a full inventory of myself. Now five foot six with a hundred-thirty-five-pound frame and the perfect size butt and set of full naturally red lips, I was the mixed version of Angelina Jolie. So I knew I had nothing to worry about.

You would have thought I had been dancing for years, the way I slowly, then on perfect beat, started gyrating my hips to T-Pain's "I'm 'n Luv (Wit a Stripper)" as soon as it blasted out of the speakers. As I seductively gave each one of the three guys my full attention, it was clear they were mesmerized by me. Before long I had danced to three songs, and it was over. Each guy had a look of total satisfaction plastered on his face. Without saying a word I exited the room. Damn, that had been easy. I practically skipped back to the dressing room. And true to his word, Kirk was standing by my door waiting on me.

At home in my bedroom, I tossed eight one-hundred-dollar bills on top of my bed. I had danced for less than thirty minutes and walked away with eight hundred dollars; the shit was unbelievable, I was over the moon ecstatic. Never in my entire life had I made money for basically doing nothing. Kirk had come through as promised.

That's why when he called me the next morning and told me to meet him for breakfast, I jumped outta bed like I had been called by the president. Once there, he told me that I must have been a pro, because the owner of the gentlemen's club wanted me to be on his entertainment schedule once a week. So already I had a permanent customer. Not to mention he already had me booked for three more nights that week with other clients. And I couldn't wait. I was counting my money before it was made.

"Where are you off to?" I occupied Isis's opened door while she dressed.

"The last place I want to go to. Work. So how did it go last night? I tried waiting up for you but I was tired."

"Better than I could have imagined." I couldn't wait to tell her all about it. "I admit I was nervous at first. But I got over it and fast. Isis, I made eight hundred dollars in less than thirty minutes."

"Really." She seemed surprised. "That's what's up." She slid into a pair of flats.

"I know, right. And that was just in one night. I just met up with Kirk, and I'm already booked for three other nights this week. And check this out. The owner of the club where I danced last night— he already have me booked as a regular for one night a week."

"Wow, for real. You must have killed it."

"Aye, I ain't one to brag, but you know me, I did my thing. I gave them niggas straight body." I giggled while twerking my butt for good measure.

"Yeah, I taught you well." Isis started twerking and looked at her butt along with me.

"Sit yo ass down. I taught you." We both laughed. "Real talk, though, if the cash keep flowing like it did last night, I'ma be able to jump a ride. Shi'd, I can't be catching no bus to my gigs."

"What y'all up to?" Penny appeared in the doorway out of nowhere. We suddenly got quiet. A few days before when Kirk had called me with the first gig, Isis and I had come to the conclusion that Penny didn't need to know just yet. I needed to see how it all went first.

A few weeks had passed, and things had been going great with the private dances. The demand for me was rolling in: I was sometimes pulling in two jobs a night, some paying me as much as twelve hundred dollars after Kirk got his cut. I had managed to save five thousand dollars, two of which I put down on a 2009 Chevy Impala. I was glad to be off heels and finally on wheels. The city bus and dirty smelling cabs could eat my dust.

"Penny, you better hurry up and get out this car

if you want to shop." It was Saturday, and I had decided to take Penny shopping, but I had made the mistake of buying her a new cell phone before we made it to the mall. She couldn't stop playing with the thing.

"I swear you have no patience, Secret. Dang," Penny complained, climbing out of the car, her eyes still glued to the cell phone.

"And you know this," I co-signed with a grin. "Time waits for no man." I laughed at the simple quote that I had heard from some movie that I couldn't even remember the name of. Two hours later we were marching out of Foot Locker; she was carrying two bags with Jordans inside and a huge grin to match.

"Let's grab something to eat. I'm hungry," I announced, already pointed in the direction of the food court. We had been out most of the day, and the only thing I had eaten for breakfast was Cap'n Crunch cereal. We both decided on Panda Express. It happened to be one of our favorite places to eat when at the mall.

Sitting down, I wasted no time going in on my walnut shrimp and fried rice. Penny followed suit. Her favorite was orange chicken with fried rice. After a few bites I started to feel satisfied and slowed down. "So how's school going?" It had been a while since we talked about school, and it was time we caught up.

"It's been cool. Just can't believe this my last year."

"I know. I be trippin' when I think about you being a senior. You growing up on me too fast."

Her mouth full of orange chicken, Penny gave me a shy grin. "Aww, are you going to cry?"

"Maybe at your graduation." I laughed. "But don't let growing up fool you. I'm still the big sister, and I'll bust your ass."

"Ha ha. Secret, you should really stop the violence," she joked, then sipped her Pepsi. Staring at me, her expression became a bit serious. I wondered what was up.

"What else you got on your mind?" I prayed it wasn't about her so-called boyfriend; I was over that. Or at least still not ready to accept it.

"I just been wondering what's up with you lately. Something is different, so I just have been waiting to see what you had to say . . . So are you gon' tell me?"

My mind shot into overdrive. I had no idea what she was talking about. "What you mean? I ain't up to nothin'. Just doing me."

"Secret, first off, the family that we come from, I didn't get to be seventeen and be stupid . . ." She paused, but I didn't respond. "Listen, I know you ain't working at Taco World no more or Chic." That got my attention real fast. She was for real calling me on my shit. I had tried to keep that from her. "Did you think you could hide that from me?" She sounded like the big sister and not the baby.

"How you know about that?"

"That's not the point. Just know that I do. And the main question is, what's up? I know ain't no man, baller, or whatever you might call him been creeping. But you dropping money around the crib like crazy, buying cars. Hell, clothes and shoes." She pointed at the bag from Macy's and the shoe bags from Foot Locker like they were evidence to prove her case.

For a minute I was speechless. I was still not ready to tell her yet. What would she think? But even I had known that eventually she would see the change going on around her. I mean cars and shopping sprees could raise anybody's eyebrows, but I still thought I had a little more time.

Not able to bring myself to admit anything, I used my one and only strategy: play dumb. "Penny, I swear you be exaggerating things. It's not like I paid for that car in cash, and I have been saving money from both jobs. Besides, those shoes I just bought you were needed." I allowed my eyes to land on the bags. I didn't want to look at her for fear she would see the lie in my eyes, even though I knew that she knew.

I could feel her eyes burning a hole in me, so I glanced up at her. She shook her head with disappointment. I can't lie; she had always been wise and very observant. Jackie had taught us that. "No, Secret, don't try it. I ain't going for that bull. Now I have been watching you come up in that house late nights. When you think I'm sleepin'." She stressed that part with a little roll in her neck. "Yes, I be woke. You be coming up in that house late nights dressed in fishnets and half naked, with a face full of makeup. So are you strippin' at one of these hole in the walls?" I almost doubled over in my seat. Was she gotdamn I Spy? I wasn't no stripper, but damn, she was close.

It took a minute for me to find my voice. That I had not been expecting. I could not believe she had been staying up late watching me slide into the house like a burglar. I made sure that I was extra quiet when I came in at night, but it was clear I hadn't been quiet enough. I swapped things around in my head that I could use in my defense.

Penny sighed. "Secret, just stop the lying. I ain't stupid." Anger slowly crept into her face. "You know I just wish you would stop treating me like some child. In case you forgot, I'm almost an adult. It would be nice if you treated me as such sometimes, and soon." She rolled her eyes.

At that moment I realized she was right. I needed to stop lying to her. "I'm not a stripper, okay." I found myself looking in her sad eyes for forgiveness. I didn't want her to lose faith in me; she had had enough of that with Jackie. I had to be honest with her. "But I have been doing some private dances." She gazed at me as if she was trying to register that, possibly the difference between the two.

"What's that exactly? I mean how it is different from being a stripper?"

"Well, I don't slide down poles for a bar full of men per se while they toss money at me. I just dance for a specific person or persons for a set fee." I really wasn't sure how that sounded.

Penny seemed to ponder what I said. "Soooo . . . is that safe? Being alone with them."

"Yeah, do you remember Kirk from our old neighborhood?"

"Of course I remember Kirk. Why?"

"Well, he is who I work for. He sets up and schedules everything for me. He makes sure everything's legit."

"Wait, is he a pimp or something?"

"Hell no, he ain't no pimp." I was shocked to even hear her say that. Damn, my baby sister had grown up on me. "Kirk just set up the gigs and make sure I get paid and that I'm safe. I can quit at any time," I stressed. "Plus he has the connection to the ballers and/or business owners that request me for the dances."

"Oh, okay . . . Well, as I can see, the money good."

"It is. And we need it," I added.

"I know just from seeing the things we have now," she agreed. "Dang, I haven't seen Kirk in years; you gon' have to bring him around."

"Bet I will. But trust he is not the same old dusty Kirk you remember." I laughed.

"Wait, you checkin' for Kirk now?"

"Uh, no. We still cool just like in the old days. But he fine as hell, though; I can't front. Wait till you see." I held my right hand in stance for a high five. We laughed. We sat and talked for a minute then went and found us a mall locker, popped in our fifty cents, and finished our shopping. It felt so good to be able to buy her those nice things. It motivated me to get back to work and dance my ass off, if for no other reason than my sister deserved it.

Chapter 11

Isis

For the fourth time I glanced at the time on my cell phone; it was now five thirty p.m. I had now been off work for thirty minutes, standing outside by the front entrance of JCPenney, waiting for Bobbi, who was supposed to pick me up at five o'clock when my shift ended. But there was no sign of him or his Cutlass. Hot and just a bit agitated, I walked back inside. Again I checked my phone: no missed calls. I had already called his phone ten times and received no answer. It was like him to be late by five minutes, maybe, but never longer than ten.

Seeing the long line of people wrapped around the cash register in the kids' department, I decided not to get too close for fear my manager might ask me to help out. It was a must that I get out of the store quickly. I almost called Secret, but

I remembered she had a gig early in the day and wouldn't be home until around eight. Realizing the bus was my only option, I pouted under my breath on my way to the bus stop in a hurry. The bus was due in ten minutes; if I missed it I would be waiting another hour for the next one.

Two hours later, I dragged my hot, tired body in the door. Riding the bus made me remember why I hated to ride it. The ride was too long, and I always ended up sitting next to weird people with bad breath who forced conversation on me. Bobbi and the Cutlass had spoiled me. But I thanked God I was finally home. Heading to my room, I kicked off my flats, grabbed a t-shirt and a pair of my girl boxers, and headed for the shower. After the dreadful heat and bus ride I had endured, it was a must.

After my shower I lay across my bed for what was supposed to be a moment of relaxation, but I fell asleep. I woke up a few hours later starving. Sliding into my slippers, I went into the kitchen to find food.

"What's up?" Secret spoke, as she barged into the kitchen clearly in a good mood.

"Making me a turkey sandwich, I am so hungry." I pulled my bread from the toaster and spread hot mustard over both pieces.

"Well, it looks good. Maybe I'll make me one."

"So why you so happy?" I asked.

"I'm always happy when I get these coins." She dumped ten one-hundred-dollar bills on the counter. "Isis, this money is too easy. I can't make this shit up."

"That is some to smile about. Hell, yeah," I

agreed. "But while you were out gettin' money, I was busy riding the hot-ass bus to the crib."

"What? Why?"

"Bobbi did not pick me up today."

"For real. Shit, he always scoop you. Maybe he forgot. Did you call him?"

"Yep, I called him several times, and he didn't answer. The phone just rings then goes to voice mail."

"You worried about him?"

"Nah, he probably at the shop busy or at home and laid that phone down. Shit, he's bad about that." Reaching for my cell phone, I hit his name again. Still no answer.

"You want to use the car to ride over and check on him?" Secret offered.

I thought about it for a minute, but I was home, had a fresh shower and a fat turkey sandwich. Going back out was not an option. "Nah, I'm 'bout to sit down and eat this food and relax. He'll call when he get straight. But he gone get this business." Wrapping my turkey sandwich up in a paper towel, I reached on top of the fridge and grabbed an unopened bag of Doritos. "I'm off to my room for the night, 'cause after this snack, I'm going to bed."

"A'ight." Secret reached in the fridge for the turkey. "If you change your mind, you know where to get the keys."

Almost knocking the still open bag of Doritos out of the bed, I woke up to the sun shining through my window. I must have fallen asleep while eating, because not only were the chips still in my bed, but my right hand was still in the bag. Sitting up, I closed the bag and set it next to the lamp on my night table. Picking up my cell, I could see that Bobbi had not called or texted during the night or morning. Again I tried calling his cell and again there was no answer, but this time it went straight to voice mail.

Sighing, I realized that Bobbi had let his phone die. He was famous for that. I was so frustrated with him. But I didn't have time to dwell on it because I had to be at work in an hour. I took another quick shower and got dressed and woke Secret up to drop me off at work, because there was no way I was getting back on that bus.

Secret was off for the day and promised to pick me up after work. JCPenney was having a grab-a-tag sale, and we were so busy that time flew by, and I had not had a break. I had no chance to call Bobbi. But with a quick view of my phone I knew he still had not called me. I was so ready to get off I damn near ran outside after clocking out. I was glad to see Secret was there and on time.

"Damn, you look stressed," she commented as I climbed into the car.

"They done worked the shit out of me." I threw my head back on the headrest for a bit of relaxation as Secret took off. "People were damn near fighting over those damn clothes."

"I remember that crazy shit from Chic." Secret laughed. "And I don't miss it one bit."

"I don't blame you. Pandemonium." I chuckled.

"Aye, but Kirk called and said he got a gig for

me, and since it's kinda last-minute, I'ma need you to drop me off and come back for me."

"Cool. I can use the car and drop by Bobbi's crib. I still ain't heard from him."

"For real." She seemed surprised. "His ass trippin', but it's cool, do what you got to."

Pulling up to Bobbi's crib, the first thing I noticed was his Cutlass parked in its usual spot. Parking Secret's Impala right behind it, I jumped out and strutted up to the front door. His ass had better been dead, because I knew he was not at home relaxing and had not called me or picked up my phone call for going on day two. I wouldn't be cutting him any slack. I knocked at least five times before trying the doorknob, which was locked. Finally, the door swung open and Melvin was standing on the other side of it.

It was brief, but he had a look on his face as if he was almost surprised to see me. "Dang, Melvin, it's about time you open this door." I stepped inside past him without him inviting me in.

"I was in the bathroom. Been eating those frozen burritos again," he tried to explain. I hated when he shared disgusting information like that. But I was not surprised; he never had any tact about himself. I didn't waste time saying just that. I was on a mission to talk to Bobbi.

"Where your boy at? He sleep again? I been blowin' him up since yesterday. I told his ass about not chargin' that phone." I kept marching toward the back. When I didn't see Bobbi on the couch, I assumed he was in Melvin's bed asleep. Sometimes when Melvin got up for the day Bobbi took his bed. Reaching Melvin's room, I pushed the door open to find his bed empty. I turned to face Melvin, who was still hot on my trail and quiet as ever. And that was not normal, because Melvin was known to run his damn mouth way too much.

"Melvin, where the hell is Bobbi?" I asked him.

Sharing the same surprised look on his face, he hunched his shoulder looking confused. "He left yesterday . . . and went out of town."

I wondered if I heard him right. "Outta town. What you mean? Where?" This was becoming crazy fast.

"I don't know. He packed some bags and left."

Nothing he said seemed to register. I stood still and silent for a second to think. Where would be Bobbi be going? Then suddenly I realized who I was talking to: Melvin. He was such a jokester and loved to play around. I knew then that stupid confusion on his face was all a part of his little joke. He was trying to Ashton Kutcher me. I started laughing.

"Bobbi, get your ass out here and stop playing," I yelled. "You got me, okay. But this ain't funny."

The look on Melvin's face still had not changed. The house was so quiet you could hear a pin drop. Still I waited. "Isis, Bobbi is not here," Melvin repeated again.

"How can he not be here? His car is right outside," I pointed out. And Bobbi never went anywhere without his car.

"He had a rental when he left." At this point my heart dropped. None of this made any sense at all. "Shit, to be honest I thought you were with him."

Finally I believed him and didn't want to hear

anymore. Without another word I walked out the front door. Inside the car I sat in silence and played everything Melvin had said over in my head. I stared at Bobbi's car. I pulled out my cell phone and tried Bobbi. Again I got the voice mail right away, no rings.

I started the car and drove straight to the bank. Inside, I asked the teller to give me the balance on the joint bank account that I shared with Bobbi. The teller typed the information into her computer then handed me a slip. "This can't be right." I handed the slip back to the teller that basically told me all the money I had put into the bank was now gone. Without saying a word, the teller typed the information into the system again. She carefully looked the account over.

"This is the balance as of yesterday, after a withdrawal was made."

I stumbled backward just a little. "Are you okay?" the teller asked, concern all over her face.

Snatching the paper off the counter, I turned and briskly walked back to the car. With each step I took it seem like the soles of my feet were on fire. Back inside the car, I sat in a daze as reality set in full speed. Bobbi, my boyfriend of two years, had taken all of my money and the money we had saved together and left town. Most of the money belonged to me. When we had started saving money, I already had six thousand dollars in the bank that I had managed to save from the money Mrs. Tate had left for me.

When Bobbi and I had decided to save together, we agreed that I would add him to my already established account, and he would just add to it. Even still, I added more than he did, because in the beginning he didn't have a steady job, and he worked when he could. But through it all we had managed to save twelve thousand dollars. And now it was all gone.

Tears rushed down my face as I hit the steering wheel and screamed out loud from pure frustration and the feeling of brutal betrayal. Both my arms were weak, but somehow I managed to start the car back up. It was time to pick up Secret. As soon as Secret climbed into the car, she knew something was up with me, and I could not hold it. The tears ran again like a faucet.

"What's wrong? What the fuck is it?" She got impatient when I didn't answer fast enough.

"Bobbi . . . he gone. He left town," I cried.

"And went where?" Secret was confused.

"I don't know, but he is gone. I went by the house, and Melvin told me. At first I thought it was a joke. But I went by the bank, and all the money we were saving is gone. He took it all, Secret. All of it." A cry came from deep within.

"That nigga took yo money? See, I told you his bitch ass was not up to shit. I never trusted his grinnin' ass." Secret pounded the dashboard with her fist. I continued to sob. I felt as if I had been beaten with a ton of bricks. "Drive this damn car back over Melvin's house. His punk ass know more than he saying." Reaching in her gym bag with her change of clothes inside, she retrieved her cell phone. "I'm 'bout to call Kirk. He gone come over there and fuck his ass up. I bet he tell where your money at then."

"No," I sniffed and grabbed her cell phone out of her hand. "Don't do that . . . I really don't think Melvin know more than what he is saying."

"Fuck that, he know! That Alabama slick motherfucker know something!" she shouted.

"I really don't think so. You didn't see the look on his face; he really seemed surprised." I continued to sob; who knew when I would stop. This had to be a dream and could not be happening to me. There was no way that Bobbi, the love of my life, could or would do this to me. To us.

Chapter 12

Isis

It had been one of the longest weeks of my entire life. Day in and day out I lay in the bed in a zone, only getting up to shower or go to work. Going to work had been like going to my own private torture. The last thing I wanted to do was deal with strangers and their needs. No, what I needed was to find Bobbi and pop a cap in his thieving, lying ass. I was angry and unsure if I would ever get over what he had done to me. Every time I thought about it, my stomach twisted and turned into knots. Already I had shed five pounds because I simply had no appetite. The only thing that would seem to go down my throat was liquids. Today had been the first day that I had actually paid attention to the growling that roared from deep within my stomach. But physically I was not in the mood to climb out of bed.

"Can I come in?" Secret stuck her head inside my door. She and Penny both had been there for me emotionally in a big way. I was lucky to have them in my life. They always had my back.

"Come on in," I said without looking up. I had my pillow rolled up and my chin buried in it.

Secret bopped down at the foot of bed. "This bed is all bad for you. You gotta get up."

"I have been up. I worked today, remember?" I reminded her. But I knew what she meant.

"Trust me, going to work does not count." She popped her mouth. "But don't worry, I got you. Wanna roll up?"

Now she had my attention. "Please, I need to be on cloud on nine." I sat up slowly and crossed my legs Indian style to face her.

Pulling the already rolled-up blunt out of the purple Crown Royal bag she had in her hand, Secret smiled. "I told you I got yo back." She pulled out a lighter and lit the blunt. The smell calmed me. "Here, you do the honors." She passed me the blunt.

I wasted no time inhaling. I had to have it. Holding the smoke in longer than usual, I slowly exhaled and watched the smoke circle above me into a thick cloud. Secret reached for the blunt. I watched her as she followed my lead. "I still can't believe Bobbi played me like that. I'm fit to kill him." I balled up my right hand into a fist. "I thought he loved me," I shrieked.

"You already know I never trusted that nigga." She passed the blunt back to me. "He was always too damn persistent. Or tryin' to slick control some shit."

Now that I sat and thought about it, she was right. How could I be so stupid? I shook my head as I thought about it. "All that fuckin' money just gone . . . Especially the money Mrs. Tate left for me. Her and her husband worked hard for that money, and I managed to give it to the devil without a clue . . . Shit, I'm stupid!" I screamed. I was so disappointed in myself.

"You ain't stupid, Isis . . . Just in love . . . That can happen to anyone." I knew she just wanted to make me feel good. But even I knew I was stupid as hell. I should have known something was up when he suggested we use my account to save the money. For one, because he knew about the money Mrs. Tate had left me and I had managed to save, and two, he barely had a job at the time he suggested it. Out of the twelve thousand in the bank, ten of it had belonged to me. Then once he had started working full-time, he always had an excuse as to why he had to skip a week here or there putting his share of money in. So he had only contributed two thousand dollars.

Tears started forming in my eyes. "I'm just disappointed in myself. I should have known better."

"Fuck all this crazy talk. And Fuck Bobbi. It's time for you to get out of this damn bed and get to work. Get, get money," she chanted with the blunt hanging from the corner of her mouth.

"I already been going to work. I'm just not feeling it enough to do any overtime." I reached for the blunt, afraid it might fall out of Secret's mouth. The last thing I needed was for my mattress to catch on fire, because I didn't have the money to buy a new one.

"I ain't talkin' about that dead-ass job at JCPenney. That shit need to be history. I'm talkin' about private dancing. That shit pays. And right now you need to build your nest egg up again. All you got to do is say the word, and Kirk will set it up."

"Secret, we talked about this already. The answer was no then, and it still is no." This conversation was sure to blow my high. This was not the time.

"Why not? What's your excuse now? Shit, the money good, your body right, you single, and all you have to do is dance."

I tried to pass her the blunt, but she was too busy making her point to reach for it. I decided to take her turn. As I inhaled the smoke, suddenly what she said did make a little sense, as much as I hated to admit it. I exhaled. "Okay, let's do it." I hunched my shoulders in a nonchalant manner. Again I attempted to pass the blunt. This time she grabbed it.

I could tell the sudden change of my answer surprised her. She raised the blunt midair and glared at me.

"I won't be a stripper, though." I had to make that clear. "Miami has enough of those."

"I already told you it ain't like that. All we do is private dances; there is no touching or anything involved. They don't even throw money at you. They pay Kirk and he pays us. No worries, I promise you will be in good hands," Secret explained with excitement. But I didn't need to hear anymore. I was in. I had nothing to lose.

*   *   *

Two days had passed since my conversation with Secret, and I still had not changed my mind. After notifying my supervisor at JCPenney that I would not be returning to work, I went in and cleaned out my locker. Secret wasted no time calling Kirk an hour after our conversation and told him of my decision; he assured her I had made a good decision. "Get the door, Penny. It's probably Kirk. He supposed to be stopping by," Secret yelled from the kitchen. I was in my room lying across the bed thumbing through an *Essence* magazine. I instantly pushed it aside. I jumped to my feet. The living room was my destination. I could hear Secret already talking to Kirk.

Kirk's eyes bulge with excitement when I rounded the corner. "What's up, Isis?" He gave me a wide grin. "Man, it's been a long time."

"Hey, Kirk." I smiled. I couldn't believe how different he looked. To put it mildly, he looked like money. Not to mention handsome as hell. Secret had been right.

"I'm glad you decided to go in with Secret. You gone be straight. I'ma make sure of it. I'm already setting up some gigs for you. I came through 'cause I wanted to give you some money to do a little shopping. Pick out some things." He handed me a wad of bills. "Take Secret with you. She can help you pick the fits."

"Cool." I gripped the bills.

"Yeah, I got her," Secret assured him. For the next half hour I watched as Kirk and Secret talked about the business. There seemed to be this unspoken chemistry between them. It was so clear that Kirk cared for Secret. But it was equally clear that she didn't have a clue. Excusing myself to my room, I counted the money in my hand. There was a thousand dollars there. I couldn't wait to go shopping just so I could spend it. I was ready for my new beginning.

Chapter 13

Isis

I had to admit private dancing wasn't all that bad. I actually dove into it head first. Not once was I nervous on my first gig. It almost felt as if I had done it before; walking into the room it felt almost natural to me. R. Kelly's "It Seems Like You're Ready" blasted out of the speakers, and it was like I turned into someone else. My body moved like silk, the lap dances I performed for my client were mesmerizing, so much so he paid Kirk an extra four hundred dollars. I walked away from the experience simply ready for the next. Not one regret. And to be honest, I'm sure all the boldness I approached it with was from all the anger I had built up for Bobbi. Either way, I took the torch and ran with it.

Four weeks had all but flown by, and already I was saving again, putting away my nest egg, as Secret called it. At the moment I had no plans what I would do with it. But one thing was for sure: it would be my plan and mine alone. I soon learned that though Bobbi had hurt me I wasn't broken, because each day I moved on for the better. Each day he grew further and further from my memory. And for that I was happy, because I was able to enjoy myself. Any contempt I held for him had to be buried deep within or I wouldn't be able to go on. And allowing some nigga to cause me to fail was not an option.

Tonight all work was turning into play. Secret and one of her friends, Trina, and I were hitting the club for some girl time. I had spent most of the day getting ready. Sliding through *Styles Beat* I let my girl Crystal hook me up with a sixteen-inch loose ponytail with a chopped-up, layered bang. Then Secret and I both hit up Macy's for the perfect outfits and some shoes. Back at the house, Secret did my makeup; she was really good at that. At ten o'clock we were ready to hit the door, taking a few selfies before leaving the house. And I think it fair to say we were beat for status. Secret struck a pose so that I could snap her; she was rocking a black Guess cutout halter dress with some royal blue platform pumps. You couldn't tell her nothing; she was knocking hos dead.

Walking back over to the hallway, I gave myself one more look in the full-length wall mirror. I smiled at myself. My milk chocolate skin glistened with my pearly white teeth. The one thing I was always sure of was my beauty, no matter how hard times were. I was five foot eight, a hundred thirty pounds, with a jawline identical to Naomi Campbell's; the only thing round on me was my perfect butt. Mrs. Tate had always told me I should become a model. I laughed at that, though; I didn't have time to be pretty. But looking at myself in the mirror dressed in an all-white crossed-back, suspender cropped at the ankle jean romper, with a sleeveless red fitted halter top, laced off with a pair of Steve Madden red two-piece pumps, I could easily be mistaken for one of America's Next Top Models.

The pleasing stares once we stepped off in the club confirmed everything we already knew. We were classified bad bitches. T.I.'s "I'm Back" blared out the speakers as we made our way to the bar, and with every step I took that's exactly how I felt. It had been a while since I felt like partying, but it was going down tonight.

"Oh, shit, I'm already ready to hit the dance floor," Secret chanted.

"I know, right," Trina cosigned. " 'Recognize I'm back,' " she sang along with T.I. "These bitches better know it," Trina added, feeling herself.

"Let's get this drank first." I stepped up to the bar.

"Let's do that. We 'bout to get lit tonight," Secret confirmed.

"Give me a shot of Crown Royal," I told the bartender.

"Damn, bitch, you going hard, quick." Secret laughed.

"I just need something strong real quick. That fire starter." I chuckled.

"Well, in that case, bartender, hit me with a shot of Hennessy," Secret instructed.

"Second that Crown Royal for me, too." Trina put in her order. "Matter of fact, make that a double for me," Trina added. Secret and I both gave her the side-eye. "Y'all bitches know I can drink. Shit, just blame it on Terry; that nigga still be puttin' me through some shit." Terry was her trifling baby daddy who for whatever reason she just couldn't seem to leave alone. He had cheated on her with just about everyone in Miami, and still she was with him. The dude was a loser for real, a nickel boy who swore up and down he ran Miami.

"I keep tellin' you to drop that nigga like a bad habit." Secret never bit her tongue, harsh advice or not.

"Trust me, I am soon, I am so sick of his shit. But for right now this Crown Royal gon' have to do the trick." She chuckled. We all knew the chance of her keeping that threat was slim to none. But if it made her feel better to say it, we would go along.

"Bottoms up then." I laughed, then tossed my shot back. The warm feeling that tingled through my body went from my head to my toes. Coincidently at that very moment Trey Songz's "Bottoms Up" blasted out the speakers. Feeling good, I pranced to the dance floor with Trina and Secret on my trail.

Doing our thing on the dance floor for the next three songs, we were having too much fun. Tired, we headed back to the bar. "That was fun," Secret said, out of breath.

"Heck, yeah. Give me an apple martini," I told the bartender.

"I'll take one, too," Secret added.

No sooner than I had taken the last swallow of

my martini did ASAP Rocky's "Fuckin' Problems" blare out the speakers. "That is my song," I chanted and wasted no time shaking my ass back to the dance floor. During the middle of the song I looked up to find Secret dancing with a tall chocolate brother with shoulder-length dreads. After a Lil Wayne song, followed by Rick Ross and Nicki Minaj's "You the Boss," Trina and I sat down while Secret was still dancing with ol' boy.

"Why y'all sittin' down?" Secret strutted over to us with a grin on her face so huge I could almost see her gums.

"'Cause we tired. Why you grinning so damn hard?" I shot back.

Trina started laughing then stood up. "These damn drinks running through me. I'm going to the bathroom." Her walk was a little unsteady but I wasn't surprised: she had consumed at least six shots of Crown Royal, not to mention an apple martini spiced with gin. She was going hard for real.

"That is a drunk bitch walking right there." Secret chuckled, as she sat down next to me.

"Nah, for Trina's walk, who was that chocolate brother you was over there twerking for?" I made sure not to get off the subject.

"Oh, him? Girl, his name Marco."

"You know you was giving his ass action. He is fine, though. I'll jump his damn bones if it were me," I added jokingly.

"Yeah, he cute. But it ain't shit poppin', though." She was nonchalant about it. But I knew better: she was all over that nigga. I had witnessed her give him a private dance off Rick Ross and Nicki Minaj's song for free. So she could keep that *"it ain't shit poppin', though"* comment, because I was not trying to hear it.

I twisted my lips up so that she knew I wasn't hearing it. "Why don't you stop playing around, Secret. You know you feelin' him, so you can stop while you ahead."

"I don't know what you talkin' about." She continued to play dumb.

"A'ight then, since you want to down play that situation. What's up with you and Kirk?" The look on her face told me that question had caught her off guard. I waited for my answer.

"What you mean, what's up? Kirk like a brother. Your ass be trippin', I swear."

"Secret, tell me you don't see how he looks at you. Shit, it's written all over his face." I kept it real. "Ray Charles could see he got it bad for you."

"You done had too much of that damn Crown Royal," she joked.

"Ha ha. You funny." I was sarcastic on purpose. "That nigga lust all over you. And you know it, too."

Standing up, she looked herself up and down. "Look at me, Isis, fine as I am. What nigga wouldn't?" She tried to make her point.

"Your ass know what I mean."

"I do." She smiled. "Real talk, though, Kirk and I are too fuckin' cool for that; it's all about stackin' this dough. Besides, being in a relationship with him would be odd . . . Remember we tried being boyfriend and girlfriend in elementary school. That shit did not work out." We both burst out laughing. Just the thought of it was funny.

"Yeah, I remember that catastrophe. It was too funny. Your ass was too bossy, just like you are now. Nothing has changed."

"Lies you tell. All lies," she denied with a laugh.

I was about to share an example when suddenly a caramel-toned fine brother stopped in front of us. "Hi," rolled off his thick lips, which were surrounded by a perfectly trimmed goatee. Looking me in the eyes, he said, "My name is Trey."

I glared at Secret. She gave me the "go for it" blink. "Hi," I replied with a bit of uncertainty.

"I was wondering if you would like to dance." He was bold and straight to the point.

My hormones screamed HELL YES! But my mouth said, "No, I'm tired."

He smiled, and I almost fell into his arms. "Well, if you change your mind, I'll be right over there." He pointed to where he was sitting with two other dudes who were just as fine as he was.

"Okay," I said in a shy tone.

We watched him as he walked away. "What the hell are you doing? I gave you the go ahead signal. Or are you blind or something?" Secret fired at me.

"No I'm not blind. But you know that already."

"Then what the fuck just happened? That nigga was like a shade darker Derrick Rose. You trippin'. I swear." She shook her head with disappointment.

And boy, was she painfully right. I could have smacked my own damn self. "Trust, I hate myself for turnin' him down . . . I felt like wrapping my legs around his waist and have him carry me up outta here."

"And you should have. The fuck." Secret appeared

appalled at my actions. "And it ain't too late." She sipped her drink.

"I'm just not ready yet, Secret."

"Bullshit, Isis. Don't let no punk-ass nigga like Bobbi steal your joy. Shit, you too bad a bitch for that."

"And that much is true." I smiled. But it was easier said than done. Bobbi had taken something from me that would be hard to get back: trust and damn near humanity. The pain he had caused me was rooted deep. But the last thing I wanted to do was make another man suffer for that. So for now I just had to chill. Hanging with my girl drinking and dancing was enough for me. Fine-ass niggas like Trey would have to take a backseat, at least for now.

But after turning his fine ass down, I had to have another shot. Two more drinks later we three took the dance floor back over and danced until we damn near passed out. Wasted as fuck, we drove home with everyone in the car on full DUI.

Chapter 14

Secret

The last couple of months had been full of change around the house, all of which Isis, Penny, and I welcomed. Private dancing was bringing in plenty of money for Isis and me, and that trickled down to Penny. For the past few months we had been preparing for her graduation, and it was expensive. She took photos; we had to pay for cap and gown and a host of other things that came along with her being a senior. But Isis and I didn't mind spending for whatever she needed, because she had done well in school. Her grades were up to par, and she had all intentions of attending college in the fall. We were very proud of her. And today was the day we had been preparing for: graduation day had arrived. I was overly excited and beside myself with joy.

"Can I come in for a minute?" Penny stuck her

head inside my bedroom door. I had just got out of the shower. I had my clothes laid across the bed for the ceremony.

"What's up?" I looked at her through my dresser mirror as I started to apply my Mac makeup. I had put hers on about an hour earlier, and she looked just beautiful. Penny was my twin; the only difference was she was a little taller than me and she had green eyes like Jackie. Mine were hazel brown. I could tell by the way she fidgeted on the edge of my bed something was up.

"Well, I was wondering . . ." She paused. "I was wondering how you felt about the fact that Jackie will not be there for my graduation?"

I should have known that was what was bothering her. Penny still had a soft spot for Jackie, and she wanted her to be there. She wanted her approval, for her to be proud of her. I felt bad that she had to deal with those emotions, while Jackie replaced all her emotions with a bottle, never once sympathizing with Penny or me. "It's cool with me. I don't expect nothing more of her anyhow. And you shouldn't, either. Remember she came to mine an hour late . . . but I wasn't shocked. I hadn't expected her to show up at all. I figured she'd be somewhere laid out drunk."

"So you don't think she'll come today?" The sadness in her voice made me angry. I hated that Jackie put her through this.

"Honestly, Penny, I just don't know. But I wouldn't bet my left kidney on it . . ." I didn't like being so straightforward about our mother's so-called love or lack thereof, but I always tried to find a way to be honest with Penny . . . "Listen, even if she does or doesn't show, Isis and I will be there for you. And we are all you need." Looking at her sad face from the mirror really bothered me.

She let out a soft chuckle. "You know I bet people look at us and think our family is really fucked up and not normal at all."

I wanted to say I agreed, but validating it wouldn't help her. I knew how our mother's neglect could hurt. I had experienced it and suffered from it early on. But over time I got over it and moved on. "Penny, baby girl . . . you can't be worried about what people think. Hell, half of them fucked up, too . . ." I turned to face her. "But I promise you this. This is your moment and can't no one take that away." I choked up. Tears rushed down Penny's face. I reached for her; she stood and we hugged it out.

"Like always, Isis and I are your family. You have two sisters, and we both got your back." I let her go and stepped back to look at her. "Look at you, you so grown up and beautiful."

Penny laughed and sniffled at the same time. "And you know this." She chuckled.

"Now go finish getting dressed. It'll be time to go before you know it."

"Right, and I don't want to be late to my own graduation." Without another word she skipped out of my room.

The graduation turned out great. By the time Penny came down the aisle and stepped onto that huge stage, Isis and I were covered in tears. Penny, on the other hand, did not have one tear in sight; she walked across that stage with so much courage my heart almost exploded from excitement. Like I said, we would get her through. We would get each other through. The three of us would be okay.

Back at work a few days later I was feeling good about the dance Kirk had set up for me. They were paying an extra seven hundred dollars because at the last minute they added an extra song to the dance. And I was always happy to get the money. Stepping into the room, I was ready to shake my natural ass. I was dancing for two guys that partnered in the tattoo business. Starting off with a slow twirl motion to R. Kelly's "Slow Wind," I was so feeling the song, slowly making my way toward the light-skinned guy with the full-body tattoo. He was engrossed in my seductive moves but the ringing of his cell phone pulled his attention away. I could tell by the way his eyebrows moved it was important. His lips mouthed the word "shit." He whispered to his partner and stood to leave. Approaching me, he leaned in and whispered softly in my ear, "Sorry," then placed four hundred dollars in my G-string. And for that I gave him a wink. Shit, they had already paid Kirk two thousand for the dance. And I loved tips. Now focusing my attention on his handsome caramel-skinned partner, I was just as eager. I made sure he got a good glimpse of every roll and shake I had to offer. I danced to one more song, and when it ended he placed five one-hundred-dollar bills in my hand.

"There's more where that came from" fell off his lips. "A thousand for sex, no oral, and no more than twenty minutes." He was detailed.

Damn, with the twelve-hundred-dollar cut I would

get from Kirk, plus the four hundred his friend had given me, and then the five hundred he had given me, I was cashing out. But even still, that thousand dollars sounded so good. "I don't do that" helplessly fell from my lips. "That's not what Kirk set up." I wasn't sure why I was explaining.

He just smiled. "What Kirk don't know won't hurt him."

I gripped the five hundred dollars he had given me so tight in my hand I thought it might disappear. Shit, shit. A thousand fucking dollars.

Chapter 15

Isis

I had called Secret's name three times, and she was not trying to wake up. She had just gotten in like three hours earlier after working late, so I knew she was tired, but I had looked everywhere and I could not find her car keys. "Secret." I yelled her name again. Then I jumped up and down on her bed.

Slowly opening one eye then the other, she glared at me. "What the hell, Isis. You know my ass tired."

"That's what you get for chasing that damn money so hard." I laughed. "Where the keys to the car? I got to drop Penny off at work." Penny had just started a new part-time job at JCPenney. The last thing she needed was to be late.

Secret ran her fingers through her hair and

sighed. "Damn, good question. Did you look on the kitchen counter?"

"Now you know I looked there first."

Secret turned over and put her face in her pillow. "Oh, God, I don't know." She pouted. "Maybe I flushed them down the toilet. Tell her to get money out my bag for a cab." She pulled the cover up over her head and snuggled up tighter.

"Secret, get yo ass up." I snatched the cover off her. "Help me find these keys."

"Dang, I swear you a pain." She reached for the blankets.

"I found them," Penny yelled from the hallway, then entered the room. "Secret, you left the keys in the refrigerator."

"See, I knew they were close by." She laughed then pulled the covers over her head again.

"Pathetic," I joked. "I'll be back later. I'm going to do a little car shopping."

"Have fun." Secret's reply was muffled into her pillow. All she wanted was to be left alone so that she could rest.

"What's up with Anthony?" I asked Penny as I pulled into the mall parking lot and drove around to JCPenney. It was early and the mall parking lot was already half full. I did not miss it at all.

"Ain't nothin' up wit' him. That's half the problem." She smacked her lips. "Ain't nothin' changed from last week when I told y'all I was done wit' him."

"I guess you serious this time." I grinned. "I mean this like the second time you declared to be done with him. So Secret and I did not take you serious."

Folding her arms across her chest, Penny sighed. "Nope, this time is different. I'm done for real. Anthony's full of shit, he thinks he's a player. And that crap only gets over on me once."

I had to look at her. I couldn't believe how much she was growing up. She was not a little girl anymore. And I was so proud of her for standing her ground.

"And besides, he ain't doin' shit with himself. He still ain't signed up for school, and he graduated a year before me. Now he runnin' around Miami with them nickel-sack boys on his block. I just don't need that anymore." The tone in her voice told me that she was giving up on the conversation. Which meant she was serious. Then she turned to me and smiled. "I bet them college boys fine anyway."

"I'm sure." I chuckled as I came to a complete stop in front of JCPenney. "Now get out before you're late."

"Later." She laughed while climbing out of the front seat. I felt bad that she was already experiencing a breakup. But I admired her courage; she wasn't allowing the fact that she cared about him to hinder the fact that he was not doing the right things. And she cared more about that than any love.

Hale's Car Shop was my first stop on my journey to car shopping but I left as quickly as I arrived. His cars were overpriced and clearly pieces of shit. I found duct tape one time too many inside his cars, supposedly holding up this or that. I was young and a woman, not stupid. He had me fucked up. Before long I had visited four car lots with no real prospects; turns out they were all peddling a bunch of junk that they were trying to pile off on the first dummy they could fool. So after stopping off at a shoe store to pick up a pair of heels for my gig that Kirk had scheduled for the night, I swung by JCPenney to pick Penny up after her six-hour shift had ended.

Back at the house, we found Secret still snoring. The only evidence that she had even been out of the bed was the smell of chronic in the air. It was lit. After taking a hot shower, I went back into Secret's room to grab the piece of blunt that was left in the ashtray, then went back to my room and got into the zone. Sliding into a pair of skinny high-waisted Guess jeans, I threw on a crop-top belly shirt over my head, and slid on a pair of pumps. Peeking into Secret's room I discovered she was still asleep. I knew she was off for the night, so I told Penny I was leaving and taking the car. Snatching the car key off the kitchen table, I headed out the door to the money.

Soon as my dance was over, I wasted no time getting up outta there. I was starving, so after sliding through Taco World and grabbing a few chicken tacos with cilantro and onions, I headed toward the house. I was ready to eat and kick my feet up. The beeping sound from my phone alerted me that had a text message. I reached for my Coach bag where I thought I had put my phone, but to my surprise the light from the phone was beaming from the side of the seat. My phone must have fallen out of my purse. I hated when that happened. I reached for it as I stopped at the red light and opened my text. The number on the text was not familiar, but I opened it anyway. Reading the text, anger flushed over me. I couldn't believe what I was reading. I also realized in that moment that I was holding Secret's phone and not my own.

Livid, I ran four red lights on my way to the house. I threw the gearshift into park and rushed inside. All the lights were off and the house was quiet, so I knew everyone must be in their own rooms. Pushing the door to Secret's bedroom wide open, I couldn't believe she was still asleep. It had been a full day. "Secret," I called her name. She stirred. "Secret, wake up." I almost yelled this time, but the last thing I wanted to do was wake Penny up and get her involved.

"Huh." She stirred.

"What the fuck is this?" I tossed her cell phone onto her bed, and it landed right next to her pillow.

"What?" She sat up.

"What the fuck does that shit mean?" My tone was aggressive and demanding.

"What you talkin' about, Isis?"

"Look at the damn phone!" Picking up the phone, she opened it up. "Read the damn text from that first number." I watched as her eyes bulged. She glanced at me for only a brief second then back at the phone. As if she needed to read it again. "Is that why you so damn tired. 'Cause you out trickin', having sex with niggas for money?" I spat with disgust.

Scooting to the edge of the bed, she threw her legs over the side of it.

"Isis, you . . ." She tried to speak, but I cut her off.

"Don't try to deny it. I read that shit over more than once . . . Yeah you left your phone in the car again." I nodded at the phone in her hand. Our phones were identical; there were plenty of times when we had mistakenly grabbed each other's phone. But Secret had a bad habit of leaving hers in the car.

The guilt of being caught was all over her face. She kept looking at the phone then back at me. That was starting to annoy the hell out of me. "Aye, you right. Okay. I been doing that shit on the side. But it's only been with two niggas." She said it as if she was trying to convince me that it was okay.

Tears kept running down my face. I had known all along that the job would be full of troubles. "I knew this job—or whatever you would like to call it"—my tone was sarcastic—"was too good to be true. Kirk on that bullshit."

"Kirk doesn't know anything about this, Isis. I set this up on my own."

"Well, good thing I don't believe that."

"Believe it. It's true, he doesn't know. I was offered and I said yes. The money was good: one thousand dollars for one round. I couldn't turn it down." She shrugged her shoulders as if it was no big deal.

"But why would you, Secret? Hell, we are not hos. Shit, at least that's what I thought."

"Listen, I'm sorry, Isis. But like I said, it was for the money. It ain't like I enjoyed it. It was a quick nut, and I was through." Again she hunched her shoulders.

I just stood back and looked at her. I could not believe what was coming out of her mouth. Never in a million years would I have guessed this. But this would not be my life; I didn't care how much money was involved. Watching my mom destroy our life gave me a clear picture as to when to walk away. This was it for me.

"Maybe you need a reality check; the shit is nasty and downright degrading. Money ain't never been that damn important. But you do what you want . . . I'm out of it. No more private dancing for me. Tell Kirk I quit." I turned to leave, but just as I put my left hand on the doorknob, I realized I had something else to say. "Oh, and you might want to tell Kirk you hoing now." I hoped it sounded as bad as it was, and I would not apologize. "I'm sure he would hate to know that he missin' his cut." With a heavy heart I turned and left her room. I was dumbfounded and in complete distress.

Chapter 16

Secret

I really don't know when I came to the point of not giving a fuck about what I did. Never in a million years would I have ever thought that I would sleep with someone strictly for the love of money. But I did. And honestly, not once after I was done did I feel sorry. Instead I just gripped the money tight that they placed in the palm of my hand. And each time I felt comfort from that. But after seeing how bad I had hurt Isis, that was the first and only time I ever felt any regret. Isis and I were like blood family; I never wanted to do anything that would intentionally hurt her.

I was sick with guilt after she confronted me with her allegations. I called up Kirk the very next morning and told him that Isis was done with the private dancing. And so was I. The last thing I wanted Isis to think was that I was continuing the lifestyle. No, I was out for good. If she was done, then so was I; whatever we did next, we would move forward together. We had to always have each other's back. After I apologized to Isis a million times for ruining things, she had finally forgiven me. That had been a week ago, and I needed to work. Time was money. I called up Kirk and asked him to meet up with me.

"What's up, big baller?" I greeted him.

"Nah, you got it." He stood up and hugged me. We decided to meet at a bar downtown called Mike's Burgers. They're famous for juicy steak burgers, and their mixed drinks were always on point. I needed a drink.

"I thought I might beat you here, but I see you checking your clock."

"It's all love. I was already in the neighborhood on business. But what's up wit' cha? You been missin' in action." The waitress approached the table. "Let me get another shot of that Hennessy. And whatever she wants." He nodded in my direction.

"Let me get a martini with three olives." The waitress smiled at Kirk before swishing away from the table. I even think she winked at him. I swear there was not a ho in Miami that couldn't sniff when a nigga had some money. And Kirk had it. "Hmmm, she doin' too much. Maybe you should pay her light bill or some," I joked.

"Shi'd, maybe." He chuckled. The ice on his wrist was shining so bright, I couldn't look at it head on.

"Bitch on thirst for real. But I can't blame her, 'cause yo ass got it." I grunted.

"I might be on that." He smirked.

I laughed at his cockiness. Kirk was the truth. "I see you goin' hard to on that hen. Nigga, it ain't even two o'clock yet."

"Yeah, but I had a long-ass night. Chasing that money ain't got no business hours. And when you building an empire you gotta stay on boast."

"No doubt," I agreed. I loved to hear him drop that knowledge.

"But what's up wit' you, though? You got me out here."

"What you think. I ain't worked in a week. A new gig is a must," I stressed.

"Yo, the set you had was it. And y'all just walked away from that. Now, I ain't trippin', but you still ain't never tell me why. The clientele was straight, and the money was good. So what?" He looked to me for an answer. The waitress set his Hennessy in front of him then placed my drink in front of me. I wasted no time taking a sip.

Biting into one of the olives, I chewed for a few seconds. I could never find the words to tell him what I was doing. So I just didn't. And I still didn't want to talk about it. "Look, like I told you, we just decided not to continue with that. But what's up now? I know you got us."

"Hey, you know I always got your back. But to be honest, I got some other moves I'm making right now. So I can't make no promises."

"Come on, Kirk. Don't bullshit me." I was disappointed as hell; this was the last thing I needed to hear him say. His cell phone started to ring, and he looked at it. He held up a finger signaling me to hold on.

"What's good?" he answered. He nodded his head a few times like the person on the other end could see him. "That shit one hundred," he replied. I just sat and sipped my drink. I wanted to roll my eyes. Shit, fuck that call, I needed his attention right now. "That play solid. I'ma get up in a flip." With that he ended the call.

"So it's like that." I was agitated, and there was no way I could hide it.

"Listen, baby girl. Don't trip, just know that we good. But right now I gotta go."

Not knowing what else to say, I just looked at him. I felt like I was being played, but what else could I do. "A'ight. Make moves." I hunched my shoulders with frustration, finished off my drink, stood and bounced.

Disappointed, I swung by the supermarket and picked up some pork chops to fry for dinner. A good home-cooked meal and a blunt would make me feel a lot better. Dropping the two plastic grocery bags I had on the kitchen counter, I pulled the pork chops out first and set them on the counter.

"What you buy from the store?" Penny strolled in the kitchen.

"Some pork chops, sweet potatoes, flour, and cooking oil."

"What you gon' do wit' all that?"

"I'm gon' cook it. What you think." I knew she was trying to poke fun. It was a known fact that I didn't care much for cooking. I was good at it but not a fan of it. "Yep, 'bout to fry up these pork chops, with some rice and butter, and steam some sweet potatoes."

"Now you got my stomach growling. And it's about time I get a good home-cooked meal, 'cause those peanut butter and jelly sandwiches constipating me." She laughed.

"Ha ha. You got jokes, huh." I placed the two-liter Cherry Coke I had also picked up in the freezer. It would be icy cold by the time the food was done.

"Well, since you in for the night, I need to use the car so I can go hang out with Erica and Shay."

"What y'all 'bout up to?"

"Just hangin' out at the bowling alley for a few hours."

"A'ight, it's cool, but no fuckin' drinking, 'cause you know I'll bust your ass," I threatened. I never really had any problem out of her when she went out, but I always threatened her just in case she forgot.

"Damn, Secret, you know I'm more responsible than that." She played offended. And she was right: I had never busted her drinking and driving.

"Yeah, you and Erica play that sneaky shit. But I know the game, because I been there done that," I reminded her. "Where Isis at?" I asked.

"In her room." She reached for the car keys. I had laid them on the counter next to the stove. "I'm out, though. Aye, make sure you save me a plate. And you know I like my pork chop really crispy. So fry it hard short of burning it. And I want two big ones." She made sure to give me precise instructions.

"Get your greedy ass outta here." I chuckled. "Isis." I yelled her name loud enough for her to hear me.

"What?" she yelled back. Her pet peeve was me bugging her when she was relaxing. I was surprised when she rounded the corner not even a minute later. "What's in the bags?" was the first thing out of her mouth.

"I'm cooking pork chops for dinner."

"Wait a minute. What?" She threw her right hand to her chest as if shocked.

"Whatever, Penny said the same thing. You two have jokes. I'm 'bout to sizzle up in this bitch. So get ready for my finger-licking pork chops."

"Aye, you know I'm always ready to eat. I was just laying down thinking 'bout what I was gon' eat."

"You need to get out that bed and get outta this damn house." Ever since we had stopped working she hadn't been leaving the house much. If she didn't get out soon, I was gon' have to take drastic measures to get her out.

"I'm cool. I gets out. Earlier today I went down to T-Mobile and paid my cell phone bill."

"Hmm, I guess, if you want to call that getting' out. But I'm talkin' about really gettin' out. Not saving your phone connection."

"I'm good. But where the hell you been? Shit, you burn up the streets enough for the both of us. Miami streets don't owe you nothin'." She giggled.

"Ha ha. You got jokes. I'll give you a slight laugh for that." I gave a soft clap along with it. "Nah, real talk, though, I stepped out to meet up with Kirk. He's clear about us walkin' away from the private dancing."

"Are you still sure that you want to walk away?" she asked. "I didn't ask you to do that."

"Like I have said a thousand times before, I'm

sure. We been besties since we were little, and it's a must that we stick together. Always," I stressed, and I meant every word. I hoped she believed me.

"I'm glad you respect that. But what are we going to do for jobs? We gotta get out here and make money. The little money we have saved won't last long with these bills constantly rolling in."

"That's what I've been thinking about. And the way I spend it, mine won't get me past another month."

Isis giggled. "It'll last a bit longer, but you gon' have to chill. It's time to think smart and spend less." She was always more responsible than I was.

"Aye, I'm wit' that, but we can't work no dead-end ass job that pays eight dollars an hour. That shit will not fly. We gotta make sure we gettin' paid."

Damn, we need Kirk is what I wanted to scream, but I chilled. "Real talk. Let's get this money and soon." I was hyped, but I calmed down quickly, because in reality I had no idea what we were going to do, where we were going to get a job making decent money. Racking my brain, I had a booming headache before I had an idea.

Chapter 17

Isis

We had been all over Miami looking for jobs for two full weeks and still we had no luck. Even still I didn't regret walking away from private dancing. And as mad as I had been at Secret for going behind my back doing the unthinkable, I was proud of her for walking away from all of it just to please me. But now I felt bad that she didn't have a job at all now. She had been out every day pounding the pavement with me. Every door that closed in my face closed in hers. Not wanting to give up, we kept our heads up and a positive attitude. When we heard that Macy's was hiring part-time starting out at thirteen dollars an hour, we scrambled our way down and put in applications. But after a week we hadn't heard anything back. We made the temp agency our destination. We began to believe that if they couldn't help us, then no one could.

"I swear, Isis, if that bitch say one more sarcastic thing, I'm going to jump over that counter and choke her ass." Secret referred to the girl whose name tag read "Tabitha" who stood behind the desk. Ever since we had walked through door she had had an attitude, and she showcased it as if she was getting paid for it.

"Ignore her. She just mad her weave jacked up. That ho don't bother me at all," I said, hoping to calm Secret down.

"That's 'cause you too easygoing. But bitch got one more time to try it. And I'm gon' snatch that matted rug off her damn head." And she meant every word.

"Are you done with your application? So we can get up out of here, Secret." I glanced up at her, and she turned red in the face. Tabitha was really getting under her skin.

"Yes, finally, all these unnecessary-ass questions; damn application look like the feds," she joked. "Let's turn this shit in and get outta here. It's too damn stuffy and somebody borderline musty." She tightened her nose and swatted at the air.

I almost laughed my guts up. Secret was crazy, but she was honest. I tried to ignore the smell, but it was getting more complicated by the second. Getting back in the growing line, we waited our turn so that we could turn in our applications. When Tabitha reached Secret, Secret glanced at me and rolled her eyes. That meant she was not ready to deal with Tabitha. But she stepped forward and placed the application on the desk.

For a moment everything appeared to be fine. I was glad we were almost finished and could leave.

After watching Tabitha look over her application, Secret turned to walk away. But Tabitha said, "Umm, you need to sign the back of this application. We can only accept completed paperwork and this . . ." Tabitha held the application up with a look of sarcasm covering her face. "This has no signature, so it's not complete."

Secret stepped back up to the desk. "Do you have a pen?" Secret sucked her teeth. It was clear she was annoyed.

"The pens for clients are out in the lobby where you filled out the application. You will need this." She dangled the paper in Secret's face. "Once you are done, get back in line and wait your turn."

I swear Secret's entire face turned bloodshot red on sight. It was about to get ugly and quick. "Bitch, who do you think you are?" Secret snatched the application out of Tabitha's hand, then threw the application back at her, barely missing her face as she ducked. Secret attempted to jump across the counter. It took me and a man in line to pull her back just as she swung a blow toward Tabitha's face. "Let me go, this bitch got me fucked up!" she barked and continued to tussle, attempting to break free of our hold.

Finally able to pull her outside, I placed my now ruined application into my purse. There was no way I could turn it in. "Secret, calm your ass down. I told you not to let that ratchet girl upset you." Now I was upset. Here I was, my clothes all jumbled up and trying to catch my breath, all because Tabitha didn't have any customer service skills. At this point I could slap her myself.

"Fuck that ho. Fuck her." Secret was beyond

pissed. I knew that in that moment she would not listen to me, so I let it go. She needed to vent her anger.

"Well, I guess we won't be getting hired up in there." I reached back inside my purse, pulled out the application, and dumped it in a nearby trash can.

"Isis, that application can kiss my ass. Why the hell y'all grab me? Damn, I wanted to hit that bitch at least once." She stomped her left foot. "I swear if I ever see her again, I'll bury her and put two bricks on top."

That was funny; I couldn't help but laugh. And it felt good: I needed laughter in my life. "Aye, don't worry about a job. We can always go down to JCPenney and get hired on the spot."

"Get the fuck outta here." Secret giggled. But it faded as she looked at the caller ID on her ringing cell phone.

"Who is it?" I asked.

"It's Kirk ass. I don't even know if I should answer. What you think?"

That explained the grim look on her face. "You might as well," I replied, but not certain it was the best idea.

"What's up?" She answered the call with a dry tone. I sat and waited to see what her next facial expression would be. "Yeah, but what's up?" she asked, then silence filled the air again. "That's cool. We are together right now anyway. Go ahead and text me the address." She looked at me.

"What?" I mouthed quietly so that he couldn't hear me over the phone.

The beep on her phone signaled a text. "A'ight, I got it." She ended the call.

"What'd he say?" I was anxious.

"He wants us to come out to his crib. Say we need to talk."

"About what, though?" I was curious.

"Guess we'll find out when we get there. Let's ride."

Thirty minutes later we had arrived at Kirk's house and boy, were we both wowed. He was living like a boss. I'm talking about a mansion compared to where we had come from. All of my life I had heard about gated communities—I had even seen them on television—but nothing compared to seeing it in real life. Pulling around the circular driveway, we stopped in front of the two grand double doors.

"This nigga out here living like Nino Brown," Secret joked, but it was the truth.

"Ain't that truth," I agreed. Climbing out of the car, we slowly made our way up to the door. "Aye, you sure you got the right address? I ain't tryin' to scare no white folks."

"Shi'd, this the address he text me." Secret quickly rechecked her text, but Kirk opened the door before she could locate the text.

"I was beginning to think y'all got lost." He chuckled.

"No, we found it fine, but we wanted to be sure this was it. We ain't tryin' to go to jail way out here. You may never find out what happened to us." Secret made her way to the door. I followed. I noticed she didn't even worry about locking her car door. I guess out here no one would steal it. In the hood she hit the locks before the car doors were shut good.

"Don't even play me. You know I wouldn't send you to the wrong address. Come on up in here." He motioned us forward with a hand gesture.

"What's good, Isis?" He spoke as I stepped past him in inside. My mouth all but flew open. His home was beautiful. The hallway was so wide and the ceilings so high, it was like something out of a magazine.

Secret's mouth was wide from astonishment just like mine. "Damn, nigga, I see who cashin' out." Her eyes had a gleam in them; I was certain mine did also.

"I swear," I concurred, shaking my head in agreement. Living lavish was the best way to describe it.

"It's cool. A nigga need a getaway. You know?" He played at being modest, because this was a far cry from the three-bedroom shack he and his host of brothers and sisters grew up in.

"Well, I want to see every inch of it." I was excited.

After taking us on a tour of the six-bedroom, seven-and-a-half-bathroom, four-car garage home, Kirk led us outside to his massive pool. We sat at a poolside table where he had a fruit tray set up. I was still in awe. But I was also ready to get down to business.

"Can I get y'all something to drink?" he asked. He treaded over to his outside bar and poured himself a drink. "And just help yourself to the fruit tray."

Secret looked at me, and my facial expression must have been what she felt. The generosity was nice, but business first. "Nah, we cool. What we want to know is why you called us way out here to Beverly Hills for?" I couldn't have said it better myself.

He downed his drink quickly, poured another, then returned to his seat at the table. "I brought you out here because I wanted to tell you about a new play I have for you. Now I know you still upset wit' Secret, because when you came to me a few weeks back I was onto something different. But like I told you, I have other ventures."

Secret gazed at me, and I looked at Kirk. I had had no idea she was upset with him, but who knew what that was all about. What I needed to know more about was the situation at hand. I was not up to the bullshit, and I was ready to make that clear. "What is it?" I asked. He wasn't saying anything fast enough for me.

"Well, it works a li'l some like this." I didn't like the way he said "li'l." That meant the shit was not legit. "You will go on dates that I will set up with professional athletes, on the rise rappers, or even successful businessmen. Pretty much anyone who pocket is laced."

"What the fuck, man. What is you talkin' about, Kirk? Dates and what not," Secret questioned. Like me, she was confused.

"Just like I said, you will go on dates. The only thing is all dates will be set up out of state. So you will have to travel, probably several times a week. But I promise you the money will be worth it. And

I ain't talking no chump change; I'm talking fourteen to fifteen thousand a job."

That got my attention full speed ahead. Secret and I both looked at each other, grins spread across our faces as we looked at Kirk. But suddenly I could feel my own grin flatten. "Wait, what will we be doing?" I asked. I was no fool, and that much money came with a price. That much I knew for sure.

Kirk looked at Secret first then at me, and all I saw was seriousness. "The thing is you and Secret will be setting them up."

"Setting them up? Setting them up how?" I sat on the edge of my chair.

"They are going to get robbed." The words slid off his tongue like a bullet and me the target.

"Oh, hell no." I all but jumped up out of my seat. "Kirk, that's some bullshit that could get somebody killed up, and I ain't gettin' involved. Do you understand what position you puttin' us in?" I looked at Secret, but her expression was blank. "Don't tell me you down for this, Secret?" Her eyes scrolled from Kirk back to me. She dropped her head but lifted it promptly. I knew then the only thing on her mind was the money. But I couldn't lie, as I declared I couldn't do it. The money was still heavy on my mind.

"Listen, y'all both know I would never put you in danger. Believe me when I tell you there is nothin' for you to worry about." He looked directly at me because he knew I was the one he had to convince. "The way the whole thing is set up, they won't even recognize they're being set up. Trust me, it will never cross their minds that either of you were involved."

"And all the jobs will be out of state?" Secret asked as if she was trying to clear things up, when in fact I think she was trying to convince me we were not in any danger, by clarifying Kirk's theory. He took the bait.

"Yeah, you will also be using fake names. Your appearance will be different. I'm going to have some real expensive wigs special made for both of you."

Secret stared at me, but my hesitation was still clear. She asked Kirk to leave us alone for a minute. As soon as he disappeared inside the house, she tried to reason. "Isis, I know this seem crazy—"

"Crazy . . ." I cut her off. "This is risky as fuck. This type of shit can get us fucked up, or worse, killed." I wanted to drive my point home. "Private dancing is one thing, hell, even having sex for money is different . . . but stealing from people. Now that's a whole other type of betrayal. Hell, all three of us are from the hood, so we should know better."

"And I know all of this. But Kirk will protect us. He has our back. Like he said, our names and appearances will be different. We will be safe, Isis. You just gotta trust. I know we can do this. Besides, the money is too good to just turn down. Shit, I don't know about you, but I want a taste of the good life. Just take a look around you." She referred to Kirk's house. "This is it. I don't know about you, but I can wake up to this type of living every day. And Kirk tryin' to lead us to it. All we gotta do is drink."

As much as I wanted to denounce her words, some of them for us rang true. And this was the only way that we might ever see that type of cash. It wouldn't hurt to at least give it a try. Or would it? Reluctantly I agreed.

Chapter 18

Isis

It had been three days since we had accepted our new gig from Kirk. For two of those days I watched a lot of movies to try to keep my mind off what I had agreed to do. I thought about going down to visit Felicia, because normally, when I saw her, it reminded me of the stupid mistakes in life that I should never make. For the life of me I couldn't drag myself from the television to do it. But today Kirk of all people dragged me away when he stopped by the house and dropped five thousand dollars apiece on Secret and me and told us to go shopping. We needed a new wardrobe to hit the ground running with our new gig.

The way he put it was we would be dating ballers, so we needed to dress the part. After we both took hot showers we got dressed and hit up Macy's. One thing was for sure: I had no second thoughts about shopping. I had a special love for new clothes and shoes. So did Secret, so spending money would not be a problem for us.

"OMG, I swear, I could never leave this store and be happy." Secret beamed while picking up piece after piece of clothing. I could relate. Everything was nice; it was hard to decide on any one thing.

"Me either," I agreed while thumbing through some cute rompers by Calvin Klein. I loved them and the way they fit my slim body. "So have you thought about what we gon' tell Penny while we're away on these trips? I mean some nights we'll have to stay overnight and sometimes two days depending on the gig. We are gon' have to tell her something."

"I know, and I have been racking my brain for a solution. But the only thing I could come up with was to tell her that we were still we dancing, and that the job is out of town. That should work, seeing as how we never really told her that we quit. Besides, she'll be starting school soon, so she'll be busy. She might not notice."

"This alibi sounds good. But what about the money? We won't be able to hide the cash for long. Penny is smart. She'll figure something's going on."

"This is true." Secret smiled. "Can't get much past that girl." She shook her head. "I say we just cross that bridge when we get to it. For now, let's focus on getting this money."

"Yeah, speaking of that, my first gig tonight is in Cincinnati, Ohio," I said, clueless. "Where the fuck is that anyway? It sounds like KKK central. I ain't got time for that." I laughed.

"Girl, stop, ain't nobody down there wearing no white sheets. Calm down." She laughed. "I feel you, but you gon' be good, it's up north. What are the details, though?"

"Some dude, he's a ball player." I shrugged my shoulders nonchalantly. "Kirk said he'll have more on him when we catch our flight tonight. It leaves at eight, so he gon' pick me around six thirty." I was glad when Kirk told me he was flying out with me for the trip. He wanted me to see that I would always be safe.

"That's what's up. I'm glad he decided to go along with you."

"Yeah," I said as I gripped the overflow of clothes in my forearm and headed toward the dressing room to try them on. I had to get a move on, because time was flying by.

Kirk and I checked into the Hilton around nine thirty; our flight had been a little over two hours; a personal driver was at the airport waiting on us when we arrived.

"You don't have much time, so get dressed. A limo will be picking you up in an hour. It will deliver you to the restaurant where your date will be waiting." Kirk gave me the run-down as the elevator stopped on the fifth floor, where my room was located.

"Dang, Kirk, a girl needs time to pamper." I smiled, rolling my suitcase off the elevator.

"Aye, take five minutes to pamper yourself." He chuckled. "For real, though, you got this. I'll be close by, so don't worry. Remember, be cool, calm, and collected. Everything will be fine." He looked me in the eye as the elevator door shut; his mouth was still moving but that was all I heard.

Wasting no more time, I dragged myself down to my room and damn near picked up my cell to call Kirk and tell him to change the time. The room was insane: plush carpet, new furniture, and a glimpse of the Jacuzzi really had me hyped. Kirk did not tell me he had rented me a master suite. All I wanted to do was get naked, jump inside, and soak. It was nothing less than a shame that I didn't have time to chill. Pouting, I undressed and slid into the shower. The Jacuzzi would have to wait.

Thank God the limo had a mini bar, because once I stepped inside I think I almost had a panic attack. When the driver shut the door, I almost felt like I had a date with doom. But the bar saved me, and thankfully it only took two shots of cognac to calm my nerves. Pulling up to the restaurant, I felt sure of myself and ready to do it. The six-foot-tall, medium build ball player seemed to be mesmerized by my appearance. But that was the goal: I was dressed in a black fitted crepe T-back dress, and it gripped all my assets. My feet were even pleasing in a pair of dusty rose colored two-piece heels. There was no doubt that I came to get the job done.

Turned out he was cute and really cool, but Kirk had already stressed the need to keep it only professional. We talked, ate, and drank a lot. The plan was to get the date to drink as much as possible. Kirk said that he would make sure that all our dates were drunks, which meant drinking would be no problem for them. Soon it was time to head back to his place, which was also a part of the plan.

Once inside, I was to search for the cameras and/or bodyguards if there were any. Then, once the coast was clear, I would seduce him as if I was ready to sleep with him, then text the person that was doing the robbery to let them know it was game time.

As planned, as soon as I began to fake-seduce him, I asked to go to the bathroom, then three masked gunmen descended on the house and held him at gunpoint. They asked him if anyone else was in the house. To my surprise he lied and said no. I'm not sure if it was to protect me or not. But one of the gunmen asked him again if anyone was in the house. He threatened that if they found out he was lying, they would kill him and whoever they found. Only then did he admit that I was in the bathroom. As planned, I was pulled out of the bathroom by the gunman; he shouted for me to get back in the same room where they had Mr. Ballplayer tied up. I was then told to lie down on the floor. They questioned him about whether he loves me or does he care what they do to me? They told him it's either him or me. He told them he just met me. They said, "Well, you don't care what we do with her then . . ." and that if he tells anyone they would kill him. Snatching me up off the floor a little rougher than I would have liked, one of the gunmen pulled me out of the room. He led me out the front door, where I jumped inside a waiting car. I was relieved when I saw Kirk. He explained that he already had all of my things. We headed straight to the airport while the three gunmen stayed behind and finished the job.

Finally, my part in the mission was over. According to Kirk, we had to leave right away. He told me that Secret had just left for Arizona for her mission, and that he would be getting on a different flight at the airport so that he could meet her there. Things were definitely in full swing. The next day I lay in bed a bit shaken as I replayed it all in my head. But the sight of the sixteen thousand dollars in cash that Kirk had delivered to me an hour before, which now lay on the bed next to me, helped calm my nerves a bit. After placing all the money back into the package that Kirk had delivered it in, I lifted my mattress and slid it under. Feeling exhausted, I climbed back under the covers and snuggled myself inside. I trembled as I felt as if I was a thief and even worse than my mother.

Chapter 19

Secret

I can't front; when I think about my first couple jobs I can't do anything but smile. Already I had completed five jobs and all went well, nothing off the course of what was planned. Talk about easy money, I had managed to make over eighty thousand dollars, and I could not believe it. Things were on the rise. We were finally getting a taste of what I referred to as the good life. We had all moved into a new apartment across town. Isis and I had thought about getting our own cribs at first but agreed we were not ready to separate. What we really wanted was a condo, but with our busy schedules, the time didn't permit the search or paperwork. So we just planned to do it later. However, what we did have time for was car shopping. I wasted no time signing on the dotted line for a 2014 all-white fully loaded Camaro, and I loved it.

Isis jumped a 2014 Challenger; we were balling and no one could tell us shit.

Today we had decided to meet up at the spa for a mani and pedi. We had invited Penny to come along, but she had a class, so she sent strict orders for us to bring back gift cards for her and Erica for another time. It had not gone unnoticed by her that our income had picked up in a major way, but when I told her the private dancing jobs out of town paid thousands more, she didn't question it beyond that. Talk about a relief.

"My feet so need this pedicure, I swear they are just dog tired. I think I have been wearing heels way too much lately," Isis said.

"I feel you. This visit was a must. I told you we should have got in here two days ago," I reminded her.

"That would have been nice, but like I told you, I had to pick up a few things for my upcoming trip. Plus I had my hair appointment yesterday. I just couldn't squeeze it in."

"I get it, but we can afford this shit now. It needs to be a part of a weekly priority."

"I can agree with that. Now I'll make it your responsibility to work it into reality." I laughed.

"Shit, don't worry I'll get right on that. You know I got this." I chuckled. "For real, though, we both been crazy busy lately. Even Penny been busy between work and school. I think we should all take a trip to Jamaica. We have earned it, and I think we all would enjoy it. Just think, a week of fun in the sun. And hopefully some fine-ass Jamaican dudes with that island accent," I added as an incentive to encourage her.

Isis had her head back with her eyes closed as her feet soaked. "That does sound nice." She opened her eyes. "Maybe we should go while Penny is out of school for her winter break. It's coming up soon."

"No doubt. I'll hit Kirk up to get the name of his travel agent. 'Cause we don't know nothin' 'bout booking no trips."

"I agree." Isis chuckled. "So how is work going for you?"

"Shit, cool. Why you ask? What's up?" I knew how she felt in the beginning, but now that money was rolling in, she seemed cool with it. But her question struck me as odd.

"Are you ever nervous while on the job? Like when it all goes down, the guys come in with the guns, the whole nine. 'Cause we kinda be in the middle of all that at first."

"Hell, no, I ain't nervous one bit. As long as I know them guns ain't for me, and it always go as planned. It should be the same for you."

"Yep, the plan always stay on course." She seemed hesitant.

"A'ight then. And it always will; we just gotta keep our head and make sure that nigga take plenty of shots before it all goes down."

"Please believe I be on that. My last guy damn near passed out before they even got inside his house, he was so drunk. While they were questioning him, he was dazed as fuck."

"That's what I'm talkin' about: keep sending that liquid down them niggas' throat. But you straight, though, right? You gotta stop worrying so much."

"I'm good, no worries over here. Besides, I leave

for Vegas tomorrow. And I can't wait to see what Vegas looks like."

"Damn, Kirk hook that up? I ain't been there yet, but when I do, I'm hittin' up them casinos. Fuck getting right out of town. I got to pull some slots first." The ringing of my cell phone cut me off. The number was unfamiliar, but I answered anyway. "Hello? Yeah, it's me, what's up?" I asked. It was this guy I had met a couple of weeks ago. I had forgotten I had given him my number. "Let's do that. Text me the address to the restaurant. A'ight, bye." I ended the call.

"Restaurant?" Isis's left eyebrow went up. "Who was that?" she interrogated me. Clearly she had been ear hustling.

"That was Marco—remember, that dude I met at the club a while back."

"That's been a minute. Is this his first time asking you on a date?"

"No, actually he called me twice after the club, but I was always busy with that private dancing. But he hit me up the other day, and I told him to call me in a few days so I could check my schedule. Hence all that bull. I'm going this time. Hell, I need a date."

"Since you about to go on a date with him, can I officially meet him then? 'Cause at the club Trina and I kinda hung back."

"Hell, naw, you don't need to meet him. Dude don't need to be gettin' any ideas. Nigga might think this love or some. And you know I ain't havin' that." I was known to dodge relationships and love. It all came with too much seriousness and this forbidden word called commitment, and I was allergic to that nonsense.

"You gon' have to get rid of that black heart because there's a guy out there for you somewhere that's worth your commitment."

"Ha ha, and with that we need to get something to eat. Because you trippin'." After our nails were dry we jumped in our whips and drove over to Real Wings.

The line inside was long as usual. Real Wings always had a crowd because they had some of the best wings in town, crispy and full of sauce just like I liked them. "This line need to get moving before I starve to death," I complained. I was truly hungry. My stomach growled for confirmation.

"We shoulda stopped off at the store and ate a sneaker for satisfaction. 'Cause it's gon' be a minute before those wings touch our tongue," Isis joked.

"I'll remember that the next time." We took a few steps forward as the line began to move. "It's about . . ." My eyes bulged out of my head at the sight of Jackie, who was about four people in front of us. She turned in my direction, looking me directly in the eyes. Suddenly I wasn't hungry. "This world is too damn small. Let's go." I grabbed Isis's arm and all but snatched her out of line.

"We gon' lose our spot. What's up?" She tried to keep up with me.

"I seen Jackie, she was in front of us." Isis turned to look in that direction just as Jackie yelled my name.

Walking as fast as our legs would allow to us go, we bolted out the door, but Jackie was right on our trail still yelling my name, clearly determined to get my attention. The touch of her hand on my shoulder proved we had been defeated. Angrily I snatched my shoulder back and turned to face her. "Don't you fucking touch me, ever." I spat the words out. I could not believe she had the nerve to even approach me.

"I just wanted to talk to you, Secret." I even hated the way my name rolled off her alcohol-smelling tongue.

"You have nothin' to talk to me about . . . We have nothin' to talk about." I wanted to be clear.

"Hey, Isis," she spoke as if the whole situation were normal.

Isis looked at me, and we both started walking toward our cars. I reached mine first, snatched the door open, and jumped inside, instantly starting the engine and throwing it in reverse. As I started to back up, Jackie grabbed my car door.

The strange words out of her mouth left me boiling. "I love and miss you and Penny. I would like to see you two sometimes," she shouted.

Livid, I screamed, "Get your hands off my got damn car, Jackie. And stay away from Penny and me with that dramatic bullshit. You never loved anyone but yourself." I burned rubber out of Real Wings's parking lot.

Jackie screamed, "I see you are doing good for yourself." I could not believe her.

Isis's name lit up on my Bluetooth in the car. "Hello?"

"You okay?"

"Yeah, damn, why did I have to see that evil-ass woman today?" I hit the steering wheel as I started to feel emotional. A tear attempted to sting the roof of my right eyelid. I wiped it away with so much force it burned. "That woman is the reason why I'm never scared. Seeing her reminds me that I have to do what I gotta do. And I'd do mostly anything to keep from going back home to her."

"And you won't ever have to," Isis tried to reassure me.

The growl within the deep pit of my stomach reminded me that I was still hungry. "Aye, meet me at Buffalo Wild Wings. Shit, I gotta eat asap." I gave a slight giggle.

For the first time I realized that I was stronger now and I could no longer permit Jackie to predict my life. Penny and I had survived despite her, despite the way she tried to break us. I would not allow the sight of her and her manipulative words to ruin me or my day.

Chapter 20

Isis

The tires on my Challenger did a circular side spin as I burned rubber pulling out of the carwash. "That was dope." Penny laughed, holding on to her seat. I was on my way to drop her off at school, but my car was dirty so I decided to stop by and let the carwash soap it off and shine my rims, because I could not be pushing through the streets of Miami looking dusty. "So you still gon' let me borrow the car tomorrow night? So that Erica and I can kick it with our other friends," Penny asked.

"Of course. But don't make me have to smack any of your damn friends about my whip."

"You know I will not let anything happen to this car. Everybody gon' be chill keepin' they hands to themselves."

"That's cool. I will be out of town working, so just take the car. I'll fill the tank up before I leave."

"That's what's up. Thank you so much." Penny grabbed her bag and climbed out of the car.

I had a job in St. Louis the next day and nothing to wear so I headed over to Macy's to find something. After an hour I had found nothing. I guess I had bought everything they had to offer with all the shopping I had been doing lately. So I ended up in Sunglass Hut trying on shades. A pair of Guccis had caught my eye. I took a step over to the mirror so that I could flex in them. I took one step backward to get a good look and stepped directly on this guy's foot.

"I am so sorry," I apologized right away. That Gucci had me tripping. I was paying no attention at all to where I stepped.

The guy whose foot I had brutalized didn't seem to be the least bit bothered, and he was noticeably cute. He gave me a slight smile. "It's cool." His demeanor was calm.

With that I turned back to posing with different facial expressions. I tried on several more pair of sunglasses before settling for the Guccis that had originally caught my eye. Since I didn't find anything to wear for my date, I decided to just wear something I already had. I still had things with tags on them, so something would have to work. But I was certain that I didn't want to go to another store to look for anything. And since I had some free time left, I decided to take a drive out to the middle-class area of Miami and take a look at a

condo that I had recently seen advertised on Facebook.

"I thought you were flying out to New Jersey earlier." I was surprised to find Secret rummaging
through the fridge when I entered the kitchen.

"Kirk canceled that about two hours before my
flight was scheduled to leave. I'll be going to Atlanta
first thing in the morning instead." She pulled
sliced turkey, Swiss cheese, honey mustard, lettuce,
and a tomato out of the fridge.

"Did he say why they cancel?"

"Something about the dude pulled out when his
wife who was supposed to be out of town returned
a day early." She hunched her shoulders nonchalantly. "I'm glad for that, too, because I don't need
to be in New Jersey locked up for beating a bitch's
ass." She chuckled while pulling out the butter-
flavored bread.

Watching her pull out the cutting board and seeing all the ingredients on the counter, I now wanted
a sandwich. "Real talk." I sighed. "Hook me up one
of them sandwiches."

"I got you. What you been up to today?"

"Nothin'. I dropped Penny off at school then
hit up the mall, got me a new pair of Gucci shades.
And they beat, you gon' be jealous when I flex." I
reached into the fridge and pulled out a bottle of
Dasani water, which had been my original reason
for coming into the kitchen. "Afterwards, though,
I checked out this dope condo. It was a two-bedroom, three-and-a-half bathroom, with a two-car

garage. I'm thinkin' about leasing it. The cost is reasonable and everything."

"No doubt. You gon' have to take me over to check it out."

"Cool, we'll go when you get back day after tomorrow."

"Aww, I don't want you to move out." Secret gave me a fake pout.

"Whatever, you can't wait until I bounce. But that was our plan anyway, remember. Eventually grab our own crib," I reminded her.

"I know, I just hate the idea."

"Me too," I admitted, suddenly sad about leaving her and Penny. My stomach growled as she passed me my sandwich. "Thank you so much; this looks good. I'm about to go to my room, eat this sandwich, and take a nap. I'm tired."

"A'ight. Wait a minute." She stopped me as I turned to leave the kitchen. "I got a call from Christian today. He said that he ran into Karen from the old neighborhood a couple of days ago and that she said your mom wants you to come down for a visit."

Instantly annoyed, I rolled my eyes. I couldn't for the life of me understand why Felicia would send a message through Karen. I hadn't spoken to Karen in years. Her sister Linda had been locked up with my mom for the last four years. And still we hadn't even managed to run into each other.

"Why that face?" Secret giggled. "What's up?"

"That's just bullshit that Felicia would send a message through Karen. Like what would make her think she could reach me through her?"

"The streets and connects, I guess . . . But when the last time you been down to see her?"

"It's been a minute, but not that long ago. I mean, I went down that one weekend to straighten out that issue about that money. But . . . anyway, I been busy and just ain't had the time." That was enough reason for me to at least excuse myself. I couldn't fool Secret, though; she knew better. "I just ain't been feeling like foolin wit' her. Real talk. Things been going good, and I just want it to remain that way for a minute."

Secret nodded her head in agreement. "You know I understand that. So you ain't even gotta trip . . . I gotta say, though, on Felicia's behalf. Growing up before she got sent up, you had it better than us. Because she might have been a thief, booster, or whatever you want to call it. But she loved you. Still do . . ." Secret's eyes watered, but no tears fell. "Penny and I didn't have that . . . Just think about that." Stunned at the real she had just given me, I exited the kitchen with a heavy heart.

Chapter 21

Isis

Although it was a hard truth to swallow and I wasn't sure if I was ready to accept it yet, I woke up early the next morning and drove out to see Felicia. On the drive down I wondered what she would think about the work I was doing now if she knew. Would she accuse me of being a hypocrite? Or if I told her about all the money, would she just tell me to keep getting it? I even taunted myself with the dumb idea that I might tell her just to get my answer. But by the time I arrived, checked in, and she walked into the visiting room, I had come back to my senses. I could never tell her what I was doing. Never did I want her to judge me in a negative way. And while I didn't know if she would or not, I didn't have the guts to find out.

As soon as she saw my face, the solemn look on hers evaporated. "Hey, sweetie." She looked as though she had been relieved of some sort of grue-some pain. "It's been a minute since you been out to see me. I missed you so much, Isis." I could hear the cry in her voice, full of evidence of the love that she carried for me. Still I fought not to soften.

Like a pro I bottled my emotions and remained my usual Isis. I didn't even give her a hello. I jumped right in. "Why did you have to send word to me to come down here? And by Karen of all people," I said her name as if a pile of shit was con-nected to it. I didn't have anything personal against Karen; I was simply annoyed by Felicia's ac-tions. "If you need to reach me, you know how. You know where I am. The same way you know I will eventually come to see you. I don't need to be summoned like some child," I reminded her like I was the parent and she was the child.

The calm look on her face confirmed that, as al-ways, she was choosing her words carefully so as not to upset me. I think she worried that if she pissed me off I might get up, walk away, and not re-turn. "So what have you been up to?" She chose to change the conversation.

"I've been busy with this or that." I kept it sim-ple. There was really nothing else I could fill that question with. But I wanted to keep my lies at a minimum, because then I would have to remem-ber what I said.

"Well, you look good." She smiled at me. "So how is school going for you?" I swear she wanted to piss me off on purpose. Not once had I told her I had signed up for school; that was just her way of getting that conversation started, when she knew that was the last thing I wanted to discuss.

"I'm not in school, but you know that already . . . So why do you keep bringing this up at every visit? It's just not the time." I sighed with annoyance. The look of disappointment hid behind the shadows. She tried her best to hide, but it was too late. I had seen it. "Listen, like I've said several times before, I am happy being what life has allowed for me to be."

"And there is nothin' wrong with that. I just want to be sure you're happy and secure. That is all." It felt good to hear her say she just wanted me to be happy. I hoped that was the truth, because at this time I had no real idea what I would do next.

"Good, so let's drop the school talk . . . I have to get going, though. I got plans for later." That was the best way to sum up what I really had in store. How could I say I was headed back home where I would be catching a flight so that I could participate in the messy scheme of robbery? Exactly, I could not. So a simple goodbye would have to do.

Chapter 22

Secret

Ever since talking with Isis about a month ago about the condo she had visited, it really got me to thinking. With the money I was making I could more than afford a condo. I was already on the come-up so why not take it to the next level. But then Isis suggested that we just find a condo together and lease for a year, then get our own. I wasn't ready for her to move out yet, so I quickly agreed. After a careful search of a host of condos in the Miami area, Isis and I narrowed it down to a downtown location that was just absolutely beautiful. A 1,495 square feet, three-bedroom, three-and-half-baths master-piece. We would have full access to a swimming pool and our sun deck. There were also free yoga classes, a state-of-the-art fitness center, and more in the building.

Today was the day that we told the manager that

we could fill out the application and sign the rental lease. Signing on the dotted line was magical; we couldn't wait to drop the down payment in the manager's hands.

"Let's go for drinks," Isis suggested to me after we walked out of the manager's office.

"Yeah, this deserves a toast. Besides, she said she'd be calling us within an hour so we may as well stay on this side of town," I agreed, but wouldn't be able to wait much longer than that. Finding a close bar and grill, we strolled inside, sat down, and ordered martinis.

"You think we're gettin' in over our heads? That rent ain't cheap," Isis asked, sipping on her drink and pointing out the obvious.

"See, there you go with that shit. Hurry up and drink that liquor down quick. Wait, no, where is the bartender?" She scanned the room like she was looking for the waitress. "Because you need something stronger. I'm 'bout to get you a shot of that brown, yep, that Hennessy," I chirped.

Isis chuckled. "I don't need a damn stronger drink. This is fine." She raised her drink like we were about to toast.

"Real talk, though. We gon' be fine, and you know we can afford that amount easy. What we gon' be out of forty-five hundred a month. That includes our rent, parking, condo fees, and all. We halve that shit down the middle and it's nothin', just like we previously discussed. We make that in a week," I reminded her.

She stirred her martini as if she was confirming what I said in her mind. She shook her head in agreement. "You right, we got this, I just want to be sure. Because we also need to focus on saving: that's equally important. Especially since we plan to get our own crib eventually."

"Hell, and I can't wait to get my own crib to get away from your ass," I joked.

"I know, right. A party will be thrown when I buy my first place and become delivered from you. With yo naggin' ass." She laughed. "But you know you will miss me."

"I guess I might." I chuckled, then finished off my drink. The waitress walked past, and I signaled her to grab me another martini. This time I asked her to add an extra shot of vodka. The first one was good, but it seemed a little too light for me. "How did the visit go with Felicia?" I asked.

"Same ol' visit. She worried about me and school, as if that matters. I told her to dead that conversation. Ain't no school for me, and it's time she accept that."

"I know, right. I can't believe she still be on that."

"Girl, yes, she does, that's the one thing she never forget to ask me about on each visit."

"I get it, and it sounds good but . . . we gotta get this money. Real quick."

"But that's just it, though, Secret, we got money now. It's time to try something different, like turn up. And I mean all the way up."

"Aye, I can get wit' that." I was relieved. I thought she was about to say something like it's time to get out of the game. And I was not down to hear that shit no time soon.

"I got an idea. How about we get with Kirk and

tell him not to book anything next weekend. 'Cause we about to shut the club down."

"Turn up," I chanted and raised my glass in the air. "But listen, you get right on that." I looked at the time on my phone and realized we had to get going soon because I had a flight to catch. "I gotta get back to the house, my flight leave soon. I need to grab my whip and my bags. You are gon' have to finish up with the process after she approves the application on your own."

"A'ight. By the time I drop you by the house she should have an answer."

"I'm sure," I assured her, then polished off my drink.

Thankfully, I landed safely. No sooner than I got to my hotel room, I took a shower and started to get dressed. Isis called to let me know that we had been approved and could move in right away. Excited, I finished getting dressed and headed out to meet up with my date, Kenny, at a bar inside another hotel.

Right away we hit it off, and I made it my business to keep Kenny tossing back cognac shots. It seemed to take a while for him to get tipsy, but eventually the drinks started to wear him down. Back at his place we both drank some more, but I was careful to only sip as I was trained to do.

Taking a seat close to me, Kenny started to slightly rub my right thigh. I teased him with a soft kiss on the inner left section of his neck. "Tell you what, you let me use your bathroom, and we can really get this party started," I whispered seductively in his ear.

Licking his lips, Kenny gripped my thigh tight and leaned in to kiss me on the cheek. "You go ahead and take your time, beautiful."

A quick search of the house and I presumed the coast was clear, so I sent the text. Hurrying back to Kenny, I returned to my spot next to him. Wanting to waste time until my relief arrived, I tried to make small talk, but Kenny wasn't having that. And instead of the alcohol making him sleepy, it made him extra frisky. It felt like his hands were all over me. I was running out of ideas and fast as I waited for it to go down. But nobody showed. Then I finally got a text on my cell phone, but he was so close to me I couldn't answer. My instincts told me that I needed to look at that text, but I had to play it off.

"Kenny, can you please get me some ice for my drink? I need a good cold shot." I kissed him softly on the nose. "The chill from a cold shot usually gets me going." I did a quick grind in my seat and smiled for good measure.

"I'll be right back." He hurriedly stood up.

Unlocking my phone, I quickly opened the text. My heart dropped. It read, *"Running behind got pulled over."* I almost freaked as I replied, *"Hurry the fuck up this guy ready to fuck and right now."* Just as I exited the text and locked my phone, Kenny entered the room. Nervous, I had no idea what I would do.

Passing me the ice, he watched as I slowly poured it into my drink. I picked the glass up and I drank. Kenny's eyes never left me. Sitting back down next to me, his hands found both my breasts as he jumped right back in where he had left off. Frustrated and fresh out of ideas, I asked him to slow down. He looked in my eyes briefly, chuckled, and continued fondling me. I tried to remain calm and prayed that he couldn't feel my heart about to jump out of my chest as his rubbing and feeling became more aggressive by the second. I could no longer take it. "Wait a damn minute," I yelled, annoyed.

Suddenly I felt the blow from the center part of his big-ass hand as a slap landed across my face. Blood flew out of my mouth. Shocked, I glanced at him, and anger covered his face. "Bitch, you being a fucking tease," he accused me. Before I could speak, he attacked me. I tried to fight back as I was met with blows and punches to my body back to back. With each lick I felt myself growing weaker as he tugged at my clothes from all directions. Feeling dazed and realizing that he was about to rape me, I gathered all the strength left inside me and kicked him in the balls. Taking both of my thumbs, I pushed forward and pressed them hard into both his eye sockets. "You fuckin' half-breed bitch," he cried out in agony.

As he struggled with the new pain I inflicted on him, I pushed him off of me and tried to get on my feet. Just as I tried to find balance on one leg, he grabbed the other leg, and I fell back to the floor. Using my free leg, I kicked at him and tried to crawl close to his built-in fireplace. I reached for a statue of a tiger that was resting there. Out of breath and panting really hard, I flipped myself halfway over and somehow hit him in the face with it.

All I heard was a loud thud, then saw him on the floor next to me. Jumping to my feet, I grabbed my cell phone and clutch purse off the couch and burst out the front door. Not sure which way to go, I raced down the street. I saw lights and realized a car was approaching. The car came to a complete stop. One of the guys called me by name as he got out and helped me inside the car. With no questions asked, they rushed me to the nearest hospital.

Chapter 23

Isis

Tears flooded down my face as I snatched the door open to find Kirk standing there holding on to Secret. I thought I would never see or hug my friend again. Kirk had called around two thirty in the morning and woke me up out of my sleep, saying that he had to fly out to get Secret, because the guy that she was setting up had attacked her. He had tried as best he could to assure me that she was okay. But I wouldn't believe that until I was able to lay eyes on her. And now here she was, all in one piece, standing in the doorway.

Kirk had told me that Secret didn't want me to tell Penny what was going on, to just let her go to school as usual. Since I had taken her out to the airport the day before to pick up Secret's car, she didn't need me to take her to school. When she stuck her head in my door as she sometimes did before going to school, I played as if I was extra tired. This way she would just leave. But really, the last thing I wanted her to do was see my face. She would have been able to instantly tell that I had been crying.

"Are you okay?" I gently wrapped my arms around Secret.

"I'm fine, really, I'm okay," she tried to assure me, hugging me back tightly. She had a bruise on the left side of her face. Her skin was too light to hide any kind of bruise. I stared at it in dismay. She looked as if she was turning into a blueberry. The right side of her face appeared to be a bit swollen. She glanced at me again; this time a slight fake smile appeared. "I'm fine," she repeated.

"Well, it don't look like it at all." I got emotional.

"I promise you it looks a lot worse than what it really is."

"Yo, Kirk, what the fuck happened to her? This shit supposed to be safe. Remember?" I was sarcastic on purpose. I reminded him of his own words that he had used to convince us that this was okay.

"I know how this looks. But I promise you are safe . . . Shit just went down wrong. Nigga that was driving the car swerved and got pulled over. I got y'all; though the nigga that was drivin', I already took care of his ass . . ." He looked at Secret's face then slowly gazed at me. "And the nigga who did that to her already pushin' up daisies."

And we all knew what that meant. Still, I was not satisfied: the danger that had been clear from day one was now even more evident. "Fuck that," I said, frustrated, pacing and rubbing my forehead. "We both quit," I spoke up for Secret and myself.

In case she didn't have the sense to do it, I would do it for her. "Kirk, I can't lie, this shit has been good to us, but our lives come first." And I meant that. Even I knew that money was no good if you weren't around to spend it.

I waited for Kirk to plead with us not to leave, but instead he declared he understood. Spinning in Secret's direction, he apologized to her. With every sorry that oozed from his lips, I knew they were sincere. Soon after, he left.

"I knew that shit was not safe." I marched over to the alarm monitoring system and turned it on. For some reason I didn't feel safe. Even though this had happened in another city, I was still a bit shaken. "We could have been killed at any moment. Damn!" I yelled. "We should have never gotten involved in this mess."

"But I'm okay, Isis," Secret tried to assure me. I knew better; the pain was colored all over her bruised face. The thought of what she had been through caused knots to twist and turn in the pit of my stomach. I wanted to run to the bathroom and throw up my insides.

"No, you're not, Secret. You are just saying that." I was painfully honest. "And what are we going to tell Penny? Or have you not thought about that? I'm sure this is going to freak her out. We lied to her about what it was we were doing. Now it has come back to bite us in the ass in a major way."

"And that's why I'm going to tell her the truth, or at least get as close to it as I can."

"Do you really think that's a good idea? She'll be mad we lied to her."

"But she'll get over it." She wiped a tear off her

lip that threatened to enter her mouth. "And you have to stop worrying, because I'm okay. I'm stronger than you realize. Jackie made sure of that long before some nigga came along and decided to punch me." She gave a slight chuckle but had to hold on to her side because of the pain. "Besides, compared to Jackie that nigga hit like a bitch." She attempted a joke.

I tried not to smile but couldn't help it. Even in the midst of turmoil Secret was cracking a joke. And I loved her for it. But even that couldn't warm my heart; I was sick with hurt, yet grateful that she was still alive. Grateful that we had another shot to get it right. There had to be something out there for us that didn't require us to sell our dignity. I just wished I knew what it was and where to find it.

Chapter 24

Secret

Months had slipped by since the incident and I had tried my best to move on from it, but occasionally I still had nightmares about it. I think what bothered me worst were the punches. It reminded me of Jackie and her abuse. The last time she put her hands on me I vowed that was the last time *anyone* would lay their hands on me. And there I was, laid flat under some stranger while he pounded his fist into me. I wished with every ounce of me that Kirk had not killed him; that should have been my job. And if anyone else ever tried it again I would kill them, but I had to get on with my life, and I meant to do just that. If I didn't allow my own mother's stupid actions to ruin my life, I damn sure wouldn't let a stranger's. It was bad enough we had lost out on our condo deal. And I wasn't about to give up on that completely; it was just not going to happen right now. But it would.

Kirk had been blowing me up for the past two weeks trying to get me and Isis to meet up with him. Once again he claimed to have a different play for us. Now that I was healed, I was bored and ready to get money again. Money was always on my mind; fuck being depressed, that shit was for the birds. Isis on the other hand was relaxed; the first time I told her Kirk had called, she waved me off. But he had just called again, and I had to try again, because I was not about to give up.

"Kirk called," I announced as soon as she sat down on the living couch. She had just come out of the kitchen; she was cooking dinner.

"What he want?" She tried to play dumb. But she knew exactly what he wanted. What else would Kirk want?

"This is Kirk we talking about, Isis. What else would he want? So what's up? It's been months since we worked. So we could at least hear him out."

"Hear him say what exactly? I don't need to hear nothin' about doing anything that involves me dealing with some nigga. 'Cause you know that's what it's about." She sighed. "I've been thinkin' a lot, and this might be time to just find a regular job. Just like the old days."

I had to give her a double take because I was not trying to hear that shit. That was not about to happen with me. "Now you trippin'. I ain't gettin' no regular job, because I ain't no regular bitch," I added. "So we can talk about something else, try again. By the way, what are you cookin' in there? It smells hella good and I'm hungry."

"I just finished frying some cabbage and fish. I just slid some homemade sweet cornbread muffins into the oven. Your greedy self can eat in about fifteen minutes." The doorbell rang just as she stood to go back into the kitchen. "I'll get it," she volunteered then walked over and opened the door. I could not see Isis's face, but I could tell by the way she gave them that extra double jointed stance that this was not good.

Kirk stood in the doorway with both his hands in his pants pocket. "Hey y'all?" He had a huge grin on his face, his white teeth glistening. "Are you going to invite me in?" He eyed Isis. She turned around to look at me and roll her eyes. I knew she wouldn't be happy. Stepping to the side so that Kirk could enter, she shut the door behind him.

"Umm, umm, it smells good up here. Wish my house smelled like this." Kirk rubbed his six-pack.

"It ain't math or science. It's called cooking, Kirk." Isis was sarcastic. "Did you invite him?" she fired at me like he was not standing right next to her.

I decided not to reply; it would only make her angrier. I could only hope she didn't stay mad long. But this meeting was a must. I had no choice but to hear Kirk out. So when he had called, I told him to come on over while she was home. It was now or never.

"Listen, I know what happened on the last gig was fucked up. More than fucked up. But I really need to speak with you two." I glared at Isis to see her reaction. It was just like I thought: that stubbornness was plastered to her face like cement.

"Isis, please, just hear him out," I begged. My eyeballs bulged out at Kirk. That look meant hurry up and say whatever the hell it was he had to say. This would probably be his only chance.

With an unsure facial expression, Kirk spoke fast. "I got something new for you. This play is not dangerous at all. And you will make more money than you have ever made." I noticed Isis roll her eyes at the mention of money. He should have known by now that money was not the selling point for Isis. I can't say that she didn't like money, but it definitely didn't move her. I would have to talk to him about his strategy next time. But I was different; money was like music to my ears, and my eyes shone like diamonds were in the pupils. I scooted to the edge of the couch because I didn't want to miss anything he had to say. Before he could say anything else, Isis jumped in.

"What else different this time, Kirk? Besides money; that's always the main factor in a scheme."

"You got a point. But this is no contact. You will be working from home from your computer."

"Computer," I repeated. Now I was confused. "What we doing with computers?"

"Money transfers. All you gotta do is change some numbers on rich people's accounts that I will give to you. Then you would just hit the send button to make the transfer that sends the money into another account. Some unknown person will go to the bank and withdraw the money. It's quick, easy, and untraceable to us. Easiest money you will ever make." With that he rested his case, but I couldn't believe my ears.

"Kirk, I can't front; that sounds easy as shit." Grinning, I looked at Isis. This was a play she could not refuse. No danger and a flow of cash. But that was not the feeling I got from just looking at her face.

"So that's it, huh . . . more fuckin' stealing." I couldn't believe my ears; she still was not happy. "And not no petty shit, either, but federal prison time." I swear she thought everything through to the point of negativity. Damn.

Now I was getting pissed. Why was she constantly going to the worst assumption? We hadn't even got started yet and already she had us in prison locked in a cell and all. "Fuck all that, Isis. As usual, you are thinkin' way too much."

"Isis, this ain't like that. This is untraceable, and the people that we are gettin' this money from are billionaires. They'll probably never know it's gone. This will be like taking chump change from them." Kirk tried to reason with her, but Isis folded her arms and shook her head with the look of disappointment all over her face. She was not making this easy. I dropped my head and waited for what she would throw at him next. Because I knew Isis, and she was not finished.

"Do you have any jobs that are legit? Something that won't get us locked up or fucked up?" she asked her question over-the-top with the dramatics. We both knew fast money didn't come from honesty. Kirk looked at me then back to her. He didn't answer the question. I didn't blame him. About to give up myself, I shrugged my shoulders.

"Thought so." She rested her case then headed toward the kitchen.

"You knew this wasn't going to be easy," I whispered to him. Signaling for him to hold on, I decided to give it one more try. Walking to the kitchen, I took a deep breath.

"Come on, Isis. What's up? This is what we need. We couldn't ask for a better play."

"Aye, doing this makes me no different than Felicia, and I'm not her; fuck that." Now I realized that was what this was all about. Isis always battled with comparing herself to Felicia, fearing she would turn out just like her. There was no explaining to her that she was not her mother, the same way I was not Jackie.

"Why are you making this about Felicia? This is not the same thing."

"Don't try and bullshit me, Secret. I think you and I both know this ain't no different. Hell, it's ten times worse, to be honest. Takin' people's hard-earned money. What does that make us? Saints?"

"Listen, I know it sounds bad but these motherfuckers got enough to share with people like us. Damn, Isis. Sometimes we gotta think about ourselves. It doesn't make us bad people. We were dealt a bad hand a long time ago. Who felt bad for us?" I fought back the tears that threatened to fall. Thinking about our lives often made me sad, but I brushed it off, only because I was determined not to allow my past to ruin me. "But this is a good opportunity for us, and if the money is as good as Kirk says it is, maybe, just maybe, we can cash out and stop doing it for good." Tears were running down Isis's face. I had struck a nerve talking about our lives. It was usually a soft spot for all three of us.

Pulling the oven mitten off her right hand, Isis said, "Fuck that. I don't need it. And this reverse psychology bullcrap does not work. I can always go back to my old job. This shit is for the birds." With that she walked out of the kitchen, leaving me dumbfounded. She wasn't even willing to give it a try.

Chapter 25

Isis

I have to be the first to admit I could be stubborn as constipation. Sometimes I could be swayed and sometimes not. It really just depended on the situation. But to be honest, some of the things Secret had said about our lives, us being dealt a bad deal coming up, hit home. Yeah, my emotions showed, but at that moment I wasn't ready to surrender. Yes, Kirk's offer was a once-in-a-lifetime thing; even I knew that. However, I was serious about one thing: the last thing I wanted to become was a thief and end up like Felicia. Then again, Secret had made another great point. If we made enough money, maybe would could get out the life for good. And that was what got my attention. I would love to be set for life. No more dirty work. Hell, no more work period, unless it was for myself. That I could get with that was worth considering.

So that was the reason that a few days later I agreed to do the job. Kirk had summoned us out to his crib first thing this morning for "training," as he called it. I was game because I was ready to get this show on the road. And hopefully over with.

"Damn, Kirk, these are Apple," I sang at the sight of the brand-new laptops Kirk had given us right out of the box. They were both silver.

"I know, right." Secret's eyes shone as she play-typed on the keys. "I swear these keys feel like butter. Make me feel like a career woman."

"But you're not," I joked.

"Ha ha, whatever." She played at being offended with a smile.

"Aye, nothing but the best for my two favorite ladies," Kirk gloated; he loved to see the smiles on our faces. "Now we're going to load these laptops up, and I'm going to train you myself."

I was surprised to learn that Kirk would be the one training us. And two hours later he had done just that. I was impressed at how precise the process was and at how fast it would be to transfer thousands of dollars into an untraceable bank account. "Now you will both be doing several switches a day. I will assign them to you most times the day before. But in some cases it might be the same day that I call you that the switch has to be made."

"So we just sit at home, wait for the call, pull out our laptops, and make the transfer right from there?" I asked. "Almost like working at a call center, huh?"

"Yep, that easy, except for the money factor. All

paydays are fat." He chuckled. I was convinced he loved money just as much or more than Secret did.

"Aye that's dope," Secret said, still fake-typing on her computer. Maybe if this didn't work out she could apply for a typing job. She would kill me for even thinking it, so I kept it to myself.

"But there is one small thing that's very important." Secret and I both glared at him. What was he going to say this time? "These computers are not to be used for anything else, no searching or browsing of any kind. These transfers must be the only activity on them. This is very important."

"That's cool. But will the people who pick up the transfer know who we are? Will anyone on the other end have any contact with us?" He had repeatedly told us that everything was untraceable, but I had to be sure from all aspects.

"No, there will be no contact. They won't know anything about you. And there will never be any contact. You two are invisible in this. I am, too, for the most part. Just think of them as the people on the other end." I liked the sound of that. This information made me feel more secure. The last thing I needed was some unknown crook knowing my identity. Secret seemed pleased as well.

"Here is your first real assignment." He passed us both a sheet of paper with an account number on it. "And remember, as soon as you hit those numbers, this sheet of paper goes into the shredders I gave you."

"You want us to do this right now?" Secret was surprised.

"Ain't no time better than the present. Besides,

you go live tomorrow. And we got some catching up to do."

"Nigga, you always got a surprise up yo sleeve." Secret sighed. "A'ight, here goes nothing." She took a deep breath. I watched her start typing in her numbers. Bracing myself, I followed suit. There was no turning back. A few minutes later when I hit the button to transfer, the pit of my stomach tingled. Just like that, we each had transferred eighty thousand dollars into an unknown account out in the universe.

"That took what? Five minutes." I was in awe.

"It's quick just like that." Kirk snapped his fingers. "Depending on demands, you might do about five of those a day, sometimes more. Some days none at all."

"Shit, if that's all it is then let the games begin. 'Cause I'm ready to cash out," Secret chanted.

"And, baby girl, you just did; when you fucking with Kirk that's just what it is." He stepped over to his desk. My jaw loosened and my mouth dropped wide open, as he handed Secret and me ten thousand dollars apiece.

"Now that's what's up," Secret said. "Get money," she sang. "And we gon' get stacks like this for each transfer we send, regardless of how many we do in a day?" I was glad she asked that question, because it was on the tip of my tongue.

"Damn right; for each transaction there's a payout. Your life about to change, boss style." He pounded his left hand into his right palm, and a smirk appeared on his face.

"Wow," was all I could say. The money was good.

And I was sold; he didn't need to say any more. I was just not happy about the situation. I wished my life was different. Possibly a little more honesty would be nice.

"Shit, I can't wait to get started tomorrow." Secret was super amped up. When it came to money, I didn't know her limit. In a way it was scary.

"And I got you. Now you two get home, get some rest, I'll hit you up tomorrow. And take these with you." To our surprise he pointed to two boxes on the floor; they were identical to the boxes he had handed us earlier that housed the Apple computers.

"You want us to take those to work on instead?" I asked, confused.

"Nope, those belong to you. Think of it as a bonus. The first one I gave you is for work. But this one is for searching, browsing, or whatever you want to do."

"See, Isis, I told you he had a heart of gold. My nigga, Kirk," Secret said.

"This was nice of you, Kirk," I had to admit. If only he could find us legit work, I would be so happy I might date him myself. Okay, I really wouldn't, but I would be happy.

Kirk loaded our cars up with the laptops and we balled out toward the crib. I hadn't been as hype as Secret while at Kirk's so I hoped I didn't seem ungrateful, but I had to see where this led. I hoped for good things, but I was learning in the life of schemes you never knew what card you might be dealt. So far our cards were not aces.

Chapter 26

Secret

"Secret, can I please have this Louis Vuitton bag? I promise I won't ask for anything else today. This will be it." Penny batted her innocent eyes at me. I had to admit the bag was all that. It was a calfskin tote. Looking at the tag, I saw it read twenty-four hundred dollars. I eyed her as she continued to pout.

"Yes, you can have it." I gave in. Now I would sit back and wait to see what she pouted for next. The girl was spoiled, and honestly, I enjoyed cashing out on her. I wanted her to have everything I never did growing up.

"Thanks, sis. I'm going to rock this. Let me get the saleslady to take the lock off this." Penny scurried off to go find the saleslady. Isis, Penny, and I were out at Nordstrom doing some shopping. It had been a couple of months since we started the account transfer scheme. And business was great. Shopping had become second nature to us; all we did is spend, spend, spend, and it never was a problem. Our pockets were laced, so why not. And Penny, for one, was enjoying it. She seized the moment and got every little thing her heart desired.

Penny came back with the saleslady and pointed out the Louis that she so desired. With a big smile she skipped over to Isis. "Isis, can I please have that cross-shoulder Burberry purse? Please." See, the girl played us both to get what she wanted, and we fell for it every time.

"Wait, and I already know, you promise not to ask for anything else?" Isis mocked her.

"See what had . . . happened was . . ." She laughed.

"I swear you spoiled." Isis grinned. "Yes, you can have it."

"Thanks, Isis." Penny waved the saleslady over to grab it also.

"What we gon' do with this shopping monster we done created?"

"Good question. Maybe we could ship her off somewhere," Isis joked around.

Another hour and ten thousand dollars later we were done shopping. And Isis and I both were tipsy. The more you shop, the more wine they bring out. It might as well have been an open bar. I'm sure it was part of the plot to get your money, because when you're tipsy, everything in the store is a must-have. Needless to say, I for one hoped they kept serving liquor, because as long as I had money, I would be in here getting tipsy and tossing cash in the air like I didn't really care.

* * *

I rolled over in my new king-size bed. It felt so good and plush. I absolutely loved having a bed so big that I could roll left to right more than four times and not be worried that I might hit the floor. Pushing my Martha Stewart chateau quilt back, I sat up and stretched. Sleeping under that quilt felt like sleeping under a cloud. I couldn't help but smile as I looked around my big new room. The natural light that came through my bedroom window was rejuvenating. Each morning I woke refreshed and feeling accomplished. Two weeks prior, Penny and I had moved into a brand-new condo just as we had planned. Isis now lived across the way in her own condo. She decided that she wanted her own space, and though Penny and I protested, in the end we gave her our blessings. Climbing out of bed, I made my way to the bathroom so that I could brush away my morning breath and wash my face. My stomach started to growl as a whiff of the bacon that Penny must have been cooking traveled up my nose.

"Good morning, sleepyhead," Penny greeted me as I walked into the kitchen. She was fully dressed, so I knew she was about to leave. "Or should I say afternoon."

"Wait, it's afternoon? What time is it?" I realized I had never even looked at the time when I rolled out of bed. I just assumed it was early morning.

"It's twelve o'clock. I was about to come check up on you."

"Dang, I must have been sleeping good, I'm tellin' you it's that Martha Stewart rockin' me to sleep like a baby. I'm in love with that set."

"I feel you. That Nautica comforter set is doing the same thing to me. The sheets are mesmerizing."

"That reminds me: I really wanted to take you out to look at some drapes for your room today. I told you I found this place where I can get them custom made. But you need to pick out your own fabric. That way I don't have to hear your mouth if you don't like it."

"Not today, Secret," she whined. "I'm about to hit the streets in my new car." She referred to her brand-new candy apple red Lexus, which I had copped for her the day before. "I still can't believe it belongs to me. Thank you, thank you, thank you, sissy." She rushed over and squeezed me tight. "I love you so much. You are the best sister in the entire world."

"You just be safe in it. Don't be texting and driving or drinking and driving. The first time I catch you or hear some crazy shit in the streets, I'ma kick yo ass then take the keys. And you know I'll do it."

"I won't do any of the above, I pinky swear." She gave me that innocent grin that she was famous for. "But please give me a rain check on the drapes. I promise I'll go any other time you choose. Erica is waitin' on me to pick her up; we are about to hit up the mall and do some shopping."

"Girl, I just took yo ass shopping yesterday," I reminded her. I didn't know if she forgot, but my wallet had not.

"I know, but I can always use something. And besides, I really just want to whip the scene in my new car and show off." She giggled while faking like she was turning a car wheel.

"I swear you crazy. A'ight, though, I'll hold off until next weekend or something, but we got to get this done. You still got some money?" I kept her pockets laced because I never wanted her broke.

"Yeah, I got about two stacks. I told Erica I was gon' get her a couple of fits and couple pairs of shoes. You know I gotta keep my girl on point, too."

"True that. Matter of fact, grab her two stacks out the safe and give it to her. Tell her I said enjoy." I had no problem buying things for Erica. She and Penny were tight like Isis and I were. I knew what it was like to want nice clothes and not have them. It felt good being able to help her out.

"Cool, I'm sure she won't mind that . . . You really are the best, Secret. I'ma grab those stacks, then I'm out. Oh, and I put your breakfast in the microwave."

"See, that's what I'm on right now." I skipped over to the microwave and retrieved my plate, which was still warm. Penny having other plans actually worked out in a way. Isis and I had a spa appointment at four o'clock anyway. So I guessed I would grab an extra hour or two of sleep before jumping in the shower.

Back in bed, sleep decided not to claim me, so I caught up on *Basketball Wives LA* before it was time for me to get dressed. Soon I was jumping in my newly purchased Audi backing out of my two-car garage. Watching the garage door close, I sat for a while and admired my new condo. Finally things were coming together. After all Penny and I had been through, we could see the fruits of my determination. From being raised by a drunk, abusive mother, to working dead-end jobs, to being brutally beaten, to finally finding a safe, secure safety net for my sister and myself, I couldn't ask for more. Except for maybe a cold iced tea from Starbucks, which was calling my name. I decided to head over and grab just that.

After placing my order, I noticed a familiar face fixing my drink. It was Tasha from my old job at Chic Clothing. How that trifling roach had got a job at Starbucks, I had no idea. Personally, I thought she was too ghetto to be on the white people's side of town working. I guess the manager had been desperate for help. I kept my eyes glued to her. She was the last person I would trust to fix anything for me. Thankfully, she wasn't a fool. Passing my drink to the cashier, she walked around the counter. As she stepped into my space, her eyes seemed to admire me as they glided up and down. She couldn't help but recognize the change. The fact that I was getting money was apparent. "Well, I must say you lookin' good." That was her piss-poor way of giving me a compliment. My confidence should have told the dumb bitch I already knew I looked good. I didn't need her two cents to know that.

I reached for my tea as the cashier passed it to me. Tea in hand, I glared at Tasha again, then looked her up and down; with a sneer on my face I replied, "Well, I think it's safe to say you look like you always do: shit." With a smile I made my exit.

Bitch had some nerve to attempt to say one word to me. I'm not sure what made her think I would act any different. Time didn't excuse all things. I made myself a mental note not to ever visit that Starbucks location again. It's like they say, be mindful of how you treat people, because you never know when you might run into them again in life.

Chapter 27

Isis

Turning over in bed, I smiled as I realized that my new boo was still in bed next to me. I snuggled up closer to him; his warm body felt so good next to mine. It felt so good not sleeping alone every night. Rico was his name. I had accidently bumped into him some time back while in Macy's trying on sunglasses. Then a few months ago while shopping at the BMW store for my new whip I ran into him again. I'm not superstitious, so I'm not sure if this was fate or not. But this time he made it his business to introduce himself to me. After he wrapped up the purchase on a BMW i8, he asked for my number. To my own surprise I had given it to him without thinking twice. He called two days later, and after careful convincing I agreed to go on a date with him. On our first date I found out that he owned a racecar part shop. One more date and three months later we were inseparable. That's part of the reason I decided to get my own condo. Since I had a boo, I needed my own space. I loved being able to wake up to him if and when I felt like it.

I felt him stir next to me. I glanced at the clock on the nightstand. I concluded I still had a few hours before I was supposed to meet up with Secret for our spa day. The spa was our new thing; we both loved being pampered. The ringing of my cell phone forced me to sit up. Reaching for the phone, I saw Kirk's name on the caller ID. When I answered, he gave me the code "push," which meant I had a transfer to make right away, which meant I needed to get to my laptop to print off the codes and get to work.

I attempted to ease my way out of bed to keep from waking Rico, but that failed. I felt his hands reach for me. He tried to gently pull me back in the bed next to him.

"Babe, I have some business to tend to, but I promise I'll be right back. Get some more sleep."

"That's just it, you know I can't sleep without you. Come on get back in bed," he pleaded. And he looked so sexy lying there with his light skin, six feet five inches tall, with a flat top and beautiful lush lips. Rico was the spitting image of Boris Kodjoe. Damn, he was fine. I did not want to get out of bed, I wanted to jump on top of him and never let go. But instead I tamed myself and settled for a gentle kiss on the lips instead.

"Listen, time is money." I kissed him again. "I promise I'll be right back." Reluctantly, I climbed out of bed. I dragged myself down the hallway to my office, where I pulled out my laptop and made the transfers. It took a bit longer than usual because Kirk called and told me to sit still on standby because he had a few numbers he was waiting on. By the time I made it back to the room, it was time for me start getting dressed. Secret hated when I was late.

I found Rico asleep. I sat on the side of the bed. "Babe," I called him gently. He opened his eyes and looked at me. "I have to get in the shower. It's late, and I'm supposed to meet up with Secret; we have a spa day planned."

"Come on, climb back into bed with me." Again he gave me that sexy look that I hated to deny.

"Trust me, I really want to do just that, but I can't. I do not want to hear Secret cursing me out for making her wait. The girl is a diva. I can hear her mouth now." I chuckled.

"It'll be okay. I promise." He reached inside my robe and rubbed my breast. Pushing the covers back, I looked at his member, and he was more than ready. And that I could not resist. Pulling my robe off and exposing my naked body, I crawled over to him and climbed on top. One stroke and I forgot all about Secret for the time being.

"Yo ass is fifteen minutes late. I almost left," Secret chastised me.

"I know, but I was on top of Rico." I grinned. Just thinking about it made we want to call him up.

"Whatever. Come yo ass on in here." She laughed. Inside we talked, laughed, got pampered, and sipped wine. "So when can I meet this mystery guy? It's been, what, three months? And not once have I even gotten a glimpse of him. But it's clear you feelin' him. Hell, and he keep a smile on yo face."

"That he does," I had to agree.

"What about Marco? You never brought him around."

"Marco. What made you think of him? Shit, you know I don't keep them around long. I done been cut that ass off. You are really late on that one."

"Poor guy." I laughed. I really wasn't hiding Rico, but I wanted to wait until the right time to introduce him to Secret and Penny. I didn't know if it would work out or not. And I didn't want to be serious just yet, but maybe it was time to at least let them meet. "Tell you what, it's been a minute since we turned up. Why don't we hit the club this weekend and I'll bring him through."

"Now you know I'm down with that. I'ma give Kirk a call and have him book VIP and pick up the tab. We gon' turn that motherfucker out." She was hyped; she always loved to party. I too couldn't wait. We had been working hard raking in the cash. VIP, music, and an overflow of drinks sounded like exactly what we needed.

Chapter 28

Secret

Tonight was the night, and I was ready to be on one. Pulling up to the club, I could see the crowd was thick. The line to get in was wrapped around the corner, and I knew half of them wouldn't even get in. Thanks to Kirk, we were known and never had to wait in line when we went out. I decided to bring Penny along with me. She claimed she was a woman, and it was time I treated her as such. She said the club was a start. Looking fly as fuck, we walked up to the front of the line.

"What's up, Secret?" Paul, one of the bouncers, greeted me right away.

"You know I'm ready join this party."

"Aye, and you know I got you." He removed the rope and motioned inside.

"This is my sister Penny. Remember her; you might be seeing her."

"With a face as beautiful as that, how could I forget?" He smiled. And just like that Penny was inside, no ID or nothing. But we did carry the fake ID I had made for her just in case the cops busted the club or something. You never know.

Inside was popping. Yo Gotti's "Five Star" was bumping. Penny looked around in awe. "Mesmerizing, ain't it?" I said over the music.

"No doubt, and I love the energy."

"Well, let's move. We VIP all the way, baby." Passing through the crowds, we made our way upstairs to our section.

"Heyyy!" Isis sang when she saw us. "Aye, aye, turn up," she chanted, moving her hips to the music.

"Aye," I chanted along. All I needed was a drink in my hand.

"Hey, Penny." Isis gave her a hug. "You lookin' good, girl. Killin' that dress—these females better bring out they big guns tonight," she complimented her.

Penny took the bait and modeled her fit. "I know, right. I came to slay. Please understand I'm the youngest but the baddest in this club tonight."

"They don't even know," I agreed; my baby sister was a beast. "Now it's time for me to get my drink."

"There is the bar," Isis pointed out. We all three glided over to the bar where, of course, I started off with a shot; it was a must. I did not believe in playing around. I ordered Penny a martini. I really didn't like her to drink, but like she said, I needed to stop treating her like a kid. So her maximum would be two drinks only for the night. "Drink that slowly. And remember what I told you. Never ever put your drink down in a club and walk away. If you put it down consider yourself done with it," I schooled her.

"Real talk. The mistake can be dangerous," Isis cosigned. But we both would be watching out for her either way.

"I got it. No worries." She sipped. "I'm just ready to dance." The way she held on to that drink I thought I saw a bit of Jackie in her. But I knew I was just being paranoid.

"So where is this mystery man, Isis? Or is he possibly invisible?" I joked.

"Ha ha. You got jokes, huh. For real, though, I just want to be sure he cool. So I thought I'd wait a minute. And you better behave." She pointed at me.

I playfully raised both my hands in defense. "I'm always well behaved so no worries." I smirked.

"Follow me." She led us over to where I saw Kirk and some of his squad chillin'. "This is Rico." She introduced this tall, light-skinned dude.

"Hi, I'm Secret." I extended my hand. "This is Isis, my best friend since we were in grade school. And this is my baby sister, Penny."

"Hey," Penny spoke as she eyed all the guys in the circle.

"It's nice to finally meet you both." Rico shook both our hands.

"And don't start that grillin' ol' dude shit," Kirk jumped in.

"Shut up, Kirk." I chuckled. "Ain't nobody about to do all that. I ain't the feds." I laughed. The word "feds" got all of Kirk's friends' attention. I quickly regretted saying that.

"Listen, the bar is paid for. I want you to turn the fuck up on me until you drop. Don't disappoint me." He came to my rescue. I guessed he could see sorry written all over my face. The word "feds" was never good to use around a bunch of drug dealers and criminals. "Fellas, who ready to get on those Don Julio shots?"

"Let's do it," Rico spoke up.

"Follow me then." Kirk led the way to the bar.

"Damnnnn, that tall motherfucker fine!" I stressed. "I swear he the taller version of Boris Kodjoe."

"He is fine," Penny cosigned. We all watched as he walked away with Kirk and his crew.

"Isis, you gon' have to beat these bitches off that nigga with a bat," I warned.

"Nah, I ain't doing none of that." Isis chuckled nonchalantly. "We ain't serious like that; we just kickin' it."

My head spun around to her like it was on a swivel. "Bitch, you crazy. That's the type of shit you hold down. But I feel you, though; my playa ways rubbin' off on you."

Isis smiled at me. "Nobody playa ways got nothin' on you."

"Yeah, you probably right." I fake popped my collar. "A bitch is one of a kind. But what he do for a livin' anyway?"

"He owns a racecar body shop."

"Shit, he stacked then. You know how much money that shit cost? Those parts be ridiculous expensive."

"Yeah, his pockets laced. Money, cars, big-ass house out in Santa Rosa, the whole nine."

"Well, damn. Get money then, bitch." I raised my glass in the air like we were about to toast. "That's what's up."

Young Jeezy's "SupaFreak" blasted out of the speakers. "That's my jam." Penny started to gyrate her hips to the beat. "I don't know about you two, but I'm about to hit the dance floor."

"Let's do it," I cosigned.

We lit the dance floor on fire. Soon I was dancing with one of Kirk's friends who introduced himself as Sway, and he was cute as shit. I had seen him a couple of times before, but this was the first time we ever had any interaction. We sat and chilled for a bit, and after our few dances I gave him my number. No doubt he was feeling me. But what nigga wasn't?

After all the turning up I had done at the club, I could not believe when Penny and I made it home. I was still restless. I downed a shot of Patrón and climbed into bed and still no effect, but I did have one thing on my mind and that was Sway. Just as I closed my eyes in order to force myself to sleep, my cell phone rang. The unknown number intrigued me so I answered.

"Who dis?" I answered with broken English on purpose

"Secret." I heard my name and noticed the voice right away.

"What's up, Sway?" I was surprised to hear him on the other end. The way he had been bending back those Don Julio shots I thought he might have been throwed.

"Just sittin' here relaxin'. I couldn't sleep, so I thought I might see if you gave me the wrong number." He chuckled.

"So are you satisfied now that you got your answer?"

"I'm Gucci." He laughed. "I can't believe you still up."

"Couldn't sleep either . . . How about you text me your address and I'll come through."

"No doubt. Check your text. I just hit the send button." He didn't waste any time.

"Keep the light on. I should be there in less than an hour." I ended the call. Springing from my bed, I took a quick shower, slid into a pair of cutoff Guess jeans, pulled an all-white belly shirt over my head, topped it off with my pink-and-white retro Jordans, and grabbed my keys. Once inside the Audi, I typed the address into my GPS and balled out. I arrived at Sway's front door in twenty minutes.

"I guess you were serious, huh?" He smiled at me like a kid in a candy store.

"Make no mistake about it, I'm a grown-ass woman. I don't do games. Now are you gon' invite me in?"

"My bad. Come on in." He stepped to the side.

He shut the door behind me. I turned to face him. "Can I get you a drink or something?" he asked. He had to be kidding me; it was four o'clock in the morning, and the last thing I drove over here for was a drink. Stepping in his space, I placed my hands behind his head and pulled his lips into mine. I sucked on his lips for dear life. Picking me up, he carried me to his bedroom. He laid me gently down on the bed, but I didn't want to waste any time. Standing up, I kicked off my jeans, stepped out of my bra and panties. I stood before him naked as the day I was born.

Placing both my breasts in his hands, he nibbled on them individually. I laid my head back and moaned; his warm lips felt so good on them. Gently he picked me up again and placed me on the bed, kissing my navel. He found my fruit and again brought me close to ecstasy. Finally, he took his pants off, and I gasped at what he was packing. I almost went crazy with anticipation. I couldn't wait any longer to feel him inside me. This time I instructed him to lie down; straddling him, I eased my way down just a bit, then rode him until he begged me to stop. And damn, Sway was worth the ride. He kissed me deeply as if he was surprised at how much of a beast I was. And he hadn't experienced the half.

Chapter 29

Isis

Driving back from the prison, the two-hour conversation I had just had with Felicia played over and over in my mind. For the first time since she went to prison we shared a real mother-daughter conversation. It had been a year or more since Bobbi and I had last seen each other, or since he had run off with our life savings, leaving me speechless. I tried not to think about it, and heaven knows I never talked about it. In some ways I assumed if I didn't mention it, I could pretend it never happened. But it did happen, and as fucked up as it was, I had moved on and found happiness. Noticeably so, because one of the first things Felicia said when she laid eyes on me was that I seemed happy. Never had she said that to me before. It was then I decided to tell her about Bobbi and me not being together anymore. I decided to

leave out the details, mainly because I didn't want
to relive them.

Felicia had never cared for Bobbi, so her reaction to the breakup was natural. She was relieved.
It was then that I decided to tell her about my happiness with Rico. But I did make it clear that we
were only friends because I wasn't looking to be in
a relationship. I did, however, assure her she would
like him. The feeling I had after talking to her was
indescribable. It felt so good to be able to share
something good in my life with her. It felt wonderful not to be angry with her the entire visit and
even angrier when I left. But when I thought about
how disappointed in me she would be when or if
she found out what I was doing for a living, I felt
guilty. After all the stealing she had done in her
past, she had always made it clear that she wanted
better for me.

Back in the city I tried to shake it all out of my
head as I pulled up to my bank. Kirk had given me
a pretty big payout the day before, and I needed to
put it into my safe deposit box. Since our money
was not legit, we kept it in a safe deposit box so we
didn't have to report it to the IRS. We had bank accounts, but we only kept about two thousand in
the accounts. But we also both had safes at our
houses, in which we kept at least five thousand at
all times just for spending money. The teller took
me back to unlock my box and walked away. I
waited a minute so that I could be certain she was
out of the room before I did a quick addition of all
of my money. All together I counted two hundred
thirty thousand in savings. That didn't include the
ten thousand I had in my purse or the five thou-

sand at home in my safe. It felt great to feel secure
on my own terms and with my own name on all of
my shit. Never would I ever be caught with all of
my money tied up in the same account as a nigga.
I didn't care if I loved his ass to the moon and
back. It wouldn't be about love or trust. It would
be about the determination to survive. I smiled to
myself, knowing that I was that much closer to
being able to start my own business. My goal was
three hundred fifty thousand.

"What's up, chick?" I answered my ringing cell
phone as I climbed back into the car.

"Where you at? I'm outside your crib." I was a
few minutes late; we were supposed to be meeting
up to do some work on Push, which was the code
name they'd given this job.

"I'm headed that way. I had to make a quick
stop by the bank. Use your key and go inside."

"Bet." Secret ended the call.

Fifteen minutes later I pulled into my garage.
Inside the condo I found Secret in the kitchen
adding grapes to the fruit tray she had put together. "That looks good. I could use a snack."

"I figured I'd make something healthy instead
of grabbing cookies. But now I think I want some
Italian." All we ever did was eat. "Maybe we could
order some takeout in an hour or so."

"I'm wit' it." I grabbed the food tray and
headed toward my office. "You already got your
laptop set up?"

"Nah, I just put it the office. I wanted to get
started on this food tray."

Inside the office we got set to pull an all-
nighter, which meant Kirk had several jobs for us,

but they would come in pieces because of time zones. Normally when he did that we worked together so that we could talk, laugh, and eat. It was always fun.

"I finally told Felicia about Bobbi and me not being together anymore," I revealed.

"Damn. I still can't believe you waited this long. But wha'd she say?"

"Happy as hell, just like you. But I couldn't bring myself to tell her about him taking the money. That would have upset her too much. So I left that part out."

"Fuckin' bitch-ass nigga." Secret always got angry when she even thought about what he had done.

"I also told her about me and Rico being cool."

"That's what's up. Sounds like the visit went well. You told her a lot."

"Honestly, this is the best visit we have ever had over the years. And it really felt good not to be angry with her, to actually open up and share with her."

Secret looked at me with a smile, but I knew that she was thinking about Jackie. "That's good," she responded.

"Enough about me. What's up with you and Sway? And don't play dumb neither," I warned her. I could tell she was feeling him because she had been chilling with him a lot.

"He cool. We've been kickin' it a bit. I can't front, though, that nigga got that bomb. Plus he spending, so he straight."

"Damn, I think him and Rico got a lot in common." We both started laughing. "So what's up with Kirk, though? Is he still gon' help with this paperwork so we can start this business or what?" I needed to know now because I was serious about it, and my money was growing and time would be of the essence.

"Hell, yeah, he better. But we need to decide what kind of business we want to open up."

"I was thinkin' a clothing boutique."

Secret nodded her head in agreement. "Not a bad idea. But I really been leaning toward a shoe store, red bottoms and all type of designer shoes. You know these Miami bitches will go broke for some heels."

She had a point; we had witnessed women in Nordstrom spend twenty thousand on nothing but shoes. It was bananas. "You got a point. And at this point I don't care, but we need to open up something so that we can clean this dirty money done made."

"Aye, I'm game. What we need to do is set up a meeting with Kirk so we can get this shit cleared up. You know what's what."

"Cool. You still stackin' and savin' that dough, right?"

"Hell, yeah."

"You better, 'cause we got to be legit so we can not only have lots of legal money one day, but a bank account to put it in. That would make us certified boss bitches."

Chapter 30

Isis

Beyoncé's "Dance for You" blasted out of the speakers of my Challenger as I sped down the interstate headed toward Rico's house in northeast Miami. He also owned a house out in Santa Rosa; that was where we spent most of our time. The beach was beautiful, and we hung out for hours on it. The sun was shining bright and I felt good. I couldn't wait to see Rico. He had invited me out for dinner; he had his chef coming through to cook for us. Rico opened the door just as I reached out to ring the doorbell. I smiled at the sight of him clearly eager to see me.

"I've been waiting by this door for an hour in anticipation of you arriving." He reached his hand out to help me step inside.

"If I were waiting on me, I would do the same," I kidded around.

"You look beautiful," he complimented me then handed me a glass of champagne.

"Thank you."

"I thought we'd sit out by the pool. The sun is setting so it won't be too hot. It'll be beautiful."

I was convinced. "Let's do it." He gestured for me to lead the way. We hadn't spent as much time together at this house, but I was still very familiar with it. Stepping outside into the backyard, I was always mesmerized. The blue water in the pool always reminded of that scene of Brandy's pool in the movie *A Thin Line Between Love and Hate*. And boy, did Rico have the mood right with Keith Sweat's "There You Go Telling Me No Again" softly playing in the background.

"That is my song," I announced. Rico took my champagne glass out of my hand and placed it on the table. Gently he pulled me into his arms, the scent of his Versace cologne putting me in a trance. He smelled so good, I wrapped my arms around his neck tightly and held on. We danced to the song, and I hoped it would never end. Rico rubbed his soft lips against the left side of my neck, and I had to stop myself from pulling him down to the ground and fucking him. The song ended just as his lips found mine. We kissed, and it was so passionate that I moaned. Damn, he was making it hard for me. He invited me over for dinner, but I wanted to tell him to skip dinner and let's go to bed. But I chilled.

"Dinner is ready to be served," Don, his chef, announced.

"I hope you ready to eat," Rico said.

He caught hold of my left hand, and we walked

back over to the table. Rico pulled out my chair, and I sat down. Don came back out and placed shrimp cocktails in front of each of us and poured us a fresh glass of Opus One Napa red wine. Talk about delicious, the wine was superb.

"This is good," I complimented after my first sip.

"One of my favorites. I selected it especially for this meal." He seemed proud of his choice.

I looked around and took in the beauty of the sun setting and the slight beam off the pool as it faded. "We've never been out here when the sun set. It's so beautiful."

"I figured you'd enjoy it. I sit out here sometimes after a busy day at work and sip on Hennessy. It helps me relax," he revealed. I loved having these types of conversations with him. Bobbi and I never talked about things like this. For him it was always how much more money we could save and how fast. But I guess he had his reasons for that.

Don brought out filet mignon next with asparagus. The meat was marinated in something so good I sucked on the meat before chewing it. God, the man could cook. For dessert he brought out homemade cherry pie right out of the oven with homemade vanilla ice cream. The choice of dessert had been at my request, and he'd done a perfect job.

"I am so full." I gave my stomach a pat.

"That was the plan." Rico walked around to my side of the table and reached for my right hand. We walked out by the pool. I kicked off my heels as we climbed into the chaise lounge so that we could relax.

Don came out and poured us another glass of

wine. This time he left the bottle resting on the table. "That'll be all for the night," Rico told Don.

I sipped on my wine and looked up at the sky. "I could do this every night. Come out here with a bottle, get tipsy, and chill. You know growing up in the hood it's like the stars in the sky never existed. Something was always blocking it. Or maybe it was the sirens that kept us from looking up."

"Probably both; that's why I take advantage. I never want to take this beauty for granted." He leaned in close, and we kissed again. I could kiss him all night and never get tired. He stared into my eyes. "We've been chillin' with each other for a while now, and I haven't been in a real relationship in a long time. But with you I'm thinkin' different. I want us to be more exclusive."

And that changed the mood for me. That one word of commitment: "exclusive." Why did he have to say it? Not only was I not expecting it, we were having so much fun. I sipped from my wineglass. "Listen, Rico, I've been enjoying all the time that we have been spending. Not one minute of it do I regret, but it's like I told you when we first started kickin' it. I'm not lookin' to be serious . . . That has not changed."

I felt bad seeing the disappointment on his face, but I still was not deterred. My decision was clearcut. With Bobbi I had done things his way, thinking I was making myself happy at the same time. I could not and would not make that mistake again. I would do what I thought best for me, regardless of whom it hurt. Rico was a great guy from what I had seen so far. The last thing I wanted to do was hurt him, but I also had to come first.

"I know this is not what you wanted to hear, Rico. And if it's a problem I can step back and give you your space." I scooted toward the edge of the chaise prepared to leave.

"Wait, where are you going?"

"I think I should get going."

"Aye, no, that's not what I want you to do. And I hear you, and I don't want to force you or make you feel obligated to do anything you're not feeling. I have all the time in the world and I will give it to you. Whenever you ready, just let me know."

I swore he was so sweet; his words were music to my ears and brought out the sexy in him. I turned up my wineglass and drank it dry. Passing him my wineglass, I stood up, thankful that Don had left. I undressed right there and watched as Rico's eyes bulged with excitement. Rico sat up and placed both of our wineglasses on the grass next to the chaise. Standing in front of me, he picked me up and laid me on the chaise. He kissed me from my lips to my breasts, and traveled down to my hot spot, where he sucked until I screamed out from pure pleasure. And just before I released, he entered me and filled me all the way up. Damn, I had to be a fool not to want to commit to all this. The man was gifted in more ways than one.

Chapter 31

Secret

Two Months Later

"Sway, don't forget to bring the popcorn back this time," I reminded him as he went into the kitchen for the third time. Each time he came back out without the popcorn. We were at his house about to watch *Set It Off*. We both declared that to be our favorite movie. I was successfully rolling up the blunt while he was supposed to retrieve the bottle of Jack Daniel's and the snacks from the kitchen, but so far he was failing. And the movie was due to start in less than two minutes. "Sway, hurry yo ass up!" I yelled again.

"I'm right here, baby. I was trying to make sure I didn't leave anything this time. Go ahead and fire up that smoke." He set the popcorn and cheese

Doritos down on the table in front us. I reached for the lighter and blazed up the blunt.

"Now that's what I'm talkin' about. That killa." Sway rubbed his hands together, all hyped as I took my first puff, then passed it to him.

"Boy, you crazy." I laughed. "Damn, I hate that bitch-ass cop, she a woman, she could have been more helpful." I referred to the lady detective in *Set It Off*. You would have thought this was my first time watching the movie. Each time I watched it I was more emotional and extra dramatic than the last.

"That's fucked up." Sway passed the blunt back to me. The ringing of his doorbell interrupted us.

"You are expecting someone? I thought we were chillin', no interruption tonight. Shit, you made me put Kirk on hold. And you were supposed to put your shit on hold, too." I held the blunt between the tips of my fingertips, prepared to smoke. He had some serious explaining to do.

"Secret, I did just what I promised. I don't know who at that damn door. But I'm 'bout to find out." He reached for the blunt and inhaled, then exhaled before heading off to the door. "Pause the movie, babe. I don't want to miss a thing." Whoever it was was becoming impatient: they rang the doorbell again. I sighed with frustration then hit the blunt, which would solve any problem I was having.

"How you get in here?" I heard Sway yell.

"Nigga, don't question me, I used a damn key. How the fuck you think? What took you so long to come to the damn door?" I heard a voice that sounded familiar. It was getting closer.

"Look, you need to give me back the key to my damn house and get out. What do you even want? Why you here?"

"I want to talk to you . . ." As she stuck her head in the den, we looked each other dead in the eye. This was the first time I had ever seen her face to face. But I had heard her voice on Sway's voice mail several times. It was his baby mama Sherri. "Who the fuck is she?" She looked at Sway with her hands on her hips.

"Technically, that ain't your business, but that's Secret."

"Secret." She said my name as if it was full of disease. "And your mama named you that." She gave a fake giggle.

"The last I checked," I said in a calm tone, looked at her, and smiled. I was not prepared to let this chick blow my high.

"Why you got this bitch up here anyway?" she questioned as if he owed her an answer, totally disregarding me even being there. Still I chilled.

"Sherri, get up outta my house with this nonsense. I don't owe you no explanation. Now give me my key." He reached out his right hand.

"Boy, you and this white bitch got me all the way fucked up." That was it: she had managed to squeeze off two rounds of bitches and I had chilled, but now she had me fucked up. She had the nerve to call me white as if she really knew my ethnicity.

"This is my last time tellin' you to leave. Now drop the key and go." Sway pointed toward the door.

"Check this, though; I don't know you, but I

swear I ain't gon' be too many more bitches up in here."

"Fuck you, Sway, put that bitch out."

Jumping off the couch, I lunged at her so fast Sway didn't see me coming. My right fist went right into Sherri's cheekbone then into her mouth. She screamed for Sway to get me off. He tried, but I grabbed her by the head and pushed it to the floor. Suddenly, I heard Kirk call my name, and I felt the force that was too strong for me to fight, which turned out to be Sway and Kirk pulling me off Sherri.

"Get the fuck off me," I yelled at Kirk and Sway as I kicked and tried to wiggle away from their grasp.

"Calm down, Secret," Kirk yelled.

"I'm calm; now let me go. I'll catch you later, bitch," I shouted at Sherri.

"Fuck you, too," she screamed back at me.

"Sherri, get the fuck out my house," Sway barked. Sway blocked my path to Sherri while she attempted to fix her clothes.

"No, she ain't gotta leave. Let the bitch stay; I'm out." I went for my keys, but Sway stood in the way.

"Aye, you ain't gotta go nowhere. She's the one gon' get the fuck out."

"Fuck that ho. What you need to be worried about is your damn daughter. Why don't you go outside and get her?"

Sway froze, then turned to Sherri. "Yo dumb ass left my daughter in the car?" he screamed. Sherri put an evil grin on her face and sucked her teeth. Sway took off running outside, all while begging me not leave.

"Bitch, you really are psycho." I laughed and grabbed my keys.

"Sherri, why don't you just leave?" Kirk was frustrated.

"Sway on some bullshit," she continued to rant, burning a hole in the same spot. "And I don't have to leave. I have his child." She looked at me and sneered.

I couldn't believe her; that's all she could think about, never mind she left her child alone in a car. All she cared about was Sway and who he had in his house. It was ridiculous, and it made her look pitiful. "Bitch, you are dick drunk . . . You can have Sway, and I hope y'all have a nice life."

Outside, I headed to my car with Sway calling my name as he held his daughter. Sherri ran outside and jumped in her Camaro. Sway called her name, but she just started the ignition and burned rubber out of the driveway.

I shook my head at him as I pulled away. This was the kind of shit I did not deal with. Crazy-ass, still stuck on their baby daddy bitches. Life was much too short and I was too damn fly for that shit. I didn't know one nigga I was willing to fight over. But I would kick a bitch's ass for getting me in the wrong.

Pissed, I dialed up Isis. "Where you at?" I asked, balling down the interstate doing a full eighty miles per hour. Tickets didn't mean shit, I had it to spend.

"Over here chillin' at Rico's shop for bit. Where you? I called you earlier."

"I was over at Sway's crib. Yo, text me that address to the shop. I'm 'bout to come by."

"It's coming your way. See you in a minute." I could hear the excitement in her voice.

After speaking the address into my GPS, I pulled up to Rico's racecar repair shop in fifteen minutes. I looked for a parking space in awe. The place was nothing like I imagined. There were racecars all tricked out and banging in every direction. Isis was outside waiting on me. She waved me into an empty parking space.

"Damn, bitch, your man is ballin," I complimented, climbing out of the car. "Shi'd, I thought this was like a regular car garage or dump at best. I didn't know it would be bangin' like this." I continued to look around.

"It's hot out here. Let's go inside." She led the way. "I told you it was racecar shop. You got everything from Nascar cars to your regular fast–and–furious tricked-out racing cars."

"And the brothers." I eyed Rico standing close by talking to a host of fine-ass niggas as soon as we stepped inside the building.

Isis looked at me and smiled. "I should have known you wouldn't miss that."

"Hmph, no chance in hell." I sucked my bottom lip. At that moment I wished I had a mirror to check myself. But who was I kidding? I was always a bad bitch. Rico started walking in our direction.

"What's up, Secret?" he said.

"Hey." I looked past him and smiled at the guys. Every single one of them was cute. "You have a nice place here. And these rides are wicked."

"Thanks. I'm glad you came through."

"No doubt."

"Babe, I'm about to run a few rounds in a car

we just got in. Be back in a bit." He bent down and gave Isis a kiss. "Secret, make sure Isis shows you around the spot."

Isis introduced the two girls at the front desk as Rico's assistants before she led me back to his plush office. Talk about nice: that Ethan Allen furniture was on point, mahogany desk with the matching hutch. And my favorite, a Hudson leather sofa that was to die for, exactly what I needed to relax and get Sway and his bitch off my chest.

"So what's up? What really brought you this way?" Isis twisted her mouth up at me. The girl knew me too well, and she knew something was wrong.

"How in the hell can you read me so well? So damn creepy." I crossed my arms, leaned back, and buried myself in the Hudson comfort.

"It's my job to know. Now drop it off." Isis sat on the edge of Rico's desk and waited.

"Girl, I just had to beat Sway's baby mama's ass. This crazy bitch gon' have me locked up out this bitch."

"What the hell happen?" Isis eyes bulged with surprise. "I didn't know she even knew you."

"That's just it; she doesn't. Me and Sway at his crib chillin', smokin' good, mindin' our own damn business. Next thing we know this bitch rings the doorbell. And when he don't answer fast enough, she uses an old key and invites herself in. Then she sees me and goes bananas, callin' me out my name. And I let the bitch get away with it twice. But after that, you already know that ass was grass. She lucky Kirk showed up when he it did 'cause it took him and Sway to get me off that ass."

"Damn, Kirk came through, too?"

"Yep. I didn't even know he was stoppin' through."

"I can't believe ol' girl doin' it like that, though. And for what, though?"

"Isis, that ain't the half. Tell me why the whole time that crazy bitch was in there actin' a ass, she left their daughter out in the car. Alone," I stressed.

"Oh, hell naw. This bitch is crazy," Isis cosigned. "Sway should have kicked her fuckin' ass for that."

"I think he was so shocked, he didn't know what to do. That shit was too much for me."

"So what happened after that?"

"Well, Sway was outside getting his daughter, I grabbed my keys to leave but that nut case jumped in her car and left first. Girl, I'm through with his ass, though. That drama I ain't got time for. I'll be in the penitentiary fuckin' wit' that ho. Bitch got the nerve to call me white," I added. I had almost forgotten about that.

"No the fuck she didn't?" Isis's mouth flew open. "So this bitch branded you with ethnicity."

"That ho tried it in more ways than one. She better pray the streets of Miami hide her, 'cause I'ma finish putting this size nine foot in her ass if I ever see her again." And I meant every word of that.

"Crazy situation. Well, I'm glad you came by. We need to talk anyway. Your boy Rico confessing his love and everything. It's all too much."

"I'm tellin' you. I could use a shot of cognac or five." I chuckled, but I was serious. "And you can tell me all about it."

"Cool, let's head over to the bar up the street. They got some fire hot wings over there," Isis suggested.

"Bet. You drive." I grabbed my Gucci bag, ready to bounce.

Chapter 32

Secret

I dreaded opening up my eyes to even look at my ringing cell phone. All I craved was the option to sleep in late. It was pouring down rain outside, with a constant roar of thunder, lightning, the whole nine. The perfect time to sleep. I pulled the comforter tighter over my head and pushed my left ear deeper into my pillow. But nothing was helping; the ringing of my phone had taken on its own cry for help. Grunting from pure annoyance, I reached my head from under the covers on top, the pillow next to me, and gripped my phone. Tossing the comforter out of my face, I glanced at the caller ID; to my aggravation, Sway's name was lit up.

He'd been blowing me up for the past two weeks since the whole bullshit charade his baby mama pulled. I had purposely ignored all of his calls, but it seemed like he wasn't good at taking a hint. Frustrated, I laid the phone back down and pulled the cover back over my head just as my phone signaled a text coming through. I assumed it was another one of Sway's attempts to get my attention, so I ignored it. Again I snuggled up to my comforter and tried to find coziness, but my phone started to ring again. I contemplated just blocking Sway. I wasn't even sure why I hadn't done it already. Suddenly, my prayers were answered when the constant ringing stopped. I was squeezing my eyes tight, all the while praying that sleep would claim me, but the ringing started again.

"Shit," I hollered. I came from under the comforter like the thunder and grabbed my phone with the intention of turning it off. "Hello," I answered and cleared my throat at the same time. I still had that groggy early-morning sound.

"Rise and shine, sleepyhead," Kirk sang in my ear.

"Nigga, ain't no sun out, so what do you want so early?" I was grumpy.

"We got Push." He gave the signal.

"Cool. And stop blowing up my phone before I kick yo ass," I threatened him.

"My bad, ma." He chuckled before hanging up.

Since there was no chance I would get any sleep, I pushed back the covers, slid my beautifully manicured feet into my comfy pink Prada slippers. Dragging my sluggish body to the bathroom, I washed my face and brushed my teeth. The house was quiet as I made my way to my office, where I geared up my laptop to handle business. But honestly, as much as I hated to give up my bed, it gave me a thrill that I couldn't describe when I hit that transfer button. I wasn't sure if that was a good thing or not, but something inside me just didn't give a fuck.

Finished, I powered my laptop down and stood up, ready for some hot coffee. Stepping back into the hallway again, I noticed how quiet the house was, which was a bit of a surprise. Even more surprising was the fact that I didn't smell any coffee already brewing or brewed. Penny always made coffee in the morning before leaving for school. Once in the kitchen I confirmed no coffee had been made. Making the decision to make my own, I powered up the espresso machine.

Afterward, I made my way to Penny's room. Just as I curled my fingers into a fist to knock on her door, I realized it was slightly ajar. Pushing the door all the way open, I saw the bed was made, and there was no sign of Penny.

"Hmph," I sighed. It was odd; normally she woke me before leaving. But it was possible that she had tried, and I was in a deep sleep. Either way, I hated missing her before she left for the day. Back in my room I noticed the sun was shining brightly now. I looked out the window and there was not a cloud in sight or any evidence that it had ever rained. Suddenly my plan to sleep in on a rainy day was ruined. I had a few errands to run, so I decided to get dressed and burn up Miami's streets.

Since my espresso was cold by the time I got dressed, I made Starbucks my first order of business after leaving the house. I dialed Isis's number as I pulled up to a red light.

"What's up, chica?" I sang into the phone. It was

nice out and I was feeling good and glad I decided to get out.

"I just left the dentist, got my teeth cleaned."

"No fun." I did not envy her for that. "Speaking of that, I got an appointment coming up. For the same damn thing." I frowned.

"Well, get ready to be annoyed. I hate them diggin' in my mouth. Ugh. But gotta do what I gotta do." She sighed. "What are you up to?"

"Shit, just getting out the house to handle some business. I hoped to stay in today, but thanks to Sway blowin' me up, then Kirk hitting me up with a push, shit, I had no choice but to get my ass up. The rain finally let up, so I'm out here."

"What's up with Sway? You talk to him?"

"Hell, naw, I told you that nigga through in my book. I gladly ignored his call."

"Cold hearted, Secret." Isis laughed. "Dude gon' kill his self."

"Well, let me drive over and take his ass the gun," I joked. "But check this out, what's up, we ain't had no fun in a grip. We need to hit the club this Saturday. Penny gets out of school on Friday for the semester. So you know we got to celebrate her first successful year of college."

"Dang, school out for the year already? No doubt then, let's do it. She deserves it."

"A'ight, I'll set it all up. You know it's VIP all day. Spendin' nothin' but them stacks all night." I got hyped as I pulled into the Starbucks parking lot. "A'ight, bet then, I'ma hit you later, though; I'm 'bout to get this latte." I ended the call.

One sip of my latte and I was back to life. I savored the first taste and wasted no time going back in for the second. Finally I was satisfied. Scrolling through my phone, I hit Penny's name, but it went straight to voice mail. I headed over to the bank to put some money in my safe deposit box, then over to Macy's. I needed to pick up some new bedsheets for Penny's bed and mine also. But of course once I was inside, I ended up doing more shopping than originally planned. I can't lie, I enjoyed buying what I desired. I was in control. I determined when it was too much, not my wallet.

I realized how long I been inside the mall when I came out and the sky was totally dark. It was past dinnertime. That's just how much spending money distracted me. Starving, I decided to stop and pick up some stir-fry. Pulling into the garage, I didn't see Penny's car.

After hauling all my things inside, I was tired. Setting the bags down in the hallway, I walked to Penny's room. Her bedroom light was off. I turned it on and looked around. I observed that it still looked the same as earlier. Flipping the light off, I started back toward the kitchen but stalled for a minute, puzzled. Suddenly I realized that Penny hadn't been home last night when I came in. I had concluded that I had beaten her home. Tired, I had lain down to watch a movie and went to sleep. Rushing back to the kitchen, I opened my Coach bag and reached for my cell phone. I pushed Penny again; it went straight to voice mail.

Chapter 33

Secret

Scrolling through my contacts, I knew just who to call, because if Penny was anywhere it was with Erica. They were attached like Siamese twins; they did everything together. And that Lexus had them tripping: they were burning Miami streets up stunting daily. "Erica, where is Penny at?" I got straight to the point. Now I was pissed. Penny knew better than to not check in, especially for this long. She was already gone by the time I woke up, nor had she called me all day. She must have been really feeling herself. I understood she was growing up and needed her space, but she was doing way too much and I was ready to make that clear.

"I have been wondering the same thing. She wasn't at school today." Erica's words sent my gut flipping.

"What do you mean, she wasn't at school?" I asked for clarification.

"She didn't pick me up for class this morning. So I called her cell, and it was going straight to voice mail. I figured she was sick or something, so I jumped on the bus." My heart dropped to the pit of my stomach. My hands and forehead started to sweat.

"So you're saying you haven't seen Penny all day?"

"Nope. The last time I saw her was yesterday at school. I didn't get a ride with her because I had a late class. I was supposed to call her last night when I got in, but I ended up hangin' out with Jeff." That was her on- and off-again boyfriend.

My cell phone nearly slid out of my hands. I couldn't believe what I was hearing. "Erica, I gotta go."

"Secret, call me when you hear from her." I ended the call without responding. For a minute I stood in silence, my mind racing. I looked up, and it seemed like the kitchen was spinning. I felt as though I couldn't think. I tried to find Kirk's name in my contacts, but I was so spent I kept scrolling past his name. My hands shook uncontrollably as I was unable to focus.

"What's up, Secret?" Kirk said into the phone. Music was playing in the background, and I heard a million voices. From the sound of it, he was probably at a strip club.

"Kirk, I think Penny is missing," I managed, not even sure of the words that flew out of my mouth.

"Aye, wait, what? I can't hear you let me step outside." I heard Trey Songz's "Bottoms Up" playing in the background. It seemed like it took forever, then finally I started to hear the music fading, which told me he was probably outside. "Secret, now what you say?" He was back on the line, and I could hear him clearly.

Tears started to run down my cheeks, my hands felt hot, and a huge knot had at some point formed in my throat. "I think Penny missin'," I repeated, my voice shaking.

"Missin'? What the da fuck going on over there?" he questioned.

"I . . . I . . ." I tried to speak, but the reality of what I was trying to say made me break. I cried so hard I could barely breathe. "Help me . . . Kirk," I managed.

"I got you, baby girl. I'm on my way. But listen, I need you pull it together and call the police. Call the police now." He ended the call. Shaken, I held the phone as best as I could and dialed 911.

Chapter 34

Isis

Lyfe's "Must Be Nice" blasted out of the speakers of Rico's Cadillac Escalade as we balled down the interstate on our way to Capital Grille for a late dinner. Looking over at him, I marveled at his good looks. I could look at him all night and not be bored. Yet, still I was not able to commit and call him all mine. Secretly I kicked myself for that. I knew chicks who would jump at the chance to have him willing to commit to them. The brother was young, fine, and rich. And here I was with principles.

"You do know that the Capital Grille ain't got nothin' on me in the kitchen?" Rico grinned at me as he attempted to brag about his skills in the kitchen.

"Oh, really, well we shoulda put you in the kitchen. I got an apron at my crib with your name on it," I teased. He would always brag, but never once had he attempted to really cook.

"Nah, a brother don't need an apron. Too fly for that."

"Damn right you are." I bit my bottom lip seductively.

"Don't do that thing with your lip; you'll make me have to turn this truck around," he warned. "And you know what that means." If I wasn't so hungry, I would have snatched the wheel and turned the truck around myself. I was hooked, and he knew it.

"You better not turn this truck around, the way my stomach growling." I laughed. "I'm ready to smash."

We were interrupted when my cell phone started ringing. Digging inside my purse, I pulled it out and saw Secret's name on the screen. "Hey," I answered. She started talking fast, but her voice was breaking up. "Secret, what's wrong?" It sounded like she was crying, but I was not sure. "Secret." I had to say her name again. "Slow down."

"I said I think Penny is missin'! I don't know. . . . I don't?"

"What do you mean, you think she's missin'?" I prayed I heard her wrong, but the constant sound of crying told me I had not.

"She's missin', Isis. I don't know where she is."

"Where are you at right now?" I felt like the truck was closing in on me. Rico slowed down. He took a few glances at me while trying to watch traffic.

"I'm at home waiting on the police."

"I'm on my way. Just hang tight . . . I'm on my

way," I repeated, wishing I could reach through the phone and comfort her. "Head to Secret's house now. Penny is missin'," I yelled, and I started crying at the same time.

"I got you, baby, it's gon' be okay," Rico said as he jumped off the E-way to find a shorter route to Secret's house. He had taken me by there a few weeks ago to pick up some papers Secret had for me, so he knew exactly where to go. My chest pounded, and my stomach churned with fear and uncertainty.

As we pulled up to Secret's house, my heart dropped when I saw all the police cars parked in front. I couldn't believe why they were there. This just could not be happening in real life. Inside, Secret was sitting on the couch trying to speak as best she could. Her whole face looked as if it was swollen from all the crying she was doing.

"Like I told you, I haven't seen her since yesterday. When I came home last night she was not here yet. But I didn't think much about it. I was tired so I fell asleep while watching television. When I got up this morning, she was already gone. I figured she had left for school. I thought it was strange that she didn't tell me was leaving. But she's nineteen now; I just figured maybe she didn't want to wake me. I tried calling her, but her phone went to voice mail. I assumed it was just dead. But when I came home tonight and she wasn't here, that's when I called her best friend Erica and found out that she didn't come to school today." She bent over like she had been punched in the stomach. Kirk, who was sitting next to her, grabbed her; I rushed over and hugged her tight.

"It's going to be okay, Secret. She's coming home."

"And you say she never goes this long without contacting you?" a chubby, red-faced cop asked.

"Hell, no, I told you we talk at least once during the day. She's fuckin' missin', okay," Secret shouted. "Just go find my gotdamn sister." She fell into my arms crying. The two cops who were standing in front of us told us they were going to file the report and would keep us posted. They told us to keep our phone lines clear just in case she called. With that they left, taking the other three cops who had stood by the front door like bodyguards with them. I rolled my eyes at their sorry asses. It had taken five of them to say they were going to file a report. The one and only reason I didn't snap on them was because I wanted to keep Secret calm.

"It's all my fault," Secret cried out when the cops had exited the condo. "I should have waited up until she came home last night. But I was tired, so I came home, had a few drinks, and dozed off." Her face was soaked with tears as she shook her head in disappointment.

"Secret, this not your fault. You had no idea." I tried to comfort her but felt as though I was weak with no breath left in my lungs.

"We gon' find her, I promise you that." Kirk walked back over to us. He had stepped away while he chatted on the phone. "I want y'all to stay put. I already done put word out on the streets. I'm about to go out looking for her. I'll let you know." He looked at Secret, bent down and hugged her.

Rushing out the door, he turned and looked at us all one last time, then shut the door behind him.

"I don't know if I can just sit here. We should be out looking for her, too," Secret insisted.

"No we have to wait here just in case she comes home. We need to stay put like Kirk said."

Scaring the shit out of me, Secret suddenly jumped to her feet. "Jackie, why didn't I think of her? Maybe she's with Jackie and thinks I'm going to be mad if I find out. She's been talkin' about her a lot lately." Hope appeared in her eyes again.

"Well, it wouldn't hurt to check," I agreed.

"Let's go then. Rico, you stay here just in case Penny comes home. If she comes, don't let her leave."

"Don't worry, I'll keep her here," Rico tried to reassure her.

Reaching for my hand, Secret grabbed her keys, and we rushed out the door. We ran at least two red lights and swerved at least four times to avoid hitting someone before finally arriving at the last place Jackie had been known to live. To both our disappointment, the house had a "For Rent" poster out front and no sign of anyone or thing living there. Secret's entire face dropped. Placing her head on the steering wheel, she cried; unable to control myself, I cried with her. Realizing that I had to keep it together and be there for her, I pulled myself together; it took me twenty minutes to convince her to allow me to drive back to her house, because she simply was in no shape to do it.

Chapter 35

Secret

Two agonizing days had passed, and still there was no word about Penny. I felt as if I might die. The only thing that kept me alive was the possibility that she would come back. I was a mess, though; I was sick with no real medical reasons. My body was exhausted from no sleep or food. I had tried to eat, but there was this huge knot in my throat that refused to move. The only thing I could get past it was liquid, and even that was a struggle. I simply felt nausea all day, at all times. Every time I attempted to close my eyes, Penny was there holding her hand out reaching for me. Her lips would be moving, but no words came out. I reached out for her, but she faded. I felt tormented and enraged all at the same time. So I decided that staying awake was best. Erica had rounded up mounds of friends and some of her family and basically set up a task force to find Penny. They had all had been out for two days pounding the pavement, hanging posters all over Miami. She had even set up a Facebook page, as well as a tip line where people could call in any information they might have. She was truly holding her best friend down. I thanked God for her. Because I wasn't able to do anything, my mind had folded up and I was sinking.

Isis and I lay around the living room on my huge sofa, wrapped in our throws, waiting on anything. She had not left my side since she had arrived two days before. In addition to going to Jackie's last known address, I had put word out to Jackie in the streets, but still had not heard from her. But I was not shocked. If it wasn't about Jackie or a bottle, she was nowhere to be found. So I decided not to hold my breath about hearing from her.

The ringing of my cell phone ended my debate with myself on Jackie. "What you hear, Kirk?" I asked right away. I had seen his name on the caller ID.

"Aye," he said, and I knew he had something. But he was taking too long, and I was not in the beating-around-the-bush mood.

"Fuckin' what is it, Kirk?" I barked into the phone.

"I don't want you to get worked up. But I just got this call from a source tellin' me where I can find Penny."

My heart leaped with joy. "Is she okay?" The mention of her being okay woke Isis. She sat up, waiting on information. "Where is she? Who called you?" I questioned as I cried with my mouth half covered.

"I'll get back to you on that later; I just wanted you to know that everything is going to be all right." He ended the call.

"Wha'd he say?" Isis was on the edge of her seat.

"He got a call, and he knows where to find her. She's coming home." Tears ran down my face. Isis wrapped her arms around me.

We sat as patiently as possible and stared at my cell phone, waiting to hear from Kirk. Finally an hour and a half later it rang. I answered so fast I almost denied the call. "I found her and she's alive . . ." He paused. "But I need you to meet me at Jackson Memorial."

I felt faint. "The hospital? What's wrong?" My voice almost faded.

"Secret, just get down here. We will talk then."

I was unable to drive, but Isis got us there in record time. I wanted to run down the halls, but I couldn't find the strength. The sight of the hospital and the fear of the unknown had me feeling sick. Isis went to the receptionist's desk to find out about Penny, but before she could get any information, Kirk rounded the corner.

"Is she okay, Kirk?" I managed.

"She will be . . . but she has been beaten badly. They got her in the back." My legs simply gave out, and I dropped to the floor.

"Secret." Isis rushed over to me, calling my name. She and Kirk both pulled me up and walked me over to a chair in the lobby.

"You got to be strong. She's going to be fine," Kirk tried to assure me. I wanted to believe him, but I was sick with doubt and uncertainty. We sat in the lobby for two hours before the doctor finally came out to give us any information.

"She's going to be okay physically," he explained. "She was beaten badly, mostly external bruises . . . and she was raped."

A gasp from deep within me slid out of my mouth. I swayed, but Kirk caught me. I tried to speak, but my whole body seems to shake. I took a deep breath and forced my vocal cords to work. "Can I see her?"

"When she came in she was in a bit of shock. She passed out and hasn't regained consciousness . . . but she will in time. Her body needs the rest. We gave her something to keep her comfortable. Only family is allowed back to see her for now."

I grabbed Isis's hand tight. "We are her sisters." The doctor nodded his head with an approving motion then showed us to her room. He left us to be alone with her.

One look at Penny lying there helpless sent me doubling over in pain. Her bruised, swollen face looked so peaceful. I just didn't understand how something so bad could happen to her. Penny had never done any wrong to anyone; she was always honest and good. In a million years she could never deserve this.

Isis tried to be strong for me, but I looked over and she was trembling. I walked over to her and helped her take a seat on the sofa in the room. Turning my attention back to Penny, I walked over to her and softly touched her bloodstained hand. My legs shook violently as I tried to stand strong. Bending over, I kissed Penny on the cheek and whispered in her ear that I loved her and she was going to be okay.

A nurse came into the room and asked us to step out for a minute. I did not want to hear that. I was not about to leave her side; she needed me. "Listen, my sister been missin' for two days, and I ain't leaving her," I cried.

"Ma'am, it will only take a minute. We are switching shifts and I need to pass my last meds and chart."

Isis walked over to me. "It's okay, Secret. We'll just go out into the lobby area and let them do their job. Then we can come back and stay all night." Giving the nurse the nastiest look I could muster, I reluctantly left the room. Each step I took away from the room seemed to hurt worse than the last. I needed to be with Penny. I was surprised to see Sway in the waiting area talking to Kirk. He approached me, and I fell into his arms with contentment and broke down. I felt so safe in his strong arms. I was glad that he had come.

After a while, we all sat down. "I just can't believe this shit. Who would do this to her?" I continued to cry.

"A fuckin' monster. That's who," Isis spat.

"Trust me, I'm going to find out who the motherfucker is. But that call that I got was anonymous. I put money on the streets to get information, but whoever this is, motherfuckers didn't bite for that right away. Which tells me this some other shit."

"But what, though? Who would want to hurt Penny? I swear when I find out who is responsible I will kill them!" I said through clenched teeth.

"Nah, you don't have to worry about that, because I'ma dead that motherfucker. Believe that. Whoever the bitch is can't hide 'cause I got a fifty-thousand-dollar bounty out for information. And you know in the hood a nigga will give up his mama for that type of cash. So we wait." The scowl on Kirk's face told me he meant business, and murder would be the case before this was all said and done.

Chapter 36

Isis

Days crept by, and Penny still had not awakened; the doctor didn't want to say she was in a coma, but she was. Secret and I had been in the room with her the entire time. I refused to leave Secret's side. She needed me, and to be honest, I needed her. I trembled inside every time I thought about Penny and what she had been through. To watch her lie helpless sickened me. Secret had fallen almost completely apart, and I feared that if Penny didn't wake up soon she would have a nervous breakdown. The three of us had been through some pretty tough times together, and through them all we had survived. I prayed this would be the same.

And I thanked God for Rico, Kirk, and Sway. With them there with us, it helped fill the void. It felt good knowing someone else had our backs since our parents were not there. There still was no word from Jackie, and at this point I prayed she didn't show up. Secret would probably attack her for showing up this late. It was sad that now was no better than the past: when they needed her the most, she was nowhere to be found.

"I think now would be a good time for you to go home and get some rest. When she awakes, someone will notify you." The doctor tried to convince Secret. The area around her eyes was dark and her eyes were red; she resembled a ghost. But even I knew at her worst she would not be moved.

"I'm fine. I'll rest when she wakes." Her eyes never left Penny.

"You need to understand that she could wake up at any moment. And when she wakes is when your work really starts. You need rest," the doctor continued to try to persuade her.

"Doctor." Secret bounced her head in his direction. I braced myself and waited, afraid she was going to curse him out. "Thanks for the concern, but I'm all my sister got. For no reason am I going to leave her side. I'll sleep when I'm dead." This time he just nodded his head in agreement and exited the room.

"I'm sooo sorry." Erica, who was sitting in the recliner across from me, let out a painful cry from deep within. It was so strong I felt it penetrate my soul like a drum beating. Secret slowly turned around and looked at her. "It's my fault this happened to her." She tried to lift her hand to point at Penny, but it just dropped to her side like a sack of potatoes.

"Erica . . ." I started to say something, but she cut me off.

"No, it is . . . When she was done with her class for the day, she came to my last class to meet up with me so that we could ride home together. But this guy Sidney I had been flirting back and forth with asked me to stay after class and said that he would take me home. And I am so fuckin' stupid tryin' to smile up in this nigga face. If I had went with her, this wouldn't never have happened. I was supposed to be there and I wasn't," she bellowed some more.

Feeling her pain, I got up and walked over to her. "Erica, you can't blame yourself."

Secret walked over, bent down, and hugged her. "You have been nothin' but a friend to Penny, the best a girl could ask for. And I'm proud of you. This is on the monster who did this to her. And whoever it is, their days are numbered. Trust it's not your fault. So you wipe those tears. Penny will need you to be one hundred when she wakes up." Damn, I was proud of Secret; in as much pain as she was in, she took the time out to be strong for Erica. But her words rang true. Lifting herself back up, she walked back over to Penny.

"You've been here with us for the last few days. Why don't you go home and take a shower, and get some rest. Like Secret just said, Penny gon' need you when she wakes up." I smiled at her.

"But I . . ." She opened her mouth to protest, but Secret intervened.

"It's a good idea," Secret said, agreeing with me. "Go home and rest up."

Reluctantly, she stood and walked away, but not before making it clear that she would be back.

Sitting back on the couch, I glanced at the overhead television as *The Price Is Right* came on. A text came to my phone from Rico, telling me he was out in the lobby. "Secret, I'm going to step out in the waiting area for a bit. Rico is here."

"Cool," she replied, still not taking her eyes away from Penny.

"Hey." Rico hugged me tight. Tears instantly poured down my face. I hugged him even tighter. I craved his comfort. "Babe, it's all right." His voice was comforting.

"I know. It's just hard to watch her like that."

"She still hasn't woken up?"

I shook my head no. "All her vitals are good. The doctor says there is nothin' physically wrong besides the bruises. He says she's just resting from the shock of it all."

"Wow. Hopefully she's up soon. How is Secret holdin' up?"

"Not good." I shook my head. "I'm worried about her. She refuses to leave Penny's side, except to use the bathroom. She was refusing to eat until the doctor threatened to admit her."

"All that will pass, though, once Penny wakes up. She's just shook, that's all."

"I pray it's soon."

"How about you? You need to go home and get some sleep. A good night's sleep will be good for you." I one hundred percent agreed with him. I was so exhausted the day before, I had started to see double, so I had taken a nap.

"Sleep sounds wonderful, but I can't leave Secret." I shook my head. "I can't leave her," I repeated matter-of-factly. "You know the three of us always had it hard in one way or another, but just . . ." I paused as the emotion swelled up inside of me, but I tried to control it. I sucked my teeth. "Just as our lives start getting better, and now . . ." My voice started to shake. "Now this has to happen." No longer able to control it, my emotions spilled down my cheeks. Rico wasted no time wrapping his arms around me, pulling me close to his chest. All the comfort I needed was in his embrace.

Secret yelled my name, getting my attention as Rico released me. I turned in the direction I had heard her voice. The light in her eyes and the smile on her face had me anxious. "She opened her eyes . . . Penny is awake."

"Really?" I rushed over to her, and we both ran down the hall back toward Penny's room. I stopped for a moment, almost forgetting Rico. "I'll call you, okay." Without waiting on his response, I continued down the hall, making huge strides.

Chapter 37

Secret

My prayers had finally been answered; Penny was wide awake; she had been for a full day. The only thing she had said was she wanted some ice. Other than that, she just kept looking around the room at us or stared at the television. Erica had tried everything she could to get her to talk, but still she had said nothing. The doctor had assured us the day before that it was normal for her to be quiet and a bit withdrawn from the pure shock of the trauma she had experienced. I tried to understand that, but I couldn't help but wish that she would say something. But even if she wasn't ready to talk, I made sure I talked to her. I told her that we had been there with her the whole time and never left her alone.

The doctor was back today to give a status report on her progress. But I wasn't even sure what that could be. To my frustration, nothing had changed. I asked him if we could speak outside the room. Isis accompanied me.

"Listen, I understand what you said the other day. But I don't get it, she's been woke for two days now. And I have talked to her, her best friend tried, and Isis here. And still she doesn't mumble spit, besides ask the nurse for some fucking ice," I screeched.

"Secret, calm down," Isis said in a gentle tone. I wanted to keep it together, but it was becoming more difficult to control my frustration.

"I get it all right. I do. But it's like I told you yesterday and in the beginning. She has been through a lot. We can only see her wounds; we can't see her pain. However, as a doctor I have seen these types of things time and time again. Now with that being said physically she will heal. Mentally it might take time. Again, she'll talk when she's ready."

I bit my bottom lip so hard I could taste the salty makings of blood. I wanted to scream at him and punch him in his damn mouth for repeating the same thing to me. But I knew he was telling me the truth. I wiped the tears that I hadn't even noticed had once again taken over my face until the cool breeze from the hallway frosted them. I gathered my composure and went back in the room to Penny. The last thing I wanted her to do was to see me a mess. I needed her to know that she was safe. And I if was crying, she might think I was afraid and wouldn't be able to protect her.

I walked back over to the bed with the plan to adjust her pillows for more comfort. With her eyes glued to mine, I was hopeful she was ready to talk.

"Who's Rupp?" slid out of her mouth, which stopped me dead in my tracks. I'm even sure my heart stopped beating. I knew exactly who she was speaking of, but what I didn't know was how she knew his name. Tears, thick tears cascaded down Penny's face in such a manner my eyelids began to burn as my tears ran like water. I instantly wiped my face again. I had to be strong.

My teeth clenched tight. I asked. "Did he do this to you?"

"Who is he?" she screamed at me with so much force she pounded the bed with her hands. Isis rushed over to Penny and tried to calm her down.

I didn't know what to say to her. I felt as if someone had just run me over with an eighteen-wheeler truck. Her eyes burned a hole through me. I had never seen her so angry in my entire life. "He is someone I used to know." I glanced at Isis as if she could help me explain.

Penny sighed, "Hmmph." Turning her eyes away from me, she focused them on the television overhead.

The feeling of hate that I had for Rupp at the moment was indescribable. "Isis, stay with Penny. I'll be back."

Chapter 38

Secret

I nearly crashed into two nurses as I rounded the corner trying to make it outside to use my cell phone to call Kirk. Once outside, it didn't even dawn on me to find Kirk's name in my contacts; instead I went to my keypad and dialed his number like a crazy person. Until that moment I had no idea that I even knew his number by heart.

He answered on the first ring. "What's good?"

I could feel my emotions trying to take over even before I started talking, but I fought them back. This was no time for crying. I had done enough of that. I had to be strong. This shit was no punk matter. "It was Rupp . . . the motherfucker that did this shit to Penny was Rupp," I repeated. And I prayed he heard me, because I did not want to repeat that again.

"You got to be fuckin' bullshittin' me. That motherfucker?" He was clearly floored.

"He did this to her to get back at me?" It was hard for me to control the tremble in my voice.

"Aye, keep yo' cool, a'ight. Don't you worry about nothin'. I got you."

That's all I needed to hear. I ended the call with the certainty that justice would prevail. But the thought of that asshole touching and beating Penny was enough to cut my breath off. And to know that it was all my fault would scar me for life. Rupp was a dude from Philly I was enlisted to set up to be robbed during our old gig. And now he was back to settle the score with an unthinkable plot of revenge. What we had done to him was wrong, but Penny had no part in that and didn't deserve what he had done to her. Unable to control it, I buckled over and my stomach spilled all over onto the ground. What had I done to my own sister? I had done bad things, and she paid for them. My past had come back to haunt me but found my baby sister instead. Would Penny ever be able to forgive me for putting her in harm's way?

A young black nurse with burgundy hair must have witnessed me spill my guts on the ground. She rushed over to me. "Ma'am, are you okay? Let me help you inside." She gently touched my arm, but I snatched it away. I didn't want her or anybody touching me.

"Thanks, but I'm fine." I refused her help.

"Well, at least come inside and let me help you get cleaned up."

"Bitch, I said I'm okay," I barked with contempt, but it really wasn't personal. People had to learn when to mind their own business. I needed to get back inside to Penny. Taking small steps, I walked away.

By the time I got back to the room, Penny was asleep. Isis was still standing at her bedside just as I had asked.

"The nurses came in and gave her something to help her rest. I think she was fightin' it, but she finally closed her eyes."

"We should talk." I signaled her to step out in the hallway with me.

"What the fuck, Secret. Who the fuck is Rupp?"

"He's one of the clients that Kirk booked and I set up to be robbed," I admitted. Her eyes bulged.

"Damn, he figured it out. So this some revenge shit?" I nodded my head in agreement.

"Where is that nigga from? And how in the fuck did he track you here and find Penny?"

"He was from Philly, or least he has a crib there, because that's where the hit was. I have no fuckin' idea how he found us, but the fact of the matter is he did." The look in Isis's eyes told me exactly what she was thinking. If he could find me, it was possible for anybody we had set up to find either one of us. "This shit is my fault for real." Again the tears started. I was so damn tired of crying that I could scream. Isis reached out and hugged me tight.

I couldn't stop sniffing from all the crying I had been doing. Taking a step back, I looked at all the nurses and people passing through the hallways. I wondered how they handled the bad things that happened to them. I knew that everyone had problems, and even if these people didn't seem as devastated as I was at that moment, the coping with shit was normal. Lucky for me, I knew that some bad things that happened to you could be handled with revenge. I turned to Isis. "Fuck that nigga, though; I just made that call to Kirk and he gon' dead this shit. Period." I wanted to be matter-of-fact. No mistakes needed to be made about it. Ashes to ashes was what it meant for anybody who ever decided it was okay to fuck with my family.

"It's on then," Isis agreed. I had to give it to her: for the most part she was a nonviolent person, but when it came to family she didn't cut the deck. I remembered when we were sixteen years old two girls tried to jump me. Isis jumped in and beat one of the chicks up, busting her eye, then a third chick came out of nowhere trying to hit me with a bat. Isis picked up a bottle, broke the end off, ran up on her, and sliced her face. And that shit was a wrap: to this day them bitches won't even look in my direction. Simply put, Isis was a motherfucking G when it came down to it. But I guess we both were.

"Aye, I'm tired, so I know you tired; you been here the entire time. So why don't you go home, take a shower, get some rest, and come back tomorrow with a change of clothes for me."

"You sure you gon' be a'ight?"

"Yeah, I got this. I'm gon' make sure Penny straight and don't upset herself."

"A'ight, well, call me if you need me. But I'll be back first thing in the morning."

"No doubt. I'll keep you posted."

Chapter 39

Secret

We were finally home from the hospital, and damn, was I happy to be away from the cold, depressing environment that the hospital carried. Plus, now that we were home Penny could begin her healing process. But we had been home for two days and still she wasn't talking much. Erica had stayed over all night the first night she had come home. They didn't talk much, but she had said a few things, so I was hopeful. Even if she wasn't ready to talk to me, I was happy if she talked to someone. I worried that she was still upset with me, and if she was I couldn't blame her, because it was well deserved. But I knew it wasn't about me, it was about her, so I was willing to wait.

When I discovered earlier in the day one of our favorite movies, *Bad Company* with Chris Rock, was coming on, I convinced her that we should have a movie night, which was another one of our favorite things to do. She agreed but only if we watched it in her room. Her room had become her new safe haven; she hadn't been out of it since she came home. She had a full bathroom in her bedroom, so other than getting out of bed to take a shower or pee, she was otherwise glued to her bed. Her eating habits were still not the best, either; the only thing she would eat was Snickers bars.

But since the movie had come on, she was eating the extra-butter popcorn that I had popped. I wasn't sure if she was enjoying the movie or not, but when Chris Rock went into the DJ booth and put on that sad country song, I noticed a smile spread across her face. It was brief, but it did happen.

I couldn't help but laugh at that part, too. It was always one of my favorite parts. "He knew better than to play that country shit in a club full of turnt-up-ass black folks." I laughed.

"For real, though," Penny said. She smiled at me, and my heart almost leaped out of my chest with joy. I practically teared up from pure delight. The ringing of my cell phone interrupted our moment. Kirk's name was on the caller ID, so I answered. We hadn't talked in a few days; he didn't even know Penny was home. I had been too busy with Penny to call him.

"I'ma take this call real quick." I got up and stepped out of the room. I wasn't sure what the call was about, so I decided not to have the conversation in front of Penny. "Hey," I said in a low tone.

"Wha'd up? What's going on with Penny?" he asked.

"She at the crib. She been here for a few days now."

"That's what's up. I been meaning to call you; shit just been a bit bananas over here. But I'm glad to hear that."

"Yeah, now it's time for the real work to begin. She still kinda quiet, and spends a lot of time in her room. And I'm pretty sure she's not ready to leave this house anytime soon."

"Li'l sis, everything gon' work out."

"I know it will. It's just hard seeing her like this. But I'm trying to remain positive . . . Oh, I just got a smile out of her a few minutes ago while watching *Bad Company*."

"See, I told you. And don't trip, that situation is a motherfucking wrap," he stressed. I didn't need him to repeat it; I knew exactly what he was speaking of, and I was amped. Once again, he had come through for us, and I knew he always would.

"Thank you so much, Kirk, for fuckin' with Penny and me the long way."

"No doubt. You all are family. And you know I wouldn't have it any other way. Believe that."

"I know . . ." The ringing of the doorbell grabbed my attention. "Aye, but I got to go. Somebody at my door."

"Cool. I'ma roll through in a day or so. I got a few things on my plate."

"We'll be here," I said, then ended the call. The doorbell rang again. With one eye glued to the peephole, I saw Isis standing there.

"I got food." She held up a brown paper bag from one of our favorite stir-fry food restaurants.

"Why didn't you use your key?"

"It's at the house." She stepped inside

"I thought you were helping Rico out today." I shut the door behind her.

"Girl, Rico's ass had me down there working like a slave. Too much paperwork. I told him he needs an assistant, then I broke free."

"Well, I'm glad you did, 'cause I'm starved for some real food. I made some pancakes and sausage this mornin', but I didn't make lunch. I can't be eating all this food by myself, because Penny has sworn off food." I all but snatched the bag out of her hand and make a beeline for the kitchen. Setting the bag on the kitchen table, I grabbed a few plates out of the cabinet.

"So has Penny been up out that bed yet?" Isis grabbed the silverware out of the drawer.

"Nah, not yet. She was still lounging around in that bed, but she did agree to have movie time today. We in her room watching *Bad Company* right now." I reached in the refrigerator and grabbed two Cokes.

"At least she watching television then. But I guess she ain't gon' eat none of this stir-fry, huh?"

"Hell, naw, she ain't, but don't worry, I'll eat her portion." I chuckled. It felt good to be able to laugh. Things weren't better, but I was starting to have hope that they actually would be.

"You are so greedy. Talkin' about you can't be eating all that food alone." Isis grinned. "I'ma go back speak to Penny real quick. Leave me some food." She headed toward Penny. I pulled the tab back on my can of Coke and took a huge swig and stood still for a second as the sweet, strong goodness gave me life. I swear it was so good. "That was quick." I was surprised to see Isis return so quickly.

"She asleep. I'm talkin' about knocked all the way out."

"Guess she tired then. She did get up early this morning, and been up all day. Well . . ." I sighed. "Let's take this food into the den; we can find a movie."

Turning on the television, we were shocked to find *Set It Off* on. "Damn, we lucky our movie on again." Isis was amped. "I bet Jada and them enjoying these checks comin' in. 'Cause they been playin' this movie a lot lately."

"Umhmm," I agreed, sliding my first forkful of food into my mouth.

"So what have you been able to get Penny to eat?"

"Shi'd, not much. She did eat a whole Snickers bar, though, and she was eatin' some of that popcorn I popped for the movie."

"Sounds like junk food ain't the problem, then," Isis summarized. "But we gotta get her to eat some real food, though."

"For real. We also gotta figure out a way to get her up outta that damn room, and next, this house. She can't stay cooped up in here forever."

Isis looked deep in thought, then a smile appeared on her face. "I know what we can do, we can take her on vacation. I'm sure she would love getting out of Florida for a minute. I know I would."

"Yeah, that's dope A. I'm wit' it." I was glad she

had come up with that idea. This would be so good for Penny, it could make all the difference. "Bet, I'm going to talk to Penny tonight."

"Cool. You do that. Next we just need to plan."

"A'ight. So guess who had the nerve to knock on my motherfuckin' door today." I hated to even talk about this; better yet, I wished I could forget, but I had to say something. Isis looked at me, clueless.

"You know I'm not good at guessing this type of stuff. Please just spit it out," she begged.

"Jackie," I spit her name out as if some disease was attached to it.

"Wait, she came here? How she get your address?'

"Bitch, now you know we talkin' about Jackie here. She always got some damn information she shouldn't have. Except for the shit that she should know. Penny was in the hospital for a damn week, and now she pop her ass up here. Fuck outta here with that." I was pissed just thinking about it.

"What did Jackie have to say?" Isis was on the edge of her seat.

"She ain't say shit that matters as usual. Nothin' but lame-ass excuses as to why she didn't come. Just some bullshit. I tuned that cramp out."

"What did you say to Penny? I mean, did you even let Penny see her?" Isis spinned more questions at me.

"Fuck that. I don't want her in my house. Ever!" I clenched my teeth. "For the life of me, I don't even know why we went lookin' for her in the first place. She don't mean us any good, and she has never cared." Isis shook her head in agreement. "You were there when we were growing up so you know."

"I know. I remember." Isis looked in deep thought again. "Damn, our life was fucked . . . Jackie a drunk and Felicia a thief, both willin' to sacrifice us for their greater good. Or so they thought it was." To hear her break it down was welcome. It brought back actual memories of specifics.

I pulled out my box with my weed and cigarillo blunts. This trip down memory lane and Jackie fuckery was a legit cause for me to roll up a fat one. "Remember that time Jackie checked me outta school in the fourth grade so that I could go home and watch Penny . . . all so that she could go out and get wasted." I licked the blunt closed as the memory played in my mind.

"Yeah, I remember that day. And I swear that was so fucked up. Do you remember the time Felicia left me in the dressing room at Macy's? I was so damn scared." Isis had a grin on her face, but she was looking out into space. "The cops took me home in the squad car. I was scared the whole ride. I thought they might take me to jail." She chuckled.

"Hell, yeah, I remember that." I burst out laughing. "Yo ass was traumatized. The next day at school you were still crying about it. I swear you were soft as hell." We both burst out laughing at my comment. "Yep, shit has been crazy for us."

"Crazy since day one. Trust I get why you wouldn't let Jackie in here. She ain't changed. But you and I both know Penny probably wanted to see her. So you better not tell her that she was here. She might be mad at you for sending her away."

"I know." I sighed, then lit up the blunt, taking the first puff. It relaxed me instantly. "In other news, Kirk took care of Rupp."

"Oh, snap, it's done," Isis said while reaching for the blunt.

"Damn right, and I'm elated. Wish I could have done it myself. But it's all good stank-ass motherfucker. I hope they put on his tomb 'Revenge is a dish best served cold.'"

"I'm glad it's over. We don't have to worry about his no more."

I inhaled the smoke deep that I had just taken in from the blunt. It was rejuvenating knowing that Rupp was no longer a factor. But I didn't want to bring him up to Penny, so I would wait to tell her once she was one hundred percent. For now I would enjoy the satisfaction for the both us of knowing he would rot in hell.

Chapter 40

Isis

My house was lit up with candles, and the scents were mesmerizing. I was a hundred and ten percent a candle whore. And I had a special connection with Yankee Candle—so special I could easily spend five to eight hundred on candles in one visit. Every saleslady in the store knew me on a first-name basis. Strolling through my living room, I took in the smell once again and smiled. The scents calmed me and boosted my energy level. Every day I would light a few of them, but today I had gone to the extreme and lit them all.

Making my way back into the kitchen, I opened the oven door to check the homemade double-crusted peach cobbler that I had made with my hands from scratch. Pleased with the golden brown crust, I licked my lips, it looked so delicious. I couldn't wait to take a bite, it was going to be delicious.

Pulling my oven mitts over my freshly manicured nails, I reached inside and pulled out the scorching hot dish. Dinner was ready. Rico was due to arrive any minute. He was coming over for dinner. It had been an entire week since I had last laid eyes on him. He had been out of town for a week on business, and I missed him like crazy. With everything going on with Penny, I hated being alone. Every time I came home my house just seemed empty, especially with Rico being gone and knowing I couldn't just go over to his place for comfort. But that would end tonight.

I almost broke out running at the ringing of my doorbell. I swung the door open, lifted myself up on my tiptoes, and threw my arms around Rico's neck. His arms felt so good around me.

"Dang, I didn't think you would miss me." He chuckled. "If this the reception I get every time I come back, I'm going back out of town tomorrow," he joked.

"Don't play . . . 'cause if you go I won't do this." I kissed him softly on the lips. He kissed me back slowly, then deeply.

He lifted his head up and gazed into my eyes. "In that case I ain't never leaving again."

"That sounds more like it." I followed up with another quick kiss. "Now get in here." I gently grabbed him by the hand.

"Dang, you got the candles going." He pulled me to him and wrapped his arms around my waist from the back.

"Yep, you like it? It's my room of therapy. Relaxing, huh?"

"No doubt, but not as relaxing as you. Damn,

you feel so good, baby. I missed you." He kissed the side of my neck, and I melted. If we didn't eat now we never would, and I didn't cook for nothing.

I turned myself around and faced him. "I cooked, so how about you go into the dining room and I'll bring the food in."

"Sure you don't need my help?" he asked.

"No, you go sit down. I got it." I smiled.

In the kitchen I fixed our plates and delivered them to the table. I placed Rico's plate in front of him and he smiled. "Looks delicious, baby." He referred to the T-bone steak, baked potatoes, and asparagus. I had thought about frying some fish and making some mustard greens, but I didn't want to mix that scent with my candles. So I decided on steak instead.

"That's not all. I made you a homemade peach cobbler. It's in there warming," I bragged. This steak dinner was nothing I could burn; he had only tasted the surface of what I could do in the kitchen. Mrs. Tate didn't play in the kitchen, and she had taught me everything she knew. So my cooking game was on point. "I'll be right back; gotta grab the wine." In the kitchen I claimed the merlot.

"This is really juicy." Rico forked a nice size piece of steak into his mouth. I loved watching him eat. His cheekbones did this cute move when he chewed. "What your secret?"

"If I tell you, I might have to kill you." I grinned, then tasted my asparagus. After dinner and dessert we moved into the den for drinks. I brought the merlot along so that we could finish off the bottle.

"Baby, the merlot is nice but gon' grab that Hennessy. I been on a long flight, and I need a shot."

"Guess that means it's time for you to unwind. No worries. I got you." I grabbed the Hennessy and a shot glass.

"So how is Penny?"

That was a question I wasn't really sure how to answer, because in some ways I wasn't sure. "She's doing okay, still not talkin' a lot like she used to, but she is talkin' never-theless. Oh, and she eats now, which is progress, because a week ago she would barely eat a piece of bread."

"Shit just fucked up. But it's good that she eating, though. Just give it a minute and everything will eventually fall into place."

"Yeah." I nodded my head in agreement. That was the same line the doctor kept forcing on us. At this point Secret and I were just waiting for it to happen. "Secret called today and said that she was going over to spend a night at Erica's house. Secret wasn't too happy about that, but she was relieved that she was going outside of the house, so she decided not to fuss about it."

"Yo, I'm glad she didn't trip, because whatever works to get her out, I say just let it be . . . I had a cousin who was raped some years back. And for long time she was withdrawn and depressed, but eventually she got better. You all just got to keep supporting her. She'll be cool."

"Thanks for caring, babe." That was what I liked about him: he was caring, considerate, and full of respect. All those qualities went a long way with me. I wished I had paid more attention to that

with Bobbi, because being with Rico made me realize just how selfish Bobbi could be sometimes.

Rico took a sip of his Hennessy. "I know I said I
wanted to take a shot, but I wouldn't mind having
an ice cube or two to put in it. Think you can grab
me a few?"

"Whatever you like, babe. Be right back."

I stopped in my tracks as I reentered the den.
Roses were spread out on the floor and Rico was
on one knee. I wasn't sure what was going on, but
I wanted answers and right away. "What are you
doing on the floor?"

"Isis, I know you are apprehensive about love,
and I respect that."

This just could not be happening. We had just
been through this speech. Sighing, I looked away.
Here we were just having a nice dinner, and now
this. I was not ready to discuss this again.

"Isis," he called my name but I fixed on the candles. "Isis," he called me again. "Baby, please look
at me," he pleaded.

His begging softened me, but only a little bit.
Reluctantly, I faced him.

"From the first time I laid eyes on you in that
mall I have loved you. I didn't have a clue that I
would see you again. But I knew then that you
were the one for me. No one else . . . And today
right here and right now, I'm asking you to please
be my wife." He pulled out a huge platinum dia-
mond ring.

I felt faint as tears flooded down my cheeks. The
look in his eyes broke my heart, they were so full of
hope. "Rico . . . I . . . I can't and I told you . . . I told
you before." I slowly started to back up. He reached

for my left hand, but I quickly moved it out of his reach.

"I know what you said, and I want you to know that I heard you, loud and clear, but it's time. It's time for us to make a move for us. I have so many plans for our life together. I want you to move away with me, leave Miami and start new."

The look plastered on his face could break anybody's heart. Every word out of his mouth he meant. But even that didn't change my stance. How could I tell him that in any other way? God knows I had tried, but he had not heard a word I said, clearly. I felt backed into a giant corner with no escape. I needed to be alone.

"Rico, I have to think about all of this. It's just too much right now. I need time . . . Just let yourself out." I dismissed him before running to my room. Locking my door, I fell into my bed and stared up at the ceiling for hours. I had to be one of the stupidest girls in the world. Constantly turning down a fine, young, successful brother. Some might even think I needed to be committed. But the fact of the matter was that I was totally sane, just unsure of when it would be okay to let go and trust again. Was the time now? I just wished I knew for sure. Damn, I hated Bobbi's ass for ruining me and my ability to find love and admit it that it was actually love and to just trust that. "Ugh." I punched my mattress, wishing it was Bobbi's face.

Chapter 41

Secret

After weeks of being holed up in her room, Penny had finally left her room and the house altogether. Erica had convinced her to spend a night at her house so they could just hang out. I was surprised Penny had agreed to go. They had been gone for about an hour, so I decided to take a hot bubble bath, roll up the kush, and relax. It had been a while since I had been able to solely lie back; from the time we came home from the hospital I spent all my time fussing over and tending to Penny. But she had made it clear before she left that she didn't want me blowing her up. So since I was alone, I decided to unwind, but not long after being in the tub and hitting the blunt a few times, I found myself drifting off to sleep. Climbing out of the tub and drying off, I oiled myself up, threw on a pair of pajamas and a white wife beater, slid into a pair of my thick footie socks, grabbed my blunt, and climbed back in my bed. Picking up the remote control, I started to flip through channels to find something on television. The doorbell rang, and I froze. I wasn't expecting anyone to come over.

Tiptoeing to the door, I took advantage of the peephole. Now that I finally had some alone time, I really wasn't looking for any company. And I was really surprised to see that it was Sway. I hadn't heard from him since he popped up at the hospital. Taking a deep breath, I stepped back over to the alarm and punched in my code to unarm it. Unlatching the locks on the door, I swung it open.

"Hey," I said.

"Aye, I was in the neighborhood and thought I'd stop by." I almost laughed at his dumb excuse for stopping by. He was too hood for a whack-ass line like that.

"Really, so who do you know in this neighborhood?" I smiled.

"A'ight, you got me." He laughed. He knew I was only fucking with him. I had to admit he was looking delicious. "Are you gon' invite me in?"

"Why not, come on in." I stepped to the side so that he could enter. His cologne ate my nostrils up as he walked past me. "Can I get you something to drink?" I really wasn't sure what else to say. I was a bit caught off guard that he showed up unannounced like that. Normally I would check a nigga for something like that. But I wasn't even feeling that.

"Nah, I'm good."

"Well, come into the living room," I invited. "So

what's up?" I asked as we each took a seat on each end of the huge sectional.

"Nothing much doing, you know these Miami streets beat. But I'm a beast, as always, so I'm still running shit."

"No doubt. I know how you do."

"I would have come by sooner, but I been busy in these streets. And you know that's a night and day job. How is Penny doing?"

"She's good. Getting better every day. She is strong. She out hanging with Erica."

"That's what's up. I knew she would be good . . . How you been?"

"Ummm, same ole, tryin' to stay busy and keep my nose clean."

"A'ight, well, you lookin' good . . . I was wondering when you might think about letting me take you out?" That was the conversation I was not ready for. Not now.

"I don't know, Sway. I stay busy and all." I really didn't know what to say to answer that question. But I was not trying to go there with him.

"We can work that out. I just want to take you out and kick it. You know, chill."

As fine as he was looking, I wanted to say hell, yes. But I had to have some self-control, and that shit just was not happening. "Listen, I wanted to thank you for coming and checking on me when Penny was in the hospital. I'll never forget it. But I can't do any more than that." I had to keep it real. I was not sure why, but he seemed surprised. I knew then that whole hospital scene had given him hope. I would be sorry to say that it was false hope.

"There is no need to thank me. I wanted to be there. I would have come by more often, but we were in a backwards place, and the last thing I wanted to do was make you feel uncomfortable. So I gave you your space."

"Either way, I was glad you came. But right now I can't be committing myself to anyone. Besides, you got that baby mama, and she clearly ain't ready to be respectful. And I don't fuck wit' none of that, because I would be in jail for attempted murder." I had to keep it real, because if that bitch ever ran up on me like she did that night, I would kick her ass on sight, no questions asked.

"Aye, I'm so fuckin' sorry about that. And you ain't never got to worry about that happenin' again."

"Listen, I know you mean every word that's comin' out your mouth, but I can't date you. I can't. You looking for commitment and I'm not. I don't know if you've noticed this, but it's mostly about a good time and sex for me. My heart has taken an oath against seriousness; simply put, I'm not ready for a relationship, and I'm especially nowhere near ready to commit. You got your baby mama behind you. And clearly she loves you."

"That might be true, but I don't love her. Shi'd, I don't even want to be with her, period."

"That may be true as well, but you don't respect me, because if you did you would have checked her for talking to me crazy." I hadn't meant to come for him, but I was not the best at hiding my emotions. More times than not, I said what was directly on my mind, taking out victims on my way down.

"Listen, that bullshit she pulled that day was the crazy, off-the-wall shit she likes to do. But I don't involve myself in that. I don't mess with her, period, unless it's about my child. She the one confused, and no, I don't do shit to confuse her." He tried to explain himself, and to be honest, I believed him, but that didn't matter. The fact of the matter was that I would end up hurting him. I didn't love him, and I couldn't love him. My heart was like ice, just like Isis had said. The only interest I had for him was in the bed or just chilling.

"Sway, you a good dude, that much I'm sure of, but I promise you, being in a relationship with me, it's just not what you want. I won't ever love you. All I do is chase money; that's what makes me happy. Trust me, this is for the better." I really wanted to say, "Sway, get the fuck out with this sentimental shit because I don't have time for it." If he wasn't a dollar bill, love didn't exist. He needed to put this relationship shit in a romance book, because a day of love in my book was a blunt.

"Well, if you change your mind, you know where to find me." He finally stood up.

"I do," I said. At this point I just wanted him to get out so I could chill alone. Sad but true. He leaned in and tried to kiss me at the door, but of course I moved my head back. Kissing him would only confuse things. The whole time we had been talking I had been thinking about taking him back and putting it on him before he left. But he was being such a damn crybaby about relationships, I said fuck it. Hell, he would only confuse that for love, so instead I turned my face to the left so that his kiss could meet my cheek. I wasted no time locking the door behind his ass. Now I was alone and had what I craved: peace and quiet.

And I swear if another nigga stepped to me with his fucking heart in his hand, I would shoot him. Fuck love; they needed to be screaming cash money. Heading toward the hallway again, I almost screamed when the doorbell sounded off. Sway's ass must have been back at my door. I didn't know what that nigga had to say, but he was about to get cussed out. I told his ass to go home. That's when I realized Sway was not crazy enough to knock on my door like that, because he knew I would curse his ass out. I paused for a brief second; the only thing on my mind was Penny. Was something wrong? Suddenly scared, I raced to the door and put my right eye to the peephole, revealing Isis. Snatching the door open, I felt relieved that it was not Penny, which meant she was probably okay. But I was just as anxious to know why Isis was trying to tear my door down. And for the life of me I wondered why she would never use her damn key.

"What's up?" I questioned. She blew past me like the wind. I followed her until she stopped at the bar. Pulling out a glass, she filled it to the top with Jack Daniel's and took it straight to the head, no flinching or throat clearing. That Jack was strong as hell, so I didn't know how she could pull that off. "You want a shot?" she asked, her eyes full of something that I couldn't define. The whites of her eyes were red, which told me that she had possibly been crying.

"I'll take one." I figured whatever was going on with her that had her in that state once she shared it with me, I would need a drink, too. She poured the brown liquid so fast that a few drops landed on the bar.

She immediately poured herself another shot and downed it, this time burping as she turned to me. "Rico proposed to me," she blurted out.

"That nigga did what, now?" I had heard her right, I was sure of it, but it was damn sure not what I wanted to hear.

"He asked me to marry him," she reiterated, like I really didn't hear the first time. Clearly she missed the sarcastic tone in my voice.

I chuckled. The whole thing was ridiculous. "Well, fuck all that, Kirk found us a new gig. A sure way for us to get paid." We hadn't done Push since Penny's kidnapping, and with our lifestyle it was a must. That money never stopped flowing. Isis rested her eyes on me, signaling she didn't like my comment. But she knew I was not one to sugar-coat anything. Her eyes continued to roll around in her head like she was on twenty-one questions but didn't have a clue.

"Secret . . ." As she said my name, she put the palm of her right hand on her forehead. "I thought you understood I'm done with that."

Now it was time for my eyes to roll around in my head, because I had no idea what "done" meant. "What is it you actually done with, Isis? We gotta get paid."

"Secret, if the bullshit is what it takes, then I ain't gettin' paid no more. I am done with that shit. Understand that?" She glared at me as if I were the one insane, even though she was the one denouncing money.

Again I laughed. I wasn't sure what dream she

was living right now. Did she not see all that we had? Or was it something else? Possibly Rico; if he was the reason, then I got it. "I see. So you don't want money no more? You want love." The word left a bitter taste in my mouth. I still couldn't believe anyone fell for that shit.

"No, what I want is to trust again . . . and in order to do that, I accept it . . . and yes, that means accept Rico's love for me."

This whole conversation was really annoying the shit out of me. But the pain was written all over her face, and for that I hurt with her. Bobbi had truly scared her, but he was the prime example that this love bullshit was not worth it. It was time she was honest with herself. I sighed. "Listen, you got all your life for this shit . . . Your fairy tale can wait. What we need to do right now is hook up with Kirk." That for me was the bottom line.

"Ain't you listenin' to shit I just said," Isis screamed at me so loud I was startled. "Read my lips, Secret. I don't want it anymore. I don't even want to talk about the shit anymore . . . Open your eyes. Can't you see what Kirk and his scheming-ass ideas done to Penny?"

I froze at the mention of that. A ball of sadness instantly started to build in the pit of my stomach, but it turned to anger just as fast. "It's not fair for you to bring that shit up during this conversation. Besides, I told you that Kirk handled that shit. He bodied that nigga on site. It's like I have said time and time before, Isis, Kirk has our back. And he gon' make sure that no foul shit like that ever happen again. He promised me on his own life of that."

Looking at me as if I were deaf and dumb, Isis started to shake her head from side to side. "This is crazy," was her only reply. Something told me that she was not changing her mind. But I had to keep trying to get her to see why she should.

"Listen, Isis, I know you want to just walk away. But we need to do this. We do this one last job and save up enough money to get outta of this life for good."

"That's just it!" she screamed. "We don't need no money; we got enough of it already."

"You right. I do . . . but not enough to be comfortable forever." She was right: my safe deposit box was on full. Money was not an issue, and I could live good for a while. But I wanted to live good for life. And there was no question about that for me.

Again Isis shook her head at me in disbelief. I waited. "Well, you do what you gotta do. I'm done." Her words tugged at my heart. I couldn't believe what she was saying. Especially after the option I had just come up with.

I was pissed off and could not fake it. "You just gone walkin' away for the love of some nigga!" I spat the words at her. I was full of disgust, and I wanted her to know it.

"Yes, because I need that . . . and so do you." She said this calmly and seemingly unfazed by my harsh statement. "It's no different than what Sway wants from you, but you keep fighting it. And I just can't figure out why you keep fighting. No, he ain't perfect, but he really cares for you." Damn, she wanted to start that Sway talk again. That had been precisely why I had not told her of his little visit. But since she was determined to bring his ass up, I guess I couldn't avoid the conversation.

"Well, that might be true, but it's equally true that I don't give a fuck about him. Nigga bringing extra drama in my life with baby mamas and all that." I chuckle at the thought of Sway's baby mama acting a fool. "I think you know me better than that. So you know I ain't puttin' up with no bullshit. No what I'm gon' do is be about me and my motherfucking grind." I know it may have sounded harsh, but it was true, and that shit would set anybody free.

"Damn, that's pretty fucked up, Secret. I mean, when you gon' be real with yourself and realize you human. Which means you ain't no different from anybody else . . . that means you do need love and I'm not talking about from Penny, or Jackie, or even me. I'm talking about from a companion. Sacking niggas ain't gon' keep you happy forever. You gon' eventually get sick of that."

"Well, I guess you got the damn answer, Isis." I was sarcastic. "The answer to love, so I'll get a pad and paper to get all this shit down. 'Cause I don't want to miss a thing." I laughed, but it was fake.

"Whatever." She waved me off. "Like I said, you need love like the rest of us. Remember that."

That statement was funny to me because I was for sure about one thing. I didn't need love or no nigga. I laughed out loud with my arms crossed across my chest. "Ain't you been listening yet to nothing I said? Fuck love. If it ain't about the money, miss me wit' it." I gritted my teeth, meaning each and every gotdamn word.

Shaking her head at me, once more full of disappointment, she turned and walked away. I was stunned. Just as she put her hands on the doorknob, I spoke. "Isis." I said her name as if it was the last of my lifelines. She paused. "I never thought I'd see the day you'd walk away from family. We have been all we have ever had." Tears stung at my eyelids, but I fought to keep them back. I wanted to be strong. I could tell by the way Isis's hand was shaking on the doorknob that I had her attention. She glanced at me briefly, her face wet from tears. With no words she swiftly turned back around, opened the door, and stepped out into the darkness.

Chapter 42

Isis

I couldn't believe the conversation I had just had with Secret. My mind was in clutter. I knew hers was, too. The only time I could remember that we had had a real argument was back in the fifth grade, about a boy name Sammie. He liked both of us but only played with one when the other was not around. Before long we were fighting for his attention. That didn't last long, though, because when we figured out what he had been trying to do, we beat his ass and made him apologize. It was then and there that we decided boys were evil and we would never allow one to come between us again. Other than that, we never really argued, at least not to that point. But I felt as if I had to be honest with her in that moment. And she was right about us being family, and nothing should ever come between that. We had each other when we didn't have anybody else, and as far as I was concerned, that would always be the case. I truly didn't know what to do. I had been driving around for hours, the whole time my face soaked with tears. I ran out a full tank of gas the whole time with the intent of clearing my mind, yet still it was foggy. I didn't know what to do. But after pulling over at a gas station and refilling my tank, my common sense kicked in and reminded me that driving all my gas out was not going to solve my problems. So I headed home.

Pulling up to my condo, I almost threw my car in reverse when I recognized Rico's truck still in my driveway. But even I knew that would not do any good. I had to face him at some point. I pushed the button from my car, and my garage door raised. I pulled inside, shut off my ignition, laid my head on my steering wheel for a few minutes to try and gather my thoughts. With no chance of that happening, I climbed out. Walking through my house I didn't see him anywhere in sight at first. Entering my bedroom, I located him lying across my bed.

Rico sat up immediately. "I've been waiting on you to come back. I didn't want to leave without us really finishing this."

I wanted to get this over with, but I did not want to give him any eye contact. It would only make things hard. But I needed to put my big girl panties. "Rico, I can't marry you." I let it flow without stalling. A single tear slipped from his right eye, then the left. I felt guilty as sin.

"Baby, you can't just throw us away like this. So don't," he begged.

I fought back my tears. I didn't want to confuse

him with them. I had to be steadfast in my decision. "Trust me, this is for the best. We can't be together. So please just go, Rico." He started to speak again, but I cut him off. I needed him to leave before I broke down right in front of him. "Just go, Rico!" This time I screamed, hoping to make myself clear.

Slowly and reluctantly he lifted himself off my bed and left my room. I stood in the same spot for ten minutes before finding the strength to lock up my house and arm the alarm system. Glancing out my window, I saw his truck was gone. My feet some-how carried me, or should I say floated me, back to my room, where I fell in my bed and cried my-self into a deep sleep. For the next two days I only showered, watched TV, and rolled blunts. I tried to eat but couldn't; I tried to sleep but couldn't do that, either. I had hit rock bottom.

Day three I woke up with Felicia heavily on my mind. My heart told me that I needed to see her. I needed her advice, something I had never had be-fore. After getting dressed, I jumped into my car and drove full speed until I arrived at the prison. I'm not sure what came over me, but my emotions filled me. As soon as Felicia sat down in front of me, I felt my emotions. For the first time I saw my mother. I thought about my childhood, when she used to hug me and I loved her without question. When I counted on her, when I couldn't wait until I got home from school to see her. Then I thought about this dark prison, and all her pleas to me to be in my life, to still have some role as my mother, only to have me bring her coldness and a stiff stare at every visit. I felt horrible for all the time I had wasted, missed, and could not and would not be getting back. I felt sick. Tears flooded my face. I started to speak, but she held up her hand and silenced me.

"I am so sorry . . ." She paused. "I'm so sorry for being so selfish all of your life. Somehow I convinced myself that all of the stealing that I done was for you. So that I could give you a better life . . ." She wiped at the tears that were running down her face. She closed her eyes and squeezed tight for a brief second in an attempt to slow them from coming down. "Really, it was for myself. I didn't know that then, but I do now. And now I know that you deserve to want something for yourself. Sometimes that means walking away from someone who doesn't want to let go of the wrong, to get to the right. Isis, what I'm saying to you is happiness comes with a smile, not with money or material things. You'll never find it that way. Baby, sometimes you have to choose."

If it had been permitted, I would have jumped out of my seat, run around the table, and wrapped my arms around her so tight. Every single word out of her mouth had rejuvenated me in more ways than one. "Thank you so much, Mama." A smile spread across her face.

"It's been so long since you called me that. I feared you never would again," she cried.

"I've been selfish, too. Always thinkin' of myself, never once putting myself in your shoes. And I'm sorry for that." It felt so good to get that off my chest. I felt like I was standing out in the rain and willingly allowing the water to refresh me. "But please don't make me call you Mama all the time. I actually like Felicia now. It's more fun."

"Fun, you say. Hmmm. A'ight then." She chuckled. "Guard." She unexpectedly yelled over her shoulder. A short, stout Hispanic lady with corn rows looking like a dude strutted over. Felicia looked up at her with confidence. "This is my daughter, Isis, and I would like to hug her. We ain't passing contraband, we ain't up to nothin' slick, just want to hold my daughter." She looked me straight in the eyes.

The guard looked at me then back at Felicia. "Permission granted."

I was a bit surprised, but before I knew it I was in her arms, and it felt so good. I didn't even realize until I felt the wetness from her shirt that I had laid my head on her shoulder and was crying like a baby. She comforted me as if I was still a baby. This was what I had been missing: my mother who loved me dearly no matter what. Who had been a single mother doing what she thought was right when it was not. But she provided for me. "I love you, Mom," I cried.

"I love you, too, baby," she said, and I cried even harder. I could feel the eyes in the room on us. And I couldn't have cared less.

The ride home was peaceful for me, mind, body, and soul. Felicia's words about letting people go and happiness had rung true on so many levels. I now knew what I had to do, and I wouldn't waste another minute to do it. I drove back to Miami in record time. I only stopped for gas and that was it. My next stop was not until I reached Rico's house.

Pulling up to the house, I noticed two cars that were unfamiliar. Climbing out the car, I made my way up to the door. I started to feel a little weird as I approached the huge double doors and realized they were ajar. Instead of knocking, I kind of pushed one of the doors open and stepped inside, unsure of what I would find.

Too my surprise I saw a guy who seemed to be leading people coming down the massive staircase. I wondered if Rico had guests over, because I had never seen them before. "Yes, hi." The guy leading spoke first. "May I help you?" he asked next.

"Not really. I'm here for Rico," I announced.

"Rico." He repeated his name as if he was unsure about something.

"Yes, I'm here for my boyfriend, I mean fiancé, Rico." I'm not sure what made me say all that, but I wanted to be clear on a few things. And I certainly didn't like the way the valley African American lady stood and stared at me. I was sure I had mustard and ketchup spread across my face. I considered going straight pork and beans on her, but I had other fish I was trying to fry. So I settled with waving her off. The guy who had decided to be the spokesperson made his way down the staircase and headed toward me.

Once he reached me, I considered asking him to step back; he was too close. "I'm Fernando Gates, Rico's real estate agent." He extended his right hand to me. I thought about smacking it. But I really just wanted to get to Rico. The rest I could care less about, but I did pick up on the fact that he announced himself as Rico's real estate agent, and people, a couple, were following him around. "Can we step over here for a bit?" He pointed toward the den across the hall. I led the way, opening the door. I stepped inside and turned to face him. All I wanted to know was what was going on."

"Okay, Fernando, can we cut to the chase?" I was tired of playing around. I was here for one thing and one thing only: my man.

"I'm not sure if you knew this, but judging by your surprise to see me or lack thereof . . ." He really was starting to annoy me. Next I would be serenading him with curse words.

"Would you please tell me where the hell Rico at?" I rolled my eyes. I was trying to keep it cute, but he was on my last nerve.

"Rico has been aggressively packing up his clothes for the past day; he left early this morning. I was summoned here to sell this house. I was permitted to get inside as of today." He talked to me as if he was trying to sell me something.

But I quickly lost sight of his words or him as it started to sink in what he was telling me. I could not believe it. "So are you saying to me that Rico is gone?" I wanted to be clear on what I was receiving.

"Yes, he left."

I felt like someone had taken a sledgehammer and beaten me in the stomach with it. I could not believe the words that were coming out of his mouth. Without another word I turned and dashed out of the door, headed for my car, where I grabbed my cell phone and dialed Rico's telephone number.

"The mailbox you are trying to reach is not accepting any telephone calls." I felt like it was the day of doom. My cell phone slid out of my hand and landed in my lap. Good thing I had sat down in the driver's seat, or it would have smashed to

the floor. The whole scene was like a playback of Bobbi. It couldn't be possible that a whole 'nother dude had run off without telling me. But this time it was my fault. I had ruined me.

Starting up my car, I hit the interstate like a maniac. The speed limit was the least of my cares. Tears rushed down my face so thick and fast it was like I was driving in a rainstorm; my vision became so blurry I couldn't see a thing. Pressing lightly on the brake, I slowed up the car and pulled off to the side of the highway. Reaching into my glove compartment, I fished out a Kleenex and attempted to wipe my face dry. I would not cry anymore. I had done enough of that over Bobbi. So I was done with that. No, this time I had made my own bed and I would lie in it with strength and boss bitch moves. Pulling down my visor mirror, I looked at my face to be sure all the tears had dried up. Satisfied, I cleared my throat. Picking up my cell, I dialed a number that I knew would always answer. My family.

"Hello," Secret answered on the second ring.

"Get Kirk on the phone. Like you said, *if it ain't about the money*. So fuck it, let's get this damn money."

"Bitch, you ain't gotta tell me but once. And you won't believe what's up next . . ."

DON'T MISS

The Safe House

Packed with "high suspense" and "memorable
choices and consequences" (*Booklist*) Kiki
Swinson's novels sizzle with brutally unpredictable
characters, breakneck plotting—and a uniquely
gritty portrait of Southern life. Now she breaks
all the rules as a young woman with two
targets on her back tries to keep those she
loves—and herself—alive . . .

Available wherever books and ebooks are sold.

Turn the page for an excerpt from
The Safe House . . .

It seemed like time was creeping by slowly. It felt like these guys had no intentions of leaving. Every time I heard one cop announce that they'd cleared one room, meaning they logged all the evidence, I'd hear another cop say that they found something else. It was like a fucking circus; everyone was juggling their own act with no intentions of leaving.

Detective Belle walked back into Mrs. Mabel's apartment with her partner, Caesar, in tow. She made an announcement and it sounded like she was making it in the living-room area. "I just spoke with one of the neighbors. Her name was Tina. She's an older woman. Looked to be in her late forties. She said that she knew Mrs. Mabel for a long time. She was like the neighborhood grandmother. She was a nice lady and everyone loved her, so it's hard to believe that someone would kill her. She also said that she spoke to Mrs. Mabel this morning and everything seemed fine. But when she saw two uniformed cops run away from this apartment, she felt something was wrong, because cops only run when they're in pursuit of someone. And you know what, guy?" Belle said.

"What?" a few cops said in unison.

"She's right. And you wanna know why?" Belle continued.

"Why?" the same cops said.

"Because within the last hour, there weren't any calls from dispatch for this area or any area within twenty miles. So tell me who were those two cops that the lady saw?"

"Was she sure that they were cops? I mean, they could've been security officers," I heard one of the guys say.

"We asked her that same question. And she said she knows what Virginia Beach Police uniforms look like. She also said that they were driving one of the city's police vehicles too," I heard Detective Caesar reply.

"Don't you think it's ironic that a murder was committed at the apartment next door and now we're investigating another one?" I heard someone ask. I couldn't make out the voice because there were over eight to ten people.

"There's a strong possibility. And also remember that we have the suspect April, who has agreed to testify in front of a grand jury and say Terrell Mason was already dead when she entered into the apartment next door. Now fast-forward to now, when Agent Sims and I tried to speak with this lady here, she wouldn't cooperate with us. It almost seemed like she had a bond with Misty Heiress, which was why she expressed her grievances with us for going through Misty's things in her apartment. So, what if someone from Terrell's family or a friend of his came by Misty's apartment to seek revenge and Mrs. Mabel got in their way?" Belle said.

"I can definitely see that," Detective Caesar commented.

"Me too," another voice said.

"Yeah, that's plausible," someone else said.

"Okay, so we may have a motive here. Now I'm gonna need you guys to comb through this place very thoroughly. Too many dead bodies are popping up. So let's get a handle on it and let's do it now," Belle demanded.

It took all those cops a total of five damn hours to collect all the evidence they needed. When they finally filed out of here, one by one, it felt like a ton of anxiety lifted from my shoulders. I let out a long sigh of relief and then I laid my head down on my duffel bag.

Thinking about everything I heard from the police got my mind racing. Okay, so they got one thing right, which was that the two guys that ran away from this apartment weren't real cops. But as far as who they think killed Mrs. Mabel, they were all wrong. Terrell's family or close friends had nothing to do with Mrs. Mabel's murder. But if they wanted to believe they did it, then so be it. My main priority was me. Not only was Ahmad, along with his henchman, looking for me, but Agent

Sims and Detective Belle were too. So, as soon as they pulled my DNA from the towel and bath cloth I left behind, they're gonna think I murdered Mrs. Mabel and they'd have me on something like *America's Most Wanted*. Once that happened, I wouldn't be able to stay in this area. Finding somewhere to go was what I needed to concentrate on.

I had no idea where I was going to go. Nor did I know what I was going to do. I had no plans. All I had were the keys to Mrs. Mabel's car. So I figured that if I could use it to get away from here, I'd have a clearer mind to be able to come up with a good plan. "Okay, Misty, it's time to go. You gotta get out of here before someone else comes here," I whispered to myself.

After building up enough courage, I finally willed myself to climb back out of the ceiling space. On my way down, I made every step carefully. I wanted to be as quiet as a mouse. Getting caught was not an option for me. Once I had landed with my feet placed firmly on the floor, I slid the closet door back as quiet as I could. I stood still for a moment to see if I could hear any movement. After realizing that there was no more movement in the house, I stepped out of the closet and tiptoed over to the bedroom door. I peered around the corner of Mrs. Mabel's bedroom and into the hallway. I looked toward the front door, where her body had been, and it was gone. I was relieved to see that. I was even more relieved when I walked around the apartment and saw that I was alone. But the cops and forensic officers had left a lot of black dust and markers around the apartment to let someone know that they had been there. It was one of those crime scenes that you'd see in a movie. I stood there and looked down at the puddle of blood and felt so bad that Mrs. Mabel was murdered because of me. I mean, if she hadn't picked me up at the freaking grocery store and brought me into her home, she'd still be alive now. Probably watching her favorite shows. But no, the moment I stepped foot into this apartment, everything went downhill from there. I had a hand in creating this lady's demise. Now, how fucked up was that?

I knew that I wasn't going to be able to leave this apartment just like that. I also knew that in order for me to leave this place without being seen, I was gonna have to move strategically. That might entail leaving here with a wig on and sunglasses. I might also need to leave here when it got dark outside. More important, whenever I did decide to walk out of this apartment, no one, including the agents, cops, or Ahmad, could be able to see me. If they did, then I'd be fucked.

Conne

Visit us online at
KensingtonBooks.com
to read more from your favorite authors, see books
by series, view reading group guides, and more.

Join us on social media

for sneak peeks, chances to win books and prize packs,
and to share your thoughts with other readers.

facebook.com/kensingtonpublishing
twitter.com/kensingtonbooks

Tell us what you think!

31901064871538